Easy TARGET

SHANNON CURTIS

A SAFEKEEPERS INC NOVEL

INFO BLOCK PRESS

ISBN: 978-0-6487541-0-7

Excerpt from *Hidden Target* © 2020 by Shannon Curtis

Published by Info Block Press, PO Box H122, Hurlstone Park NSW 2193, Australia
Infoblock.com.au

Cover and internal art by The Wordable Writer
Editing and typesetting by Debbie Phillips, DP Plus

Dedication

*For my mother, and her mother, and my husband's mother—
such amazing, beautiful, formidable, empowering, strong
and generous women.
I'm so blessed to have you in my life, and I continue to be
inspired by you.
Robin. Mavis. Hedi. This one is for you.*

Prologue

"Mic, it's about to go down."

Michaela 'Mic' Robson stopped pretending she was working and glanced up from her computer screen. Special Agent Jenkins stood at her office door, wearing the black cargo shorts and red polo shirt that was the Eagle Express operations uniform. He'd been working undercover for three weeks in her department. The man lifted his cell phone, and she nodded. She rose from her desk—it wasn't like she'd been doing anything important, anyway. Ever since she'd turned up at her usual time—because it was vitally important to make things look like it was business as usual *today*, of all days— she'd been going through the motions. She was finding it so damn hard to concentrate, to act as though everything was normal, when it so wasn't.

She strode out of her upstairs warehouse office. Her fingers curled into her palms as the federal agent followed closely behind her. She quickly jogged down the metal stairs and led the way across the warehouse floor to the doorway that led into the general offices of the Eagle Express Freight Company. She took the stairs to her left two at a time, then led him through the labyrinthine hallways to the smaller boardroom she'd booked out for the past two days.

She pressed her access card against the reader, waited to hear the click as the door unlocked, then stepped inside, Jenkins close behind her. She made sure the door was closed before turning back to the room. FBI agents were crammed into the space, with a number of laptops, and other surveillance equipment spread out across the boardroom table and on some desks she'd brought in under the guise of clearing out some space in the warehouse for a temporary dangerous goods staging area. The agents had used a material screen as a complete blockout across the window that ran along one wall and looked out over the warehouse. She'd told the company she was in discussions with a potential client, a security firm that shipped high-value items, in an attempt to explain the number of people coming in, and their equipment. Nobody had so much as batted an eyelid.

She eyed Tony Veneziano, the IT guy she'd conscripted, under deceit and protest from his manager, Rafe Perez. She'd told Perez she needed Tony to assist with systems gateway creation and management for this potential client. She just hadn't mentioned that client was the FBI working a bust. Tony flicked her a look. He looked distinctly uncomfortable, surrounded so thoroughly by law enforcement.

"Mic." Her colleague nodded in greeting.

She hid her tension behind a mild but confident smile. "Tony. How are you doing?"

He gave her a thumbs-up and a weak smile, but she didn't miss the way his gaze drifted to the holstered weapon of a passing agent.

She gave him a reassuring wink. They were the only two Eagle Express employees who knew what was going on. The FBI had cleared Tony's participation, but had wanted to keep the number of staff involved to a bare minimum. She hadn't even been able to inform her CEO of the activity—not until they made sure they'd apprehended everyone involved in the lucrative drug-smuggling operation she'd discovered at the company she'd joined as operations manager just eight months ago.

Tony was instrumental in locking down the boardroom from any wandering staff, providing access cards for the agents, and pulling records from all of the systems—exports, imports, accounts ... She'd had to access her own records of manifests, declarations, consignment notes and driver logs—and now it was going down. She looked up at the large TV screen on the wall. It was normally used for videoconferencing, visual presentations to clients and the like, but today it showed some very different activity. The screen was divided into six blocks, all showing different video feeds. She eyed the top right corner. The GPS tracker map showed all her vehicles on the road. Red dots were vans in the metropolitan areas for pickups and deliveries, and blue dots showed the trucks transporting freight to and from the airport, or the various hubs she'd help set up around key areas of Los Angeles.

"Patch me into the radio room," she told Tony quietly. "I want to hear this."

He did as instructed, and handed her a set of headphones. She held up one headphone to her right ear. She also wanted to hear what was going on in this makeshift command center for this sting.

She listened to the chatter in the radio room. Lyn, the grandmother who manned the radio base at Eagle Express with her neatly coiffed titian hair and steely blue gaze, was barking orders to the drivers on the road like a general in a war zone. Sending through pickup orders, special delivery instructions just in, and traffic hazard alerts, the woman managed to keep thirty-six Eagle Express vans in check to ensure on-time collections and deliveries.

Michaela pointed to the GPS screen with the dots. "Run thirty-one is pulling into Encino Drive," she said quietly.

Jenkins nodded, and reached for the radio on the table. He lifted it to his mouth. "All agents, stand by. Target is two blocks away from drop site." The agent turned to one of his co-workers. "Can you pull up the dashcam feed? I want to see this in real time."

The agent nodded, and Mic blinked as the large screen on the wall flickered; suddenly it was the dashboard view of van #31 driving down the street that filled the screen. The GPS tracking map minimized to a small block in the top right corner, and she bit her lip as the red dot drew closer and closer to the address she knew was on the shipping label.

She'd stumbled across the first shipment two months ago. She'd hoped it was talcum powder, or maybe even baby formula—she'd seen stranger things—but she'd used a drug testing kit and had been dismayed at the positive results for MDMA. She'd had to contact the FBI, as per the requirements for air transport companies under those circumstances, which had led to a two-month-long covert operation between the LAPD, FBI, DEA and more alphabet soup agencies she couldn't keep track of.

Mic watched as the van turned onto Hacienda Street.

"Thirty-one to base, I'm stuck in traffic on the Santa Monica Freeway, between South Le Brea and Venice. I'm looking at a red zone. Possible accident."

Mic's lips tightened as she listened to the lie her courier driver told the radio operator. She couldn't believe the audacity—or stupidity—of Adam Hollison, the driver. Did he not think his movements were trackable? The rollout of GPS trackers had been one of her first projects on joining the company, as a result of a stolen van, and the freight it contained. Did he think that because the van wasn't stolen, nobody would look? Admittedly, Hollison was probably unaware of the route-assessment project she was working on with the ground operations supervisor; it was her involvement with the fuel-efficiency and delivery-time reporting that had drawn her attention to the delays this particular driver regularly faced.

"Base to Thirty-one, thanks for that, I'll pass it on to others in the area. I'll re-assign your two-thirty and two-forty-five pickups. If it's longer than that, let me know and I'll reassign your others." Lyn responded, and then Mic heard the woman calling other drivers in the area to avoid the I-10 where possible.

On screen, van #31 pulled into an industrial complex that was nowhere near the location the driver had given Lyn over the radio.

One of the roller doors slowly rose. Jenkins murmured instructions to his agents over the radio; all eyes were fixed on the dashcam feed. The van slowly edged through the warehouse roller door. The automatic headlight sensors of the van kicked in, and lit up the area directly in front of the van. Two men, heavily tattooed and wearing bandanas and grubby, white tank tops, moved forward. One slipped a pallet jack underneath a wooden pallet, jacked it up a little, and dragged it toward the van.

Jenkins murmured quickly into his radio, something about zooming in. Mic glanced over at the screen in front of one of the tech agents. From the viewpoint position, it looked like more agents were stationed across the street, set up for surveillance. The camera zoomed in to provide a clearer image of the warehouse door and the area visible just inside. She could clearly see the Eagle Express van, the license plate, and Adam Hollison as he came around to the rear of the van. She automatically noted his shirt was hanging out of his shorts, and looked decidedly wrinkled, and a little grubby. She had to quash her instinct to make a note for a meeting to discuss appearance and impressions with Mark Feinberg, the courier supervisor. This driver would not be getting another shift. Within seconds the bandana guys joined him, and they started to unload the large boxes in the back of the van directly on to the pallet.

Mic put the headphones down and folded her arms. Her fingernails bit into the flesh of her upper arms as she watched. Jenkins kept murmuring 'hold' into the radio but, admittedly, Mic's attention was focused on the screen, and not on the agent nearby.

They watched as the bandana guys packed the cartons onto the pallet, and then started to drag it back into the warehouse. Hollison pulled his scanner out of his belt holster and scanned a barcoded consignment note as the pallet passed him, then typed in some commands. He scribbled something on the screen, and Mic pursed her lips. He was even signing for the delivery himself, which went against so many internal procedures, it wasn't funny. Although if the guy was part of a MDMA smuggling ring, she shouldn't be surprised he wasn't following ethical delivery guidelines.

She frowned when Hollison strode around to the front of the vehicle, and the dashcam feed rocked as the driver climbed in. She glanced over at Jenkins. When were they going to make their move?

"Delivery accepted, *go, go, go*," Jenkins stated clearly into the radio, and her shoulders sagged. For a moment, she thought they weren't going to do anything, and that would mean this whole cloak-and-dagger situation had been for nothing. All the lying and subterfuge …

Tires squealed, and it took Mic a moment to realize the sound wasn't just coming from the screens, as agents pulled up to arrest her driver at the delivery site, but coming from the warehouse below as well. She turned to look at the screen-covered window. That activity wasn't on screen, it was happening right here, right downstairs. Shouts from down in the warehouse could be heard, and she frowned as she hurried across to the screen, pulling back the dark drape. Her eyes widened at the red-and-blue flashing lights of the unmarked cars that had driven into the warehouse. Three of them.

Agents spilled out of the vehicles, all wearing dark jackets with the letters 'FBI' emblazoned across the back. All of the operational activity abruptly stopped, and she saw her air operations supervisor, Luis Montenegro, step forward cautiously, a puzzled frown on his face. A van pulled up outside, blocking access into and out of the freight facility. Doors were flung open and more agents appeared, this time with dogs.

Mic's jaw dropped as two employees turned and bolted. They were chased by agents and tackled to the ground. She turned to face Jenkins, who shrugged.

"You didn't think this was just one driver acting on his own, did you?"

She blinked. She hadn't wanted to think more staff were involved … Jenkins turned toward the door, and Mic hurried after him.

"Wait—how did you know? What did they do?" She jogged along behind him as they made their way through the corridors toward the stairs and warehouse entry.

"They sorted freight and ensured certain parcels went through undetected."

She trotted down the stairs behind him and followed him out into the warehouse. "Are you sure they're involved?" She eyed the two men who were now being cuffed where they lay on the ground. They'd seemed so nice …

Jenkins nodded, then turned to her. "Yes, they're involved. Their bank accounts and spending habits suggest more than a one-off job." He held up a hand when she took another step forward. "Don't worry, Mic. You've been a great help, but we'll take it from here."

He turned back toward the warehouse, then hesitated. He looked at her over his shoulder, and grimaced. "Sorry, we're shutting down this operation while we get the dogs to search, in case there's more evidence."

Mic's eyes widened, then watched in horror when the agents waved her staff away from positions along the conveyor belts and freight chutes that snaked their way through the warehouse. It took a moment for her to lift her gaze from the conveyor belt that now stood stationary and silent, loads of freight waiting to be sorted and dispatched, to realize all of the staff were staring at her.

They'd heard the agent, she realized. They'd heard she'd helped him. She turned, then halted when she saw the figure who now stepped through the staff entry door from the main building into the warehouse.

Doug Danvers—and from the furious glare in his eyes as he stared at the unmoving freight, the Eagle Express CEO was not happy.

Her shoulders sagged. *Crap.*

# Chapter 1

"Hey, Mic, we're not going to make the cut-off."

Mic glanced up from the documents she was feeding through the scanner. The noise of the scanner and photocopier, as well as the data entry staff tapping furiously on keyboards, still didn't quite mask the noise from the warehouse beyond the office.

Two months since 'it' went down, and work was almost back to normal.

Almost.

Luis stood just inside the door, and she frowned as a forklift slowly trundled past behind him. The fork was moving way too slow.

She beckoned to Kelly, the data entry team leader, to take over the scanning. "These are nearly done, and the rest of the paperwork for Frankfurt is there," she said, pointing to the neat stacks of consignment notes and customs declarations on the large sorting desk. Other staff were pushing documents into pigeonholes, all marked with various destinations. Some of their customers were fully digital, and could complete their shipping notes and supporting paperwork online, but there were still a heck of a lot of customers who used hard copies—and airlines and customs preferred the printouts, just in case systems crashed. That way, the freight could still move out. And today, there was a lot of freight to move, and very little time to move it.

She strode over to the doorway and glanced out into the warehouse. Her lips firmed. Her guys were moving at about half the pace they usually did. Their subtle way of expressing their displeasure at the arrests of Adam Hollison, Jerry Pavlovich and Vito Garcia, she supposed.

Like she had any choice, damn it. Smuggling ecstasy was a crime, and if she found evidence of her staff doing that, she *had* to report it; she sure as hell wouldn't feel guilty about it. She could understand, though, that the staff here had been working together for years, and still doubted that their co-workers could be involved in such a racket.

But right now, she had other problems. Namely, getting approximately six tons of airfreight out of her warehouse and down to the airport in time for evening flights.

She checked her watch. They had thirty minutes, and way too many boxes were sitting on the conveyor belts waiting to be pushed and sorted. She had tried to hurry the staff along before but had met with some resistance. One of the guys had even flipped her the bird behind her back, and didn't realize she'd seen his reflection in the windows of the office at the end of the warehouse. It had taken quite an effort not to turn around and give him a dressing down.

She could understand her staff were angry, but they were directing their anger at the wrong person. Still, she knew she had to claw back some trust, and that was going to take patience and time. She glanced at her watch again. Patience, she could work with. Time, she didn't have any of.

She'd moved heaven and earth—and several tons of freight—to clear out their backlog so that only a skeleton staff would be needed to process the weekend freight while the rest of the company attended the annual retreat at the Deer Ridge Ranch about halfway between here and Big Bear Lake. When they got this freight away, they had enough time to clean up the warehouse for the weekend shift, and hit the showers before the bus arrived.

She dug her phone out of her trouser pocket and crossed over to the PA system. Sliding the phone into the digital speakers' dock, she loaded up one of her playlists and hit play.

The intricate guitar strumming of an AC/DC song blasted from the speakers around the warehouse, and she rolled up her shirt sleeves as several staff looked up in surprise. She strode over to the head of the main conveyor belt, clapping in time to the music. She noticed some of the staff exchanging looks, while others—mainly the younger guys—started to dip their head in time to the beat. She shoved some of the cartons along the belt, sending the runners reeling, and gradually the air ops crew started moving again.

"If we get this freight out in time, I'll make sure you all get a round of drinks at the retreat," she yelled. It was Friday, and perhaps they needed something to celebrate. Bring some light and fun back to their roles. She hoisted a box off the belt and walked it over to the AKE freight container. She ducked inside and handed the box to the team leader, Andy, then turned and walked back to the rollers.

Luis met her gaze from the other side of the belt, his lips pursed. "No heels in the workplace, Mic." The supervisor wasn't happy with her being on the warehouse floor. Well, tough. He could damn well get used to it.

She gave him a mock frown. "When have you seen me wear heels, Luis? I'm steel toes all the way, baby." She reached for another carton and dragged it down the roller bed. A large pair of hands grabbed it before she could lift it.

"Here, let me get that one."

She looked up as the deep bass timbre rolled over her ears, trying to ignore the spark of awareness at the sound. Green eyes met hers, with a polite smile of inquiry giving a curve to sexy lips.

Knox Jones, her new start. She'd hired him five weeks ago to replace Jerry. She should have known. The guy seemed to have a knack for always being nearby. She slapped her hand on top of the carton and smiled just as politely.

"No, it's fine, I've got this. You get the next one." If she wanted the guys to see her as one of the team, she had to do her own heavy lifting. She grunted a little as she lifted the parcel off the end of the conveyor. Good golly. This sucker was heavy, damn it.

His eyebrows rose a little, then he shrugged and lifted the next box as though it weighed much less than the forty pounds the consignment note on it indicated. She eyed the bulging biceps beneath the red Eagle Express polo shirt. For him, it probably didn't take much effort at all.

She lifted her chin and pasted a relaxed expression across her face as she lugged her own box toward the container, praying she could get it packed before she dropped it. Staff walked around her. Maybe Knox's efforts had spurred the others into action. Whether it was the music, the dangled carrot of post-shift drinks, or the new guy putting the others to shame, she didn't care. As long as her men got themselves into gear and cleared the freight without her having to give any of them a warning for not doing their job, she was happy.

The song transitioned into *Rescue Me* by Fontella Bass, and she heard one of the guys up on the conveyor cry out in surprise and satisfaction. By the end of the song, those in the warehouse were striding along to the beat. Luis even did a quick-step shuffle and turn as he handed the box he was carrying through to Andy inside the container. Mic hid her smile. Wait until they heard the rest of the playlist. She'd picked the songs with each of her staff in mind, but also with an ear to the bass and rhythm to promote activity. It was maybe unorthodox but, damn it, it worked.

Twenty-seven minutes later Mic stood at the roller doors, hands on her hips as she watched the tautliner truck pull out of the driveway on its way to LAX, with containers destined for Frankfurt, London and Sydney safely locked, loaded and dispatched.

Thank God.

She didn't know how Doug Danvers would react if they had missed the freight cut-offs at the customs clearance house. Now, hopefully, she wouldn't find out.

She exhaled, her cheeks puffing out. She glanced down at herself, and grimaced. *Note to self: don't wear white shirts to work. Just … don't.* She slid her hands around the waistband, tucking the blouse back into her navy trousers. She wasn't taking this outfit to the retreat. It was dusty and grimy. She might talk to Doug about a new standard of uniform for some of the operations leadership team, herself included. Something that carried through the Eagle Express colors, that was practical for both pushing freight in the warehouse and for greeting clients for walk-throughs or attending management meetings. Something that would make her look like, and her guys think that, she was part of the team.

She turned back to the warehouse. Music still blared from the speakers, and her staff were divided between doing the warehouse close routine, cleaning up after the busy day's freight movement, searching the warehouse for any parcels that may have slid off the belt, or under trays and chutes, while others were off to the showers before the coach arrived for their pickup. Her phone was still in the dock, blaring out music from a variety of artists. Her guys didn't seem to want to turn off the tunes.

She dipped her chin. She was hot, just a little sweaty, and due to spend an hour and a half on a coach. She needed a shower.

~*~

Knox eyed Michaela Robson as she stepped carefully down the metal stairs from her second-story office as the coach pulled into the wide driveway of Eagle Express. She was loaded up with her suitcase, laptop bag and a box. She'd showered, just like the rest of them, and now wore a pair of jeans and an oversized red top that dipped to reveal the smooth expanse of her shoulder and the strap of a white camisole beneath. When she reached the bottom of the stairs she pulled out the handle of her small, wheeled suitcase and hoisted the large box she was carrying to rest on her hip as she walked over to the group of people waiting to be picked up, her laptop bag bumping against her other hip with each step she walked in those steel-capped boots.

Her hair was still damp from her shower, pulled back into some sort of bun and anchored in place by two pencils.

His lips quirked as he walked toward her. He'd never seen her without the pencils in her hair. He'd thought she was wearing chopsticks like some weird new fashion trend the first time he'd met her, when she'd interviewed him for the role of freight handler. He'd learned since, though, that Michaela Robson was more than ready to sacrifice fashion for practicality.

He tried not to eye her up and down as she walked across the warehouse floor. Those jeans looked almost spray-painted on, yet the top draped over her body, hiding her curves. Modest, casual, but damn sexy.

And we'll just shut down that train of thought right there. She was the package. Not sexy. Well, sexy package. He blinked. Nope. Just package. Code name: Sparrow. He had to remember that.

"Would you like me to help you with that?" he asked politely as he approached from her side. She startled, her head whipping around. He pretended not to notice how jumpy she was. He gestured to both the box and the suitcase, and he glimpsed the strap of her laptop bag cutting across her chest, from shoulder to hip. He was pretty sure she hadn't intended it to draw attention to the soft curves of her breasts but, well, it did.

And his job as her undercover bodyguard was to notice things. He forced his gaze to her face.

She smiled, but it was only fleeting. A flash, and then it was gone.

"No, I've got this, thanks." She adjusted her grip on the box, settling it more comfortably on her hip—although it still didn't look at all comfortable. She'd loaded herself up like a packhorse.

"Are you sure—"

"Yep."

She strode past him. He shrugged as he adjusted the strap of his duffel bag on his shoulder. The woman was independent. He got it.

Mic brought her suitcase to a halt at the roller door, just as the passenger door to the coach opened. She reached into the box with her now free hand and pulled out a—good grief, a backpack? How many bags did one woman need? Knox watched as she turned to Luis. "I'll be back in a minute, I'm just going to drop this stuff in my car." She set her small, wheeled suitcase close to the baggage bay doors.

For a moment, Knox didn't think the man was going to acknowledge her, but the air operations supervisor finally nodded. Mic's tight smile broadened—she hadn't missed the man's reluctance to respond—and she walked out into the dark parking lot, carrying the box, the backpack and her laptop bag. Alone.

Oh, no, she didn't.

He scooted after her, and made sure she could hear him approaching so he didn't startle her again.

"Please, let me carry that," he told her, and managed to maneuver the box out of her hands before she could stop him. "It'll be quicker," he interjected when her mouth opened in protest.

She sighed. "Thanks." She slung the smaller backpack over her shoulder. He followed her down the row of parked cars toward the rear of the lot. She pulled her car keys out of the front pocket of her laptop bag, and he noticed her jingle them in her hand until she had three keys poking out between her curled fingers, like mini-daggers. He hid his frown. A rudimentary set of brass knuckles. Sparrow was definitely cautious.

"It's pretty dark out here," he observed, his frown deepening. All he could see were hiding places for potential threats, which was how he guessed the woman by his side also viewed the parking lot, judging by her improvised knuckle-dusters.

"Yeah, one of the lights has blown," she said, pointing to a dark pole in the far corner. The keys in her hand jangled with the movement. "I've put in a request to the facilities manager for a replacement. Should happen next week."

He glanced about casually. "Which one is yours?" he asked, as though he hadn't been following her to and from work every day since he'd started working at the company.

She slowed, lifting her hand to point at the silver two-door Jeep Wrangler. "Right he—"

They both halted when they saw her car. A puddle of liquid and gory matter sat on the hood, and he could smell the metallic stench of blood, the rot of gore. Guts—he couldn't tell from what creature—had been dumped on her car. A sheet of paper was held in place under the windscreen wiper. Knox's lips tightened when he read it.

BITCH SNICH was scrawled diagonally in large letters across the paper in red marker.

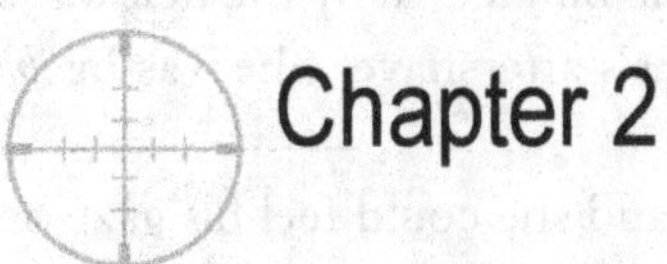# Chapter 2

Mic felt the breath freeze in her chest. Again. It had happened again. She swallowed noisily as she looked at the mess on her car. It looked like something—or someone—had been gutted on the hood of her car.

She glanced around the darkened parking lot. So many hiding places. Was the person who did this still here, lurking, watching, maybe even waiting for her? She wasn't about to admit it openly, but she was grateful for Knox's presence. She clenched her teeth. Damn it. She wasn't going to let this frighten her. She shouldn't have to be grateful for a man's company when going to her car in the parking lot. She shouldn't have to glance furtively over her shoulder to see if someone was there—that implied she was scared, and she wasn't going to let these folks scare her.

She depressed the button on her keychain to unlock the car, and opened the door, then folded the front passenger seat forward. She shoved aside the gym bag she'd used earlier that morning, and dropped her backpack with her clothes she'd just changed out of into the floor space behind the driver's seat. She turned to Knox, who still carried her box of manifests and shipping volume reports.

"If you could please put that on the back seat, I'd appreciate it." She was taking her laptop bag with her. She had some work to complete for the retreat, anyway, and she still had to finish the slide presentation before her company address the following morning.

She stepped back to allow Knox access to the vehicle, but she was still close enough to catch a whiff of his aftershave—something woodsy and subtle, with maybe a hint of something citrusy—Mic blinked. Why the hell was she trying to decipher Knox Jones's aftershave? She was his *boss*, for crying out loud.

He stepped back, and she could feel his gaze on her as she closed the door and locked the vehicle. She avoided meeting his gaze, but lifted her chin to stare at the mess on the hood. *Ugh*. It was really, really gross.

Knox glanced about. "I know there's a hose here somewhere…" He snapped his fingers when he saw the coiled hose in the garden bed that ringed the parking lot. He strode over, uncoiled the hose and leaned over to turn on the tap. Mic looked at her car, and that blasted, fluttering note caught her gaze. She reached over and carefully plucked it from beneath the windscreen wiper. It must have been added after the mess, as there were no stains from the gore on her hood.

Knox tested the hose's attachment, directing it into the flower bed. When he was satisfied with the spray, he turned to her car, and Mic stood back as he washed the mess off her hood. He then used the force of the water to direct the mess into the grate that lay across the edge of the parking lot. Mic glanced behind her toward the coach. Some staff had already boarded the bus, but the rest were still on the other side, oblivious to what had happened to her car. Her lips tightened. No, that was wrong. At least one person on the bus knew exactly what she'd find when she went to her car.

She'd been out to her car during a late afternoon lunch break, ostensibly to check if she'd left her wallet in there, but really to avoid making it obvious that she sat alone in the break room most days when she ate at work. Her car had been fine, then. No, this had happened after the morning shift had departed for the resort, and after the afternoon shift had commenced. Someone she worked with had done this to her, to her car.

She grimaced. What if she hadn't gone to her car, but just left her clothes and reports in the office? Two days of that fetid putrescence on her car would not only wreck the paint job, but it would be caked on and require—*ugh*. She shuddered at the thought of getting up there and scraping that mess off.

Knox was being quite thorough, though. He leaned down so that his eyes were on level with the hood of her car to make sure he'd gotten the last of the gore. Apparently he had, because he switched off the hose and started to loop it back through his hands as he walked over to the tap. She noticed that he didn't ask any questions. She didn't know if she should feel relieved at not having to answer uncomfortable questions, or embarrassed as he didn't seem too surprised people called her a snitch—sorry, snich.

The horn of the coach blasted. Two short toots to rally the stragglers. She took a deep breath and tried to think past the clench of muscles in her gut. She had to get in there, and travel for an hour and a half until the staff reached the resort for this weekend's retreat.

Ninety minutes, stuck on a bus, with someone who was waging a war of intimidation and fear against her. And then a weekend with said person.

She lifted her chin. Well, she was a Robson. She didn't scare easily.

Knox gestured to the note in her hand as they walked back toward the waiting coach. "Want me to get rid of that for you?" His voice was deep, gentle. She knew that he, at least, hadn't worked at the company when the bust had gone down, and probably wasn't involved in the series of incidents that had been plaguing her ever since.

Unless he was connected somehow to the guys who had been arrested, and had applied for the job just to screw with her mentally on behalf of his friends and cohorts. The FBI had hinted that there may be others involved … Her lips tightened. Okay, now she was being paranoid.

She smiled tightly and shook her head. "Nope, but thanks." Her hand clenched around the piece of paper as she walked around the front of the bus. The driver was closing the baggage bays. God, she hoped Luis had made sure her bag had been packed into the bus, and hadn't tossed it back in the warehouse out of spite. It would be a petty thing to do, but after what she'd seen on her car, she wouldn't put that kind of behavior past anyone; at least, not until she figured out who was behind this campaign of threats. It didn't matter, and it wouldn't matter—she'd still be testifying at the trial, damn it.

She climbed up the steps of the coach and halted on the driver's platform. The afternoon teams—both those who worked in the operations area as well as those who performed the data entry and administrative tasks inside the office, were making themselves comfortable and exchanging light-hearted banter as they settled in for the ride. She cleared her throat.

The noise continued. She could feel a presence behind her, and she didn't need to turn to know it was Knox Jones at her back. She didn't want to question why she could sense the man, or the impression of reassurance, of support that she felt.

"Can I have your attention, please," she called out. Again, the talking didn't stop, but she saw Kelly, her data entry team leader, give her a tentative, curious glance before she was dragged back into conversation with a colleague.

Hurt speared her, and just a little embarrassment at their casual disregard. But that's what this was all about. Notes, late night heavy-breathing phone calls, nasty little deliveries. She got the message: they didn't like her tattling on their friends. Well, it was time she delivered her own message. Okay, then. Mic took a calming breath, placed two fingers in her mouth and blew a long, ear-piercing whistle. The conversations stopped abruptly, and everyone turned their attention to her. Mic smiled to cover her nerves, her wariness—her unease. But she wasn't going to hide this anymore.

"I just wanted to thank you for the note that was left on my car. Truly, it was a lovely surprise," she said, smiling brightly. Yes, she was being passive-aggressive, but she needed to hit just the right tone. She held up the note to everyone, and she didn't miss the gasps, and Kelly's eyes rounding at the offensive note. "But, if I may point out—*snitch* is actually spelled with a T, much like bitch," she said, pointing to each word. "See? This needs a T." She turned and faced the bus again. "For next time."

Because this had been going on since the arrests, and she was fairly certain there would be a next time—at least, until the trials were done, and a verdict was in. She scrunched up the paper and shoved it into the bus bin at the front, then walked down the aisle, everyone now silent and glancing at each other in shock. Sadly, she couldn't trust that their reactions were honest ones. She found a vacant bay of seats and slid in, taking the seat near the window. She took a deep breath. Okay, so she did feel better after that.

She kept her gaze fixed out the window, and tried to ignore Knox as he took the seat in front of hers. She tried not to stare at the back of his neck, or at the way his short hair was getting just long enough on top, and was now damp enough, to tighten into springy brown curls. Nope. Wasn't going to stare.

She glanced back at the co-workers still staring at her. She made direct eye contact until they dropped their gazes. Shock and hurt were giving way to anger, and she didn't want to do or say anything that could cause irreparable damage with her staff. She didn't know who was involved, or how many— there could be more than one. But not everyone was involved, and she didn't want to ruin her working relationship with those who weren't part of this ... conspiracy of horror. She rolled her lips inward. She wanted things to work out here, at Eagle Express. She wanted to prove that *she* was right, and not her father, that she *could* do the job, that she was good at what she did—no, damn it, she was excellent. That she *was* suited to this role, to this company. But right now, someone was leaving notes, someone was calling her in the middle of the night, multiple times, and someone was trying to scare her out of her job.

She was determined not to give 'someone'—or her father—the satisfaction of caving in, either by withdrawing from testifying at trial, or by leaving the company altogether, her tail between her legs. She sighed. Maybe this weekend was exactly what was needed, for all of them. Some team-building exercises, some honest and frank discussions … really, with the whole company there, what's the worst that could happen?

She turned to the aisle, and noticed Aidan Cleary, the youngest employee on her team, staring at her warily. Mic smiled. "Hey, Aidan, how's it going?"

~*~

Knox shouldered his duffel bag and followed the tired group into the reception area of the hotel. Eagle Express CEO, Doug Danvers, was just inside, greeting each employee as they entered.

"The rest of the company is already here, so once you've checked in, you have the choice of coming down to the bar for a quick meet and greet, or turning in early. We have the bar until midnight." Danvers smiled at the cheers of the staff, and held up a hand. "Just remember, play up, show up. Have a great time tonight, but not too great that you can't participate in the real reason we're here. First session starts at eight-thirty tomorrow morning, and breakfast is served from seven a.m. in the restaurant."

Danvers led everyone over to the group check-in area, and stood back as hotel staff greeted the Eagle Express employees.

Knox eyed his surroundings briefly, and made the same shocked-but-pleased reaction the other employees were presenting at the understated luxury of the ranch-style resort. Amber Simpson, an intelligence officer at SafeKeepers Inc, had done a reconnaissance, and called it 'western lux'—whatever that meant. He could see lots of timber and glass, as well as marble tiles and polished brass trim. Western-style blankets hung on the walls and were strategically placed on the floors throughout the foyer and accompanying lounge. Some Eagle Express staff were already clustered in small groups in the lounge area, some sitting in the thickly cushioned brown leather lounges and armchairs. A massive stone fireplace took up nearly one entire wall, flames flickering cheerily to ward off some of the Californian autumn night chill—such as it was. Knox had already gone over schematics and aerial satellite imagery to assess threats and risks with other SafeKeepers staff. While he was just arriving, he knew he was probably the last of the SafeKeepers team to turn up, all of them ready to monitor the package.

A package who had managed to shame most of her staff with a seemingly casual comment. He'd seen the looks cast by the operations and office teams. Some had been stunned, some had been embarrassed—and a couple had been outraged. He eyed Luis, and Eddie Guyer, another freight handler. Both had made it very obvious during shift breaks how they felt about their boss. He wouldn't put it past either of them to have put that note—and the entrails—on Mic's car.

The queue at the reception desk shifted, and he took a couple of steps closer. Mic stood ahead of him in the line, separated by two more people. She was chatting casually to Kelly, a woman he'd learned had a good sense of humor—once she felt comfortable enough to share it with you. Until then she was happy to bust you down to size if you gave your job less than your full attention, thus making her job harder to do.

Mic stepped up to the reception desk and gave her name to the clerk.

"Ah, Ms. Robson." The clerk quickly tapped into the keyboard below the desk level and eyed the screen. "Here you are. You have room 212, on the second floor."

"And my roommate?" Mic asked as she accepted the room keycard the clerk held out to her.

Knox tried not to look like he was listening intently.

The clerk smiled. "Good news. You have the room to yourself."

Mic frowned. "Really? We're supposed to be sharing rooms ..."

Danvers approached the desk with a smile. "Ah, some of the executives have individual rooms, Michaela. In case we need to hold some impromptu meetings and such."

Mic smiled tightly and stepped aside, and Kelly strode up to the desk.

Knox tilted his head, as though stretching, and not really eavesdropping on Mic and Danvers as they passed.

"I thought we were reducing costs by sharing rooms," Michaela murmured to her boss. "Wasn't there some mention of using shared accommodation as another team-engagement opportunity?" She tugged her rolling suitcase behind her as she stepped beyond the queue and in the direction of the elevators.

Danvers pasted a smile on his face. "Yes, but we had some odd numbers, and ..." Danvers hesitated, then glanced over his shoulder toward the others. Knox kept his gaze on the exposed timber beams in the cathedral ceiling. "Some of the staff were reluctant to share a room with the operations manager," the CEO said to Mic in a hushed voice.

Knox's gaze slide to Michaela's face and he saw her blanch, then nod. "I see," she said in a low voice.

"I'm truly sorry, Michaela," Danvers said as he pressed the button on the lifts. He gave her a reassuring smile. "Don't worry. We just need to give it some time."

Michaela nodded. "Oh, yeah, of course. No, I understand." She waved a hand in casual dismissal as the elevator doors slid open, and she stepped inside.

"Will I see you down at the bar?" Danvers asked as the doors started to slide closed.

Michaela smiled. "Yes. I promised the afternoon shift that the first round of drinks was on me. I won't stay long, though. I need to finish my presentation."

Danvers gave a half wave as the elevator doors shut.

"Sir?"

Knox turned around to find the reservations clerk smiling at him expectantly. He stepped closer to the desk and gave her his cover name. He waited. SafeKeepers' tech wiz, Smithy Johnson—and yes, everyone at SafeKeepers knew it wasn't his real name, but Smithy had managed to obliterate any digital record of himself, and so they just accepted his newly created identity—had checked in earlier and gained access to the resort's systems. If Smithy was any good at his job, Knox should be—

"You're in Room 214, Mr. Jones. Second floor." The clerk smiled brightly as she handed him his room card. Knox smiled. Next door to the package. Yep, Smithy was good at his job.

"Thanks." He didn't bother to ask about a roommate. He started to walk toward the elevators, but halted when Danvers waved at him.

"You're new here, aren't you?" Danvers said, smiling warmly.

Knox nodded. "Yes, sir. I started five weeks ago."

Danvers eyed him narrowly. "Jones, right?"

"Knox Jones," Knox said, holding out his hand. Danvers shook it, and Knox noted how tight the man's grip was. He'd met enough men in suits to know some viewed the handshake as some sort of pissing contest. He normally didn't bother to engage, but after seeing the kind of culture that was bred here at Eagle Express, he decided to exert a little pressure of his own in return. He saw a flicker of surprise in Danvers' eyes, then curious assessment.

"Why don't you come to the bar and I'll buy you a drink?"

Knox jerked his thumb over toward the elevators. "Uh, I was thinking of taking my bag up to my room." *And check in on Sparrow.*

Danvers waved over a bellhop. "This guy can take your bag up, that's fine. No, come to the bar. Let me introduce you to some of the staff. It must be a little daunting, being a new start and attending one of these company kickoff events."

A figure moved in Knox's peripheral vision, and he glanced briefly in that direction. Dan Demetre, a SafeKeepers agent, was bearing a tray of glasses and napkins toward the bar, and gave Knox an infinitesimal nod.

Knox smiled at Danvers. "Sure, why not?" It would give him a chance to touch base with his colleague. He handed his duffel bag to the bellhop and turned to follow the Eagle Express CEO into the bar.

It took about ten minutes of nodding, shaking hands, and multiple introductions, accompanied with desultory chit-chat, before Knox finally made it to the bar by himself. Dan was waiting for him. The dark-haired guy grinned at the group of ladies he was flirting with before making his way over to Knox.

"Well, aren't you Mr. Popular," Dan commented as he slapped a coaster down on the bar and placed a glass filled with dark liquid on it. Knox raised an eyebrow at the women who now followed Dan with eyes full of invitation, then shook his head. The guy really was a Casanova. Knox sipped, then grimaced. Coke, without the bourbon.

"Seriously?" He eyed the bottles of spirits on the shelves behind his friend. Dan smiled brightly.

"You're still working, you know that, right?" Dan grinned.

"I know. Speaking of which …" Knox fished the scrunched-up paper out of his jeans pocket and dropped it casually on the bar. Dan grabbed an unused trash bag from beneath the sink and used a cloth to 'wipe' the wad of paper off the bar and into the bag. "That was on Sparrow's car tonight when she went out to the parking lot." He grimaced. "Along with what looked like pig intestines."

Dan arched an eyebrow. "Well, that's charming."

"I want it checked for prints. I've handled it, as has Sparrow, but hopefully we can get something from it." They already had Mic's prints on file, and his, and could quickly dismiss those.

"How did Sparrow take it?"

Knox took a sip of his drink. "She was … surprised." He grimaced. "Then she proceeded to give the team a spelling lesson."

Dan shot him a curious look, and Knox shrugged. "You'll understand when you read it."

"Okay, then." Dan stepped away to serve someone further down the bar—Penny? Patricia? Knox knew she worked in accounts, but couldn't quite remember her name. The woman smiled tentatively at Knox, then gave her order to Dan.

In less than a minute Dan had the woman smiling at him instead, as he served her drink with a remark that made the woman blush and tuck her hair behind her ear. Her smile broadened into a grin, and Dan gave her a saucy wink as she stepped away from the bar.

Knox shook his head as his colleague approached. "You're terrible." His friend had the dark good looks of his Greek father, with the blue eyes of his American mother, and used them to his advantage.

"Hey, I'm working here," Dan protested innocently, then waggled his fingers as the woman turned to look back at the bar in general, and him in particular. "So, where were we?" He snapped his fingers. "Oh, right. Smithy is in, hooked into the security and surveillance systems—he says this hotel's location means internet connectivity and cell coverage sucks, and some areas don't have any coverage at all, by the way—"

"Don't care."

"Me neither, but it apparently matters to our friend. Fitz is here as part of the team-building staff, so you'll see him tomorrow afternoon, and Smithy's hacked into Danvers' assistant's schedule for the weekend and made sure you're with the package for each activity block."

"Good. Anyone else?"

"Nope. Walker reckons four of us covering the package this weekend should be plenty," Dan said, referring to their boss, Jesse Walker.

Knox nodded. He agreed with SafeKeepers Inc's president. If the worst they had to deal with was some poorly written notes, then four SafeKeepers operatives were probably overkill. Mic would be their safest package yet. His mission was to get Michaela Robson safely to trial, and so far the operation was, well, easy.

Dan eyed the bar area and shook his head. "Why doesn't Walker ever do one of these events for us?"

Knox turned back to survey the lounge area. It looked like the Eagle Express employees who'd arrived late-afternoon had spent most of that time in the bar, and the chattering was gradually increasing in decibels.

"This is a company kickoff, Demetre. Walker doesn't do the kickoff, he kicks ass." Knox wasn't altogether sure this wasn't just an excuse for staff to get drunk in a tax write-off, but he wasn't one to judge. No, he was just here to watch his package.

A figure moved on the fringe, and his eyes narrowed. Speaking of …

Mic stood at the entrance to the bar. Silence rolled over the crowd like a tsunami, and her eyebrows rose slightly at the cloud of tension that arose at her appearance. Luis Montenegro was closest to her, and turned to face her, his feet planted as though to bar her entry.

Chapter 3

Knox watched as Mic took purposeful steps toward Luis, her gaze level. The man was forced to shift, otherwise face the risk of being walked on—and she was still wearing her steel-toed boots. The supervisor gave her a dark look, and Mic lifted her chin as she walked through the crowd, stopping occasionally to speak to her co-workers. She didn't stop for long, and it took Knox a moment to notice that she moved fluidly past people as they were turning their backs on her. It was very subtle, and she had a smile and a relaxed expression on her face, but the brief flash of hurt in her eyes, the slightest tightening of her lips … she was moving on before they had a chance to turn their backs on her. She read the room, read the people, and adapted so quickly, so casually, that many were left frustrated that their cold shoulders couldn't quite get delivered.

The growing decibels from moments before had dropped like a stone in a pond, and now there were whispers and hushed conversations as the large group eyed the operations manager in their midst.

Her eyebrows rose when she saw Knox at the bar, and she smiled at him briefly, politely, before turning to Dan. Her smile broadened when the bartender winked at her, and Knox shot him a dark look as she turned back to the crowd.

"It seems a little quiet in here," she called out airily. "Hardly the way to start off the weekend. I made a promise back at the depot to my team for getting the job done, and I'm here to deliver. Come on, guys, line up!" She turned to

Dan, whose eyebrows rose at the crowd who now cheered and moved as though in a wave to the bar. "Do you need a hand with this lot?"

Dan shook his head and grinned at Mic. "Nah, I'm good. I'll set you up first. What can I get you?"

"I'll take a Manhattan, thanks," Mic said, and she stepped aside to allow more room at the bar, her movement bringing her closer to Knox.

"I thought you had to do a report," he commented as she accepted the tumbler glass from Dan.

She shot him a surprised glance, and he gestured toward Danvers, who was watching the crowd from the entrance to the lounge. "I overheard you talking with the boss."

She nodded, then took a long sip from her glass. "Yep, but I wanted to hang out for a little. I'll head up shortly."

He didn't miss the determined glint in her eye, the slight tightening of her lips as she surveyed the crowd. It had been important to her to be here, in front of everyone. To show she wasn't cowed? That no nasty little note on her windscreen would stop her?

She turned as someone called her name. One of the couriers … what was his name? Pedro? The man lifted his beer and grinned at her in thanks. In minutes she made her way through the throng, and this time most of the staff smiled at her, nodded, and even stopped to talk. In just a little bit longer she was surrounded by a small group of couriers, and had them laughing as she shared a joke with them.

Knox had to retreat a little as more people gathered at the bar. He shook his head. She was good. The noise of the crowd was starting to creep up, and people were definitely more relaxed than when she'd first entered the bar. He heard a soft whistle, and turned. Dan held another Manhattan in a tumbler toward him, then jerked his chin in Mic's direction. Knox nodded, and accepted the excuse to get closer to their package. Not that he expected anything to happen, but, well, alcohol and anonymous enmity never mixed well.

~*~

An hour later Mic leaned forward to press the button to call an elevator.

"Leaving so soon?"

She whirled at the deep voice near her ear, heart hammering, and Knox held up his hands, eyebrows raised.

"Whoa, sorry, I didn't mean to startle you."

"Oh, my God," Mic exclaimed softly, clutching her chest. Her heart beat so fast. "Why do you keep doing that to me?" She swallowed, trying to calm herself. She swatted him gently on the arm, then had to curl her fingers into a tight little fist. His arm had felt firm. Strong. Wonderful. She wanted to swat at him again. And not just his arm.

"I don't mean to," Knox protested. "We're in the lobby of a hotel, for crying out loud. Why wouldn't you expect people around you?"

"I wasn't—I just—" she took a deep breath and exhaled slowly. "Sorry." He was right. She should expect to have people around her here, who would occasionally speak to her. She'd gotten so used to everyone trying to avoid her, it was a surprise to turn around and find him there. And it annoyed her that she was so damned spooked.

The elevator doors opened, and they waited for guests to exit before stepping inside.

"You know, you're beginning to give me a complex," Knox murmured as he stepped inside the elevator. "Thank God not all women freak out when I'm near them."

She could appreciate that 'freaking out' wasn't the usual reaction women had with him. She eyed his frame. Tall. Muscled. Gorgeous. Yeah. She could think of way better reactions. "I didn't freak out," she muttered. She eyed the panel. He hadn't pressed anything. She reached forward and pressed the button for the second floor. "You just …
surprised me."

He winced. "Not sure if that's any better." He turned to face her, and Mic's eyes widened slightly. He was so … big. Broad. Her gaze flicked between the expanse of his shoulders and the floor indicator above the doors as the elevator started to climb. He braced his hands on the rail that ran around the elevator at waist height. The move seemed to emphasize the broadness of his shoulders, and the narrowness of his hips.

He looked at her in inquiry. "You're not staying longer in the bar? I thought that was the purpose of this team-building weekend, all that face time, all that social networking among staff …?"

She shrugged. "I have some work to do." God, this elevator was taking forever, and she was trying not to drool all over her employee.

He tilted his head to the side, and she became supremely conscious of his intent stare. He was silent for a moment, and she looked up at him.

"You work too much," he told her quietly.

Her eyes widened. "Sorry?" The look he gave her was so serious, so focused.

Knox folded his arms, and for a moment she was distracted by the bulge of muscle beneath the soft fabric of his long-sleeved T-shirt. It was a pale gray-green V-necked top, and the color of the fabric seemed to highlight his green eyes. Her gaze dropped back to the biceps that stretched the fabric, just ever so slightly, and her hand rose. That fabric looked so soft.

Oh. Dear. God. She hastily smoothed a loose tendril of hair behind her ear to cover her slip. She'd been about to touch him. She was seriously reaching out to touch the man's arm, pat him like a soft kitty and purr all over him. An employee. Good golly.

She cleared her throat. They'd been talking. "What did you say?"

"You work too much," he repeated. Calmly, quietly—as though completely oblivious to her fascination with him.

Thank God. "You're the first one into the office, and the last one to leave …"

She frowned. "What, are you keeping tabs on me?" For a moment her brain halted, not knowing whether to be creeped out by a potential stalker, or secretly pleased a good-looking man paid attention to her.

His lips quirked, and he reached out to brace his hand against the wall of the elevator. She stared at his arm. The cloth clung to him like a second skin, gliding over the dip between bicep muscle and elbow. *Secretly pleased it is, then.*

And she was staring at his arm. She blinked rapidly, and forced her gaze away from that strong, muscular limb.

"No, not keeping tabs." He shrugged, and she watched the drag of cloth over his broad chest, noticing the line between his pectoral muscles. Man, what would he look like, shirtless? "People talk."

Her gaze dropped at his remark. She just bet they did. "Uh, well, I can't control what people say about me …" She didn't even want to contemplate what kind of conversations went on behind her back at the moment. Her mouth turned down at the corners. She didn't want to think what Knox had heard about her, what he might think of her … and then didn't know why it mattered.

The soft ding heralded their arrival to the second floor, and the doors slid open.

"It's not all bad," he told her quietly.

She smiled as she stepped out of the elevator. "Liar." She walked down the hallway, her shoes silent on the plush carpet. "But thanks for trying."

She could sense him following behind her, and she glanced briefly over her shoulder. Yep, he was following her. She started to slow as she approached her room, and he slowed, as well. She swallowed. Oh, dear. Had she given him mixed signals? She'd tried to be utterly professional around the man, but, well, damn, he was gorgeous and sexy, and it was really hard not to stare at his body. Or salivate. This wasn't something she'd expected. In all of her horrific visions of this weekend, it had been about her being alone, about trying to find someone to talk to—not having to fend off unwanted advances from an employee.

She ignored the little voice that was whispering any advances from Knox Jones would be oh, so very much wanted.

"Uh, I'm fine," she told him over her shoulder.

His eyebrows rose. "Good to know."

She took another step closer to her door. "Uh, I mean, I'll see you tomorrow morning." She didn't think she could get any plainer than that.

He nodded, although the look he gave her was a little confused. She halted at her door, and he took one step past her, then paused.

Oh, God, this was getting awkward.

"Uh, look, you're very nice," she started tentatively, and tried not to wince. Nice? *Nice?* The guy was smoking hot. "But you and I—" she gestured between them, "we can't— I mean, I'm sure it would be good," *great*, really, "but we, uh …"

Knox's brows rose, and he folded his arms—oh, God, those arms, and he tilted his head to the side as he waited for her to finish what she was saying.

Like she could remember how to frame a proper sentence.

"We can't," she said simply, and smiled apologetically. "It wouldn't be appropriate." The last came out in a choked whisper.

Knox dipped his chin, then pursed his lips. Great. Now she was staring at his lips. "Uh, this is my room," he said, and leaned his shoulder against the door.

Mic blinked. "What?"

"214. That's my room." He frowned. "Wait," he said, straightening. "You didn't think I—" his hand gestured between him and her, "that we—"

She tried to laugh casually, but winced when she sounded more like a hyena on helium. "Oh, no," she said, waving dismissively. "What? No." She wanted to die. *How. Very. Embarrassing.* "Uh," she chuckled, or tried to, but the mortifying lump in her throat made her gag briefly. "Nope, just kidding around with you." She forced her lips into a broad smile, and he blanched, just a little. She realized she must look like The Joker, grinning maniacally. She tried to tone it down a little. "Heh, heh. Nope. Wow. So, you're in 214, huh?" She gestured to her door. "I'm here. 212."

He nodded. "So, I see." He held the keycard against his room lock, and there was a faint click as the lock disengaged. Yep, that was definitely his room.

She gestured to her still-closed door. "I should … go." *And die quietly inside my room.* She pulled her room keycard from her back pocket, and lifted it toward the door.

"Oh, uh, Mic …?"

She turned toward him, and realized he'd taken a step closer. Her gaze dropped to that visible line separating his pectoral muscles beneath that soft, smooth shirt. "Yes?" *Stop staring at his chest. Stop staring at his chest.* She lifted her gaze toward his eyes, but found herself distracted by his lips. *Oh, God. Seriously?*

"You don't mind me calling you Mic, do you?"

Had he meant that to sound sexy? Because, watching the words coming out of those lips, they sounded sexy. All low and husky and rumbly. Did she mind? What?

"Uh, no." He could call her anything he wanted. She'd answer to—she blinked. Boss. He was staff. And she was being a not very good boss at all. She was being a naughty boss. Bad boss. She forced herself to meet his eyes. His green gaze was intent, his expression so … focused.

On her. She swallowed.

"You're right about one thing," he said in a low voice, and braced his hand on the door, just above and to the side of her head. He leaned closer, and again that scent of his caught her attention. It was warm and rich, without being overpowering. Sandalwood, with that hint of moss and citrus, curling toward her like sneaky, seductive threads, ready to entangle her in the temptation of him. She eyed that broad chest, so close to her now she could easily reach out and touch, caress—she cleared her throat.

"I a—I am?"

"Uh-huh." He nodded, but that just made it seem like his head was lower. Closer. If she so much as inhaled, they'd have lip-to-lip contact. Her eyes widened slightly, her gaze fixed on his lips. She might have even puckered up a little.

"What—what was I right about?" she asked, the words coming out as a rasp.

"We would be really, *really* good," he said, drawing the words out as he dipped his head to the side. His breath gusted against her bare shoulder, and she shuddered. *Holy Miss Moley.*

"Oh …?" She caught her bottom lip between her teeth. Heat bloomed everywhere. Her cheeks, her chest, and spreading out from between her legs. Soooo warm.

He nodded, and she closed her eyes when she felt him exhale against her neck. "Yeah. Really good." He stepped away, hesitated, then stepped right back up to her again. "Oh, and I can be very, *very* inappropriate," he murmured huskily. Her eyes flickered open, and he drew back to meet her gaze.

"Huh." She blinked. "That's two things," she whispered.

His lips curved, and he winked, then stepped away. He didn't drop her gaze though, but pushed open his room door. *Very*, he mouthed again as he stepped inside his room, and the door closed with a quiet snick.

Mic's shoulders sagged against her door. *Good golly, Miss Molly.* That man was dangerous. She swallowed, then fanned herself with her keycard. Phew. Dangerous. Hot. Sexy as all hell. She took a deep, calming breath. And he worked for her.

She turned to press the card against the lock. He could be as inappropriate as he liked, but she could never find out how very inappropriate that was. He worked for her, she was his boss, and that was where things would stay. She already had enough talk going on behind her back. She didn't need gossip linking her with an office affair.

Damn it.

She stepped inside her room and closed the door behind her. *Close the door. Yep. Close that door and shut it tight.* Because opening that door, and then opening the door next to hers— well, that would lead to all sorts of mistakes and drama.

And a whole lot of fun. Sexy, wicked fun.

She shook her head as she tossed her room keycard onto the dressing table. What a crying shame. Her hands grasped the hem of her top and she lifted it up over her head as she walked around the side of the bed toward the table lamp.

A body slammed into hers, forcing her back onto her bed, her wrists above her head. Blinded, the red top still covering her face, she tried to struggle, kicking out with her feet. She opened her mouth to scream, but a fistful of material was shoved inside, preventing anything more than a muffled cry from escaping.

All she could see was red. Darkening red. Whoever it was straddled her body, and jerked her arms out of the sleeves and down by her sides. She cried out in pain when knees pressed into her forearms, pinning her to the bed. She heard a faint rip. She tried to fight, bucking and twisting and flailing out with her feet. The material blocked her mouth and nose, and a hand pressed hard against her lips. *Can't breathe!* Her eyes widened as her assailant's other hand squeezed at her throat. *Can't breathe!*

She tried to scream again, but she couldn't push any sound past the hand pressing against her throat. Her vision began to gray at the edges. Her legs moved as though pushing through sludge. Her foot caught the harder frame of the lamp table. She heard a crash.

Tears filled her eyes as she struggled for oxygen. *I'm dying.*

# Chapter 4

Knox stood next to his bed, head tilted to the side. Was that a thud? After a moment he pulled his wallet and phone from his jeans pockets and placed them on the desk in the room. Must have been his imagination.

He pulled his shirt over his head then flopped down on the bed. Fitz and Smithy would swing by as soon as Dan could step away from his undercover bartending duties. He closed his eyes for a moment, but frowned when he thought he heard a faint cry. He sat up on the bed, and leaned closer to the wall. Mic had probably turned on the television.

Something thudded against the wall, and then he heard a crash, like glass or ceramic breaking.

He swept up his phone as he bolted out of his room. He tried the handle on Mic's door, but it was locked. Damn it. He typed a dial code into his phone.

"Yeah?" Smithy's answer was immediate, his tone bored.

"Open Mic's door," Knox ordered, rattling the handle. The small light turned from red to green, and Knox shouldered open the door. His eyes widened when he heard the soft, muffled sob, the harsh grunt. He ran past the bathroom wall and door. A masked man was holding Mic down, her red top over her head, one hand covering her mouth, the other hand pressing down on her throat.

Red-hot rage rose within him, along with that anxiety, that dread that maybe he was too late. Again. *Kayleigh* …

Knox launched himself at the intruder. "Get off her," he yelled, tackling the man across the bed. The man twisted, rolled, and they both fell off the edge of the bed. Knox landed on the floor, beneath the intruder.

Knox grunted when he felt a fist punch him in his stomach. He brought his elbow up and over, smashing the masked man in the jaw, before twisting his wrist and punching with the back of his hand.

His opponent jerked back, giving Knox enough room to shove at the man's chest, which allowed him to bring his legs up. He kicked with both feet, and the intruder fell back against the wall, his arm knocking a painting off the wall.

Knox rose to his feet, and the man launched himself forward, hunched slightly, and caught Knox in the sternum with his shoulder. Knox was propelled back against the bedside table.

Knox raised his elbow and brought it down hard on the intruder's shoulder, then jerked his knee up into the man's stomach.

He heard the man wheeze, and shoved him away. Bringing his fists up, Knox readied himself in a defensive pose, ready to punch.

The intruder lurched back toward the balcony door, slid it open roughly, and ran out.

Knox chased him. The intruder braced one hand on the balcony rail, and tried to jump, but his foot clipped the rail. He let out a strangled scream that ended suddenly in a clatter and a sickening thud below. Knox ran through the doorway and braced his hands on the railing, glancing down.

The intruder had landed on a set of table and chairs on the terrace below, and from the angle of the man's neck, Knox decided he was no longer a threat to anyone. *Ouch.*

A stream of light spread across the grass as a door on the lower floor opened, and Knox watched as his SafeKeepers colleague, Fitz, stepped out onto the terrace. His shoulders sagged. Smithy must have alerted him. Fitz looked at the very dead body on the ground, then up at Knox, and shook his head.

Knox turned back to the room. He needed to secure the package.

~*~

Mic blinked at the little penlight the doctor flashed into her eyes. He smiled apologetically, then gently examined her neck. She eyed the other men in the room.

Her hotel room wasn't tiny—it had a luxurious queen-sized bed, a desk built into the wall below an impressive TV screen, and two large armchairs and a table between the bed and the sliding door that led to the balcony.

Inside her room she currently had two deputies who'd taken her statement and were now talking to a half-naked Knox, the hotel's security manager and two of his staff, the doctor, and her boss. Doug managed to look both concerned and annoyed, which was quite a feat, she thought. She glanced at Knox. He didn't look annoyed. No, he looked grim, fierce, and just a little ruthless.

And *really* good without a shirt.

She blamed that last thought on oxygen deprivation. Or avoidance. It would be so nice to think a half-dressed man was in her room because he wanted to be in her room, and not because … someone tried to kill her—and had wound up dead on the terrace below. She blinked back the hot prick of tears. The county's forensic investigators were already attending the scene below. From what she'd overheard, there was no identification on the 'victim'—damn, wasn't that ironic? He attacks her, and *he* winds up the victim. One of the first things the county sheriff had done on arrival was view the exterior CCTV footage, and it was clearly established her attacker had tripped in an attempt to escape and accidentally fell to his death, with nobody near him at the time.

Which meant Knox wouldn't have to be arrested for murder or manslaughter. *Thank God.*

She trembled, and the doctor sighed. "Your throat is going to be sore from the swelling for the next few days, but from what I can see, you're a very lucky lady. You survived." He smiled a quick, polite, professional smile, but his brow dipped when he saw that she was losing the struggle to be poised and calm and not lose her mind.

Lucky. He'd called her lucky. Her head ached as though it was expanding from the inside and pressing against her skull, her neck throbbed, and her throat felt like she'd been chugging battery acid down in the bar. She'd found talking painful, but whispering like a true two-pack-a-day smoker seemed to be tolerable. Her arms were bruised and sore, too; she looked as though she'd been grabbed by a finger-painting kindergartner.

Lucky wasn't quite the word she'd use.

"If you like, I can arrange some tests at the hospital—" the doctor hesitated, then dipped his head. "Is there someone I can call for you? Family? A partner?"

She shuddered. The first person who came to mind was her father, and then almost immediately was the mental shout of denial. Her father didn't think she was up to the job, hadn't wanted her to take on the role at Eagle Express ... this would be just one more thing to convince him she really wasn't ready to work in his industry on her terms.

If she told her mother, Mom would tell Dad straight away. If she told either of her brothers, they'd rat her out immediately. And a partner? No. Not since Sebastien, the jerk. She couldn't remember the last time she'd had a date, like a real, honest-to-God, dress-up-with-heels, eat-a-nice-meal-with-awkward-conversation date. She'd gotten to the stage where she thought her Mr. Right was vacationing in the same rainbow realm as the unicorns. Her gaze flicked briefly toward Knox, then back to the doctor. She shook her head.

"No," she whispered. "There's nobody to call—and I don't want to go to the hospital." No. She was sore, she hurt, but she was going to be okay. She didn't want, didn't need, to go to the hospital to spend hours in a drafty cotton gown, getting poked, prodded, scanned and … whatever else they did in this sort of situation. Good grief. This sort of situation. How the hell did she get herself into this sort of situation? She blinked. She just wanted to curl up, have a good cry, and pretend the people she worked with actually liked her.

"We'll look after her," Doug said reassuringly as he stepped toward her. "I can't believe some random burglar broke into your room."

She eyed him for a moment. "Random? You think this was random?"

"Of course, Mic," her boss exclaimed softly. "You don't think that mess would follow you all the way up here, do you? We're nearly two hours away from the city." He patted her gently on the shoulder. "I know things have been tough, but don't get paranoid about this. I think this is more a case of you surprising a break-in. They wouldn't have known who was in the room, just that maybe there was something of value in here."

She frowned. "How did he get in?" She turned to Knox. "How did you get in?"

Knox looked up from his conversation with the uniformed cop, and raised his eyebrows. "What?"

"How—how did you both get into my room?" She winced as she tried to raise her voice above a low rasp.

Knox glanced from her to the door, and then back again. His gaze dropped. "Uh, it wasn't quite latched."

She frowned. She was positive she'd closed the door … Hadn't she? Or—oh, hell, had she made it easy for that man to get into her room?

"Well, I believe we're done, here," the doctor said. "If you don't want to go to hospital, I can prescribe you a sedative—"

"God, no," she rasped. While sleeping like a baby sounded almost orgasmic at the moment, she didn't want to be out of it, and vulnerable to … anything else. She wanted to be able to wake up, to function—to fight, if necessary. Her fingers clenched on the top she held in her lap—the top that guy had tried to suffocate her with. Knox had pulled a shirt from her suitcase before anyone else had arrived, so she was at least decent for company. Still, she kept remembering the fear, the terror, of being caught with her top off and a man straddling her body. She sucked in a breath.

The security manager came back from his inspection of her door. "It's closing now, but I'll get maintenance up to check it to be on the safe side."

Doug sighed. "You may not have closed it properly when you left to come downstairs, and this person could have found that just by trying it." He shrugged. "An opportunistic crime, from the looks of things … and then you've come back to surprise him in the act."

He glanced up at the police officers, and one shrugged, before nodding. "It happens."

"Do you have CCTV in the hallways?" Knox asked the security manager. The man shook his head. "No. Just in certain spots on the exterior—like the terrace and the drive, in the elevators, and at the halls near the elevators. Those cameras only have a field of vision up to the bend in the corridor, as we can see all entry to and from the floor from the elevators."

Knox frowned. "What about the fire exit stairs?"

The security manager grimaced. "No, sorry. This is a recently acquired site, and we're still making improvements to bring it into line with our other resorts." He lifted his chin at one of his colleagues bearing a tablet, and the man hurried over. "We need to move Ms. Robson to another room—this is now part of a crime scene."

Knox frowned. "Perhaps she might want to go back home?" He glanced at her. "I mean, after this, do you still want to stay here?" He shoved his hands in his pockets.

Mic hesitated. In a word, *hell, no*. Okay, that was two words, but … *hell, no*.

Doug raised his eyebrows. "Uh, let's not panic." He held up a soothing hand toward her. "Look, if you want to leave, after what's happened, I completely understand. I can do your presentation for you … Your staff will be fine with it, too."

Mic glanced down at her clenched fists. Damn it. This would be another line of separation between her and her team. Another illegal snafu she'd managed to be party to. She couldn't begin to imagine what they'd say about her—or maybe she could, and none of it was good. There was already so much tension, so much distrust between her and her team. This was supposed to be a team-building weekend, the opportunity to repair working relationships. But … here? She trembled as she glanced about the room.

The man tapped on the screen of his device, and after a few minutes winced as he showed the man the screen. "We're nearly fully booked." He tapped a few keys, then pointed to the screen. "There's that one, two doors down, or we can move her up to the fourth floor."

The security manager shook his head. "No, that's tiny. I believe Ms. Robson will be more comfortable on the fourth floor."

Knox's frown deepened. "Don't you want to leave, Mic?"

She glanced up at him and shook her head. "No." Someone had attacked her. Whether it was because of the upcoming trial, or because some random douchebag decided to try her unlatched door, she didn't care. She was tired of being scared, of looking over her shoulder, of trying so hard to make her staff like her—she was just tired, damn it, and she wasn't going to be run off, or drive another ninety minutes to go hide in her bed like a turtle retreating into its shell. No. She had a job to do, and sooner or later, every damn person that was trying to get her to quit would realize she wasn't a quitter.

But she was too spooked to stay in this room. She glanced over at the security manager. "Fourth floor, huh?" She hadn't unpacked much—just her toiletries to freshen up before heading down to the bar, and her laptop, which still sat on the table by the window. She frowned. Funny. Nothing had been stolen. She must have interrupted the douchebag before he got a chance to make off with any of her stuff.

And it wasn't like Knox had given him a chance to pick up anything on his way out.

"Uh, wait—it's late," Knox said, casually gesturing toward the clock on the bedside table, with his bare chest and broad biceps and—good grief, his shoulders were magnificent.

Mic blinked, then shook her head slightly. *Whoa.* So wrong on so many levels.

Knox said something, and she watched his lips move, but what she heard in her mind didn't quite make sense.

"What if I sleep with Mic?" he suggested.

Visions of him, and her, and no sleeping, filled her mind. Mic blinked. "What?"

"What if I swap rooms with you?" he said, as though repeating something. She flicked a gaze at Doug. He looked calm, thoughtful, and not like a member of his staff had just improperly propositioned one of his managers. The cops looked at each other, and one shrugged, then nodded. Either they were just as happy for her to get some action as she was, or she had seriously phased out for a moment. She needed to focus on what was being said, and not what she wished was being said, damn it.

"Swap rooms? You said, swap rooms?" she asked. Just to be sure … because that could be a rather awkward conversation, otherwise.

He nodded, his gaze slightly curious. "Yes. Swap rooms. You can have mine, I'll take the smaller one two doors down—that would be next to mine, now? Or in the other direction?"

The security manager pointed in the direction of Knox's room. "It's on the other side of your room."

Knox nodded. "Yeah, I'm fine to move my stuff in there, if Mic would like to stay in my room … I'm not sharing with anyone."

He wouldn't be. These bookings had been made months ago, and Knox had only just started at Eagle Express. She eyed the wall. It would mean she'd only have to drag her case to the next door, as opposed to trundling around the hotel at nearly two in the morning. "You'd—you'd do that?"

He nodded. "Sure. It makes no difference to me. I could sleep in a broom cupboard."

She tried to smile. Truly. Even felt her lips curve, but she could only manage the barest semblance of a smile. Too tired, too … shattered. She nodded. "Thank you," she rasped, then winced at the scratch in her throat.

Within minutes she'd packed her things, and Knox returned from his room, duffel bag slung over his shoulder. He'd found the time to don a shirt, too. *Pity*. Doug and the security manager saw her into her new room, after an exchange of swipe cards, and it was with a sense of relief that she finally closed the door and she was left alone. She tried the door. Yep, that sucker was definitely closed and locked. She shook her head. How could she have left her door unlatched? That was next level carelessness, a damn invitation to anyone to enter her room. If she wasn't already so sore, she'd kick herself for that kind of sloppiness—but she was a walking dot-to-dot of bruises, and decided to beat herself up over it another time.

She glanced about the room. It was as though Knox hadn't been in there at all. She leaned her suitcase up against the wall, and folded her arms to hug herself as she wandered through the room. She was finally by herself.

Alone.

Her hands clutched her arms as she walked slowly to the sliding doors that led to the balcony beyond. The curtains were drawn. She pulled one aside, just a little, to peek out. The balcony didn't have lighting, but the tented-off area on the terrace below was lit up like a football field on a Friday night. Despite the shadows those blinding lights cast, she could clearly see there was nobody lurking there.

For now.

She swallowed, then reached for the latch on the sliding door. She noticed her fingers were trembling. She clenched her fingers into a fist. *Calm down.* Half the county law enforcement was either in the room next door, or right below her balcony, and from what she could gather, they'd be there for hours yet. Surprisingly, not many people in the hotel had noticed the commotion. The hotel had erected cloths across the terrace to shield the scene from view of the guests, and the county forensics team were working quickly and quietly to process the scene. She took a deep breath, then quickly checked the latch. It was secure. She flicked the curtains closed, then turned back to her room. She was tired— exhausted, really, but she was tense, wired. She wasn't going to be able to sleep. Her shoulders kept tensing as she remembered the man pushing her onto the bed, straddling her, choking her.

She blinked back the hot burn of tears. She was safe, now. She was okay. And she had a presentation to complete for tomorrow. She pulled out the laptop, climbed onto the bed, and plumped the pillow up against the headboard.

A soft scent, sandalwood and citrus, embraced her.

Knox. He must have lain down, briefly.

He'd saved her life. She settled herself slowly against the pillow, inhaling his scent. He'd burst into her room, and fought off her attacker. She looked at the wall across from her, the wall that separated her from the man who'd risked his own life to save hers, and a warmth bloomed inside her.

At least there was someone she worked with who didn't want her dead. Someone she could trust. She opened her laptop and focused on her presentation. Still, his scent was a beautiful distraction. She yawned, and blinked at her screen, but all she could see was a half-naked Knox in her mind's eye, looking fierce and protective and wickedly hot. She blinked, then shook her head. *Work.* Focus on work.

# Chapter 5

A light tap at the door had Knox hurrying over to answer it. Angus 'Fitz' Fitzgerald and Smithy stepped inside, and Knox closed the door quickly, not wanting anyone else to see his visitors.

"Where's Dan?" Knox asked.

"He can't get away at the moment. I'll bring him up to speed," Smithy said, looking around the tiny room, and Knox followed his gaze. The security manager hadn't lied. It was a glorified closet. "I don't think he'd fit in here, anyway."

"Thanks for freeing it up." Knox had surreptitiously dialed up Smithy from his jeans pocket, and his colleague had been listening to the conversation. They'd blocked out three rooms together, just in case the need for another room, command center, storage room, or so on arose. Or for a handy haven after an intruder attack, apparently. Smithy must have released it to the accommodation block when he heard security looking to relocate Mic. No, *Sparrow*. There was a reason they code-named their packages. *Keep that distance.*

"What happened?" Fitz asked. His colleague was tall, blond, grim, and straight to the point.

"Sparrow had a visitor waiting for her when she got back to her room." He clenched his hands. The gut-twisting moment of dread still haunted him, that momentary flashback …

"Damn. This undercover bit sucks."

Knox nodded in agreement. In a normal situation, they'd go in, clear the room before the package could enter. "The woman is supposed to be my boss. I can't weasel my way into her room to clear it without it being completely inappropriate."

Fitz grimaced. "Yeah, every excuse I can think of is just … wrong."

"What do we have on the access logs?" Knox turned to Smithy. His friend wore his dark hair tied back in his customary man bun, and it looked like he'd decided to ignore razors. Again. He wore small round glasses with lenses that had a slight blue tinge to them.

Smithy sighed. "Maria Lopez, housekeeping, entered the room almost an hour before Sparrow's return."

Knox shook his head. "That was no Maria Lopez." The person he'd wrestled with, although masked, was definitely male.

Smithy nodded. "I've checked the shift schedule against access logs. Maria Lopez isn't due in today, and her pass was only used to gain access via the staff entrance, and through to Sparrow's door."

"I don't suppose there's CCTV on the staff entrance?" Knox asked hopefully.

Smithy shook his head. "Nope. But I'm already putting together a breach report. This hotel's security is woefully inadequate. I know I'm good, but gaining access to pretty much all of their IT infrastructure was child's play."

"You're modest, too," Fitz observed dryly.

Smithy shrugged. "It is what it is. I'm awesome." He turned to Knox. "So, what are we talking here?"

"Well, contrary to the theory Danvers floated with the cops and hotel security, I don't think this was a random thief taking advantage of the opportunity of a room door that wasn't closed properly."

Fitz frowned. "Sparrow didn't close her door properly?"

Knox grimaced. "No, she did, but I couldn't very well tell them that our tech whiz here hacked into the security system and unlatched her door so I could get into my boss's room."

Smithy nodded. "Yeah, that would have been awkward."

"Well, that wasn't a random thief down there," Fitz stated, pointing to the sliding door that led to the balcony. "That guy was kitted up like a professional," he said, his expression serious. "Clumsy, but professional."

Smithy eyed Knox. "You think this is related to the case?" he asked. "That's pretty extreme …"

"I think someone is trying to intimidate her, maybe scare her off from testifying." Knox told them about the note on Mic's car.

"Still, going from leaving notes to physically attacking her—" Smithy commented.

"He covered her face with her own top while he tried to strangle her," Knox said through tight lips, anger still clenching his gut at the memory of the moment he'd seen Mic struggling on the bed beneath the masked intruder. "Regardless of what Danvers told the cops, I don't think he was here for her wallet. Just to have the strength in his grip to strangle …" Despite what most people might think, choking the life out of someone wasn't so easy, from a physical perspective—especially one-handed.

"Any man who lays violent hands on a woman is scum," Fitz said, clenching his hand into a fist. "This guy knew what he was doing. Random thief, my ass."

Knox eyed his friend. They all hated it when women and kids got hurt, but it was a sore spot for Fitz, especially. Something they both had in common. Memories of Kayleigh returned, and Knox turned away. He didn't want to think what his father would say if he knew what had happened to yet another woman on his watch, under his protection. His lips tightened. He had to do better.

"Yeah. He had some quality moves. I'd say ex-military, but can't say for sure which one." The moves the man had used were rough, effective. And then the guy had tripped over his own feet trying to escape. Go figure.

Smithy frowned. "International, huh?"

Knox shrugged. "Not sure, but even his attack on Sparrow was unusual." Not that he wanted to dwell on it, but there were more effective ways to quickly and silently kill a woman in her hotel room.

"I'll check out the preliminary autopsy report when it's lodged," Smithy said. "There might be some identifying tattoos, or something else that can pinpoint this guy's identity." Knox didn't ask how his colleague was going to access the report—the less he knew, the better.

"He didn't bargain on a bodyguard to interrupt him," Fitz said sourly.

"I'll check all CCTV around the terrace and grounds to see if we can get this guy on approach or retreat," Smithy said, pulling out an endoscopic inspection camera from his pocket. "In the meantime…" He slid the camera underneath the door, adjusted it for the best view of the hallway, and then rolled it down into the corner so that the door could open and close unhindered. "I've set this up to trigger on motion detection. You can view it on your phone."

Knox nodded. "Thanks."

"Do you want me to stay here with you?" Fitz asked.

Knox shook his head. "I'll take first watch, but you can come back later, if you like." He didn't expect any more attempts on Mic's life, but they had a job to do, and he wasn't about to take any chances. Fitz nodded, then joined Smithy at the door. "I'll take a look around the grounds when daylight hits and the squints have left, see if I can pick up any tracks. Otherwise, I'll see you in a few hours."

Knox nodded. Fitz's cover was as one of the team building trainers overseeing the corporate activities in the afternoon. Dan would be on hand in the morning as backup, and Fitz would be present for the afternoon. His lips firmed. He would make damn sure nobody hurt Mic again. He checked his phone, then gave Smithy a thumbs up when Fitz passed Mic's door and triggered the camera's motion sensors.

Resolution was good, and his phone buzzed and pinged with an alert. Smithy gave him a casual wave, then left.

Knox settled himself on the bed, his hands behind his head. His phone was next to him, ready to capture video of anyone passing his and Mic's room. He stared at the wall opposite. Mic was on the other side of that wall. Scared, traumatized … he sighed. He wanted to be there with her. He wanted her in his direct line of sight—hell, within reach would be better. For now, though, she was safe. She had half the county law enforcement moving in the room next door to hers, and on the terrace below, and the source of her threats had been … neutralized. Knowing that she wasn't in any immediate danger wasn't making him relaxed, though. He tried to tell himself that wanting to reassure himself by seeing her, holding her, comforting her, was purely from a professional standpoint. That's all.

Yeah, right. If he wasn't so focused on her, he'd be disgusted with his 'professional' self.

~*~

Mic jolted awake, heart pounding, beads of sweat on her forehead. She glanced around wildly, then sagged back against the bed's headboard. *Just a dream. Calm down, it was just a dream.* Well, okay, nightmare. Or memory. Whatever. The point was, she wasn't under attack, wasn't choking, wasn't suffocating. Wasn't dead. She was safe.

She swallowed, then winced at the tight burn in her throat. It was mildly better than last night, but she wasn't going to be making much noise today. She went to roll out of bed, and caught her laptop before it tumbled to the floor. Darn. She'd fallen asleep while working on the presentation. With her steel-toed boots still on.

She switched on her laptop and checked the presentation. Yeah, it would do. At this point, and at this time, and after what happened last night, she was just happy to be in a position to deliver a report. God, was she really doing this? Acting like today was normal, that something so bizarre and terrifying as an attempt on her life hadn't occurred the night before? That a guy hadn't died jumping from her balcony? She shook her head. *No.* She wasn't going to think about it. She'd spent most of the night fighting off visions of what had happened, and what it must have looked like down on the terrace—Knox had prevented her from stepping out on the balcony to see. A dark-clothed body, all twisted and broken— she sucked in a breath. *No, stop it.* She wasn't going to go there. She wasn't going to be terrorized, damn it. That bastard, the one who'd pancaked on the terrace, he'd tried to stop her, kill her. Well, she was not stopping. She brushed at the tear that rolled down her cheek. *No. Today was a new day, damn it.* She could get past this. Oh, she wasn't deluding herself. She was scared, she was exhausted, but she was going to put her game face on and face her staff.

Her eyes widened. Wait—if that guy was the one behind the threats, that meant her staff wasn't, right? They hadn't been able to identify the guy, but Doug had confirmed he definitely wasn't an employee of Eagle Express. Relief had her tilting her head back for a moment. All this time she'd been blaming her co-workers, when it was this guy who'd been leaving those notes and calling her at night. Some stranger she was pretty sure she'd never met.

Hot tears blurred her vision. That stranger, that guy she'd never met, had made her life a living nightmare. From calling her in the middle of the night, to leaving gross crap all over her car and writing nasty spelling mistakes, to actually attacking her in her hotel room. He had invaded every space she'd considered safe.

Mic's hands shook, and her fluttering fingers typed a mess of letters on the screen before she lifted them away from the laptop. She sucked in a shaky, panic-stricken breath. Was he truly behind everything? Was he the puppeteer? Or the puppet? Her eyes widened. *Oh, my God.* What if he wasn't behind it all, but just acting on someone's orders? What if there were more out there, waiting for her, wanting her dead? Her gaze flew to the curtains, her heart pounding, and she could feel the shakes start from deep inside her.

She squeezed her eyes shut. *No. Get a grip. You're being paranoid. Don't look for a bogeyman behind every curtain or under every bed.* Her eyes flew open, and she shoved her laptop aside as she rolled and peered under the bed. Okay, so the bed pretty much went to the floor, and *nobody* was getting under there.

She sagged back on the mattress. *Get it together, Robson. You're stronger than this.* At least, that's what her father would say, every time she baulked at something. She took a deep, shuddering breath. *Face it. Deal with it. A man tried to kill you.*

And now he was dead. He couldn't hurt her anymore. Couldn't jump out and freak the living crap out of her. Everything she was afraid of was inside her head. Yeah. She nodded, moving her laptop to the side. It was over. All of this—the culprit was dead. The realization that he couldn't hurt her anymore, couldn't scare her, couldn't threaten her … or pounce, hit, attack—it was like a weight lifted off her shoulders. It. Was. *Over.*

She eyed her laptop. She really could do this. She could stand in front of her staff and not think someone there wanted her gone … Of course, she'd far rather go cuddle a bottle of white wine on her sofa at home, but that would have to wait. She was a professional, and she had work to do.

She climbed off the bed and placed the laptop on the table near the window—and she refused to look out to see what was happening with the crime scene. She had to get ready for her presentation. She'd put as much information as she could in the graphics so that she wouldn't have to talk too much. All she had to do was touch on the statistics of her department, show the areas to target for improvement or growth, and then finish up with some positive and well-deserved backslapping. Despite the crime issues, her team had managed to move a veritable mountain of freight in the last few months, and it was an interdepartmental collaborative effort the whole company could and should be proud of.

She was nearly ready when she heard a soft tap at her door. Her gaze flew to her reflection in the mirror, eyes wide. She clenched the light voile fabric scarf in her hands, and her heart picked up in pace.

"Who—who is it?" Ugh, her voice sounded pathetic, and about as loud as a squeaky dog toy—or a phone sex operator. She crossed to the door and warily peeked through the peephole.

Knox stood outside her door, wearing dark jeans and a black long-sleeved T-shirt with a V-neck that nicely framed the indent of his collarbone and that line between his chest muscles. His green eyes looked dark and serious, and he was checking the hallway.

She rested her forehead against the door. Knox. Her shoulders relaxed. She took a deep breath, pasted a bright friendly smile on her face, then frowned and replaced it with something she hoped looked polite and reserved. She cracked the door open a little to peek out.

Knox turned at the sound of the door, and his mouth curved in a small smile when he saw her.

"Hey, Mic. I was just heading down for breakfast and wanted to check in on you."

She hesitated. After last night, everything felt … different. Something had shifted. She was the boss, but he'd completely taken charge last night. She'd needed him, in a way that she couldn't manage by herself, which was all kinds of frustrating and frightening—and maybe just a little embarrassing, although why she felt embarrassed by being attacked, she had no idea. She hadn't done anything wrong—had she? Well, if you put aside apparently not closing her door properly … She didn't like being the ditzy one, or the vulnerable one, the woman who asked for it, or the victim who needed rescuing … it kind of robbed her of control; until it was stolen from her she hadn't realized how desperately she wanted to maintain it.

And yet there was a sense of relief at the sight of him, an assurance that made her relax on a subliminal level, despite her consciousness wanting to maintain alertness and tension. He was strong, and he made her feel safe.

And horny. She eyed his dark frame, all muscular and fit and oozing gorgeousness way too early in the morning, damn it. Hell. She was definitely going to boss hell.

She gave him a thumb's-up signal, to save her throat. His eyes narrowed, and his gaze dropped to her neck. She heard his swift intake of breath. Yeah. It wasn't pretty. She'd been stunned when she'd seen the marks on her neck when she'd stepped out of the shower. The purple bruising went so well with the lightweight navy sweater she'd donned.

"Uh, if you're ready, I'll catch the elevator down with you," he suggested gently. She hesitated. She still felt a little … awkward. She eyed his broad shoulders, his narrow hips. She could suck it up, though. Be brave. Catch the damn elevator with the sexy man. She nodded, then glanced briefly up and down the hall. She didn't need anyone to think anything inappropriate was going on between her and Knox—because there wasn't. There couldn't be. She was a professional, and so was he. And if she kept telling herself that, eventually her subconscious would have to behave.

She stepped back, opening the door wide, then hurried back to the mirror to drape her scarf around her neck as Knox patiently waited at the door. She bit her lip as she concentrated. There was probably a YouTube clip for how to make a scarf look casual and chic while covering up a thwarted strangulation, but she didn't have the time to search for it, so she did a quick figure eight knot, with fingers that were shaking just a little. She clenched her hands into fists for a moment, trying to steady herself. She had to stop being a wuss, damn it. She reached for her laptop on the table, then strode to meet Knox at the doorway.

"How do I look?" she rasped anxiously.

He surveyed her slowly from head to toe. "You look good."

Mic fought her blush to shoot him an exasperated glare, and pointed to the scarf.

"Oh, you mean the scarf?" he asked innocently. He held up a hand to halt her, then gently tweaked the scarf behind her ear. He grasped her shoulders and turned her, and her eyes widened slightly as he adjusted the fabric at the back of her neck, his fingers touching her skin briefly before turning her back to face him. He nodded. "You're good to go."

Mic gave up fighting the blush, and kept her gaze on the carpet as she closed the door behind her. "Thanks," she muttered in her new phone-sex-operator voice.

"Anytime," Knox said in a light tone as they walked toward the elevator.

It seemed to take ages for the lift to arrive at their floor. Mic hugged her laptop to her chest. Each time she flicked a gaze in Knox's direction, it was to find him looking at her.

"How are you feeling?" he asked in a quiet voice.

She glanced back up the hallway. She didn't really want any more Eagle Express staff knowing about her 'incident'. She didn't want to be the topic of yet more gossip, but, also, she didn't want the staff to view her as weak, or a victim, or worse, getting her just desserts after what happened to Hollison, Pavlovich and Garcia.

"I'm fine," she said, and then met his gaze. "I'd like to keep what happened, um, just between us," she said in a low voice. "And Doug," she added.

His brow dipped, just a little, but he nodded. "Okay. I won't tell anyone else at Eagle Express what happened."

She smiled. "Thanks, I appreciate that."

The elevator dinged, and the doors slid open. The chatter of conversation stopped immediately, and the group inside stared at her. Apparently, a lot of people were heading down to the hotel restaurant—or so it seemed as she and Knox had to cram themselves into the crowded car.

And he smelled just as good this morning as he did last night.

She forced herself to drag her gaze away from Knox's broad chest right in front of her nose, to greet the others in the elevator with a broad, bright smile. Show time.

"Hey, Mic," Pedro said from the rear, craning his neck to catch her gaze. "Did some guy really take a dive off your balcony?"

Mic's smile faltered. Damn. So much for keeping this under wraps. She should have known the presence of law enforcement would get chins wagging. The silence in the elevator was stifling, and she felt the weight of everyone's stares, drilling into her as they waited for her response.

And how should she respond? She blinked, and instinctively shuffled back a little. She trod lightly on Knox's foot, and his hands steadied her.

"Uh …"

"The police are trying to figure out exactly what happened," Knox inserted smoothly, and she felt him shrug—that broad chest moving against her back, oh, Lordy—"It's still a mystery."

She pasted a smile on her face as she, too, shrugged. *Yeah. What he said.*

Chapter 6

Knox folded his arms as he watched Mic give her
presentation. Doug Danvers had organized a microphone for
her and, although Knox normally couldn't give a rat's behind
about freight stats, he found himself listening intently to her
low, husky voice. He knew why she sounded slightly hoarse,
but her speech was even and calm, as though she gave these
sorts of talks all the time. Despite being very nearly murdered
the night before, Mic—no, *the package*—was surprisingly
poised, and had even managed to crack a joke before she'd
revealed the last year's weight volumes. Instead of her
customary pencil-bound bun, she'd tied her hair back in a low
ponytail at the base of her neck. She was wearing those
painted-on jeans again, with a voluminous navy top, and the
scarf that hid her bruises.

She was very good at acting as though nothing happened.
Staff had been gossiping at breakfast about the scene on the
terrace. It appeared most of the staff were still in the bar and
had missed witnessing the actual incident, but it sure hadn't
stopped the curiosity—or the Chinese whispers. There was
the usual macabre curiosity over a death nearby, but as none
of the Eagle Express staff were 'missing' or arrested, most
assumed it had been an unfortunate medical episode. Or Mic's
jilted lover. Or a cat burglar. Or a corporate spy from a
competing company, or—his particular favorite—an alien that
didn't want to beam up Mic. He guessed when folks didn't
have the facts, they made up their own to suit the story.

He glanced over at Dan. His colleague was very good at making doing nothing look very busy, and he was currently adjusting the cloth on the back table where all the glasses and water carafes sat. Dan met his gaze briefly, then glanced back at the package, before carefully surveying the collected Eagle Express staff packed into the conference room.

Knox eyed them as well, although he was a little more relaxed. A man was dead. Maybe Doug Danvers was right in his assertion that the attack was completely random, a crime of opportunity?

That theory didn't quite sit well with him. The man was too good to be an opportunistic thief.

Either way, the fact that the package didn't want anyone else to know what she'd experienced puzzled him. He didn't think she'd told her boss about the threatening letters, or the harassing phone calls she'd received. SafeKeepers hadn't tapped her phone out of respect for her privacy, but they were monitoring her call logs and he knew about those late-night calls that lasted only as long as it took Mic to hang up on the caller.

He was damn sure she hadn't shared anything with her family.

He glanced down the row of seats in which he sat. Luis Montenegro was staring at Mic intently, his chin jutting forward, his expression grim. The man had a beef with his boss, Knox could tell—but would he team up with someone else, someone prepared to do bodily harm to Mic? He made a mental note to ask Dan to check out his background.

He glanced back to the stage. Mic was wrapping up her speech, and raised three cheers for all staff involved in moving freight, from the customer service representatives who took the initial bookings, to the couriers and freight handlers, and the office administration and accounts staff who followed up payment and customs brokers who cleared the freight, and the IT staff who kept all the systems working. He couldn't help but notice the operations team were a little less enthusiastic than the other staff when cheering back, and he sighed. There was some very real antipathy toward the operations manager. He frowned. Did Smithy have a point? Was the leap from notes and calls to a direct physical attack so big that perhaps it was a random attack? Were they connected—or not? Either way, he was damn sure he and his team would keep the package safe.

Knox watched as Doug Danvers took to the stage to conclude the company overview and announce lunch. After lunch the team activities were scheduled. He'd catch up with Fitz there. Some of the employees would be doing archery, football, rope obstacle courses. He knew Mic was in the orienteering team, and that Smithy had made sure he was too. With Fitz running the activity they would both be able to keep watch over her.

They broke for lunch, and Knox followed Mic at a safe distance, not wanting to call attention to his proximity to her. Well, actually, he did want to call attention to his closeness. He wanted everyone there to know that if you messed with Mic, you messed with him, and his colleagues—but that didn't quite serve the purpose of their undercover operation.

He chafed at the restriction placed on them by Mic's father, but the man was insistent—she couldn't know about her security detail. He sighed as he loaded his plate up with food from the buffet. He'd noticed a slight distance with her this morning, a stiltedness to their conversation. He, Fitz and Smithy had taken turns with the watch overnight, but he'd wanted to be closer to her, to keep her in his view and make sure she was safe.

He should have checked her room, damn it. Logically, he could tell himself, and Fitz and Smithy could tell him, that what happened last night wasn't his fault, but the simple fact was that a package in his care, a woman, was hurt and nearly killed on his watch. At least this time, she hadn't died. He briefly eyed the scarf she'd tied around her neck. It cleverly hid the bruises that marred her skin.

He'd been a little shocked this morning when he'd seen the extent of her injuries, and realized just how close she'd come to death. He stabbed his fork into a morsel of beef. That bastard. He'd tried to choke the life out of Mic—Knox took a deep breath. He was getting angry. Angry at the man who'd behaved so violently toward a woman, particularly one within his care. Angry at himself, for Mic being in that situation—in danger, at risk. Nobody had expected that, nobody had seen it coming. There had been nothing to suggest, in all of their briefings from the client, and in their own investigation of the circumstances, that the situation would escalate like that, and so suddenly. The change in behavior was unexpected, and puzzling. From heavy breather phone calls and anonymous notes to … trying to strangle the life out of the woman.

But that one act had revealed so much. Mic's attacker had known exactly what he was doing. He'd gained entry to her room, avoided CCTV cameras, and lain in wait for her. He'd surprised her—undressing. Knox's fingers tightened around his fork, and he speared another morsel of beef. And then he'd had the strength and resolve to try to suffocate her with one hand while his other squeezed her throat. No, he didn't subscribe to Danvers' random thief theory. This guy was a professional, a cold-blooded killer.

"You do know that cow can't get any deader, right?" Dan murmured as he leaned over Knox's shoulder to top up his glass of water. Knox took a deep breath as his friend topped up the other glasses at the table, then moved onto Mic's table. Dan was right. He was filthy angry about what had happened to Mic, and he needed to calm down. He forced a smile on his face and turned to the woman next to him—he thought she was from customer service.

"Hi, how are you doing?"

~*~

Mic looked up in surprise as she stepped onto the hotel terrace. She'd tried to hurry, but it looked like she was the last to arrive for the afternoon's team-building activity. She'd had to drop her laptop off, change her shoes to more appropriate footwear—steel-toed boots, of course, and grab a jacket, because—lucky her—she was doing orienteering this afternoon, along with nineteen other staff. She'd ditched the scarf, though. The jacket collar came up high and covered her bruises, and this was California, not Colorado in the winter. She'd sweat like a Sweaty McStinky if she wore the scarf on the hike.

She glanced about the group. Honestly, she didn't know why Doug had suggested she participate in this exercise, but he'd assigned each manager to a different activity in order to create more connections between staff and management. She watched as Graham Appleton, the accounts manager, walked off with his group. They were doing arts and crafts. She, on the other hand, would be traipsing through the surrounding forest wilderness with a partner in the vain attempt to spot yellow flags. Ugh. She eyed her group. Some were from her team—she tried not to stare at Knox Jones too long. He was in a side conversation with the trainer leading their activity. She sighed. She was spending more time with Knox over this weekend than she had over the five weeks he'd been working at Eagle Express. Doug was also in the group, and he smiled as he talked casually with the courier driver at his side.

The trainer, a man with sandy-colored hair and blue eyes, stepped forward, smiling despite the serious glint in his eyes. "Ah, good, we're all here. My name is Gus, and I'm your coordinator for this afternoon."

She eyed Gus. He was tall, good-looking, and very, very fit. With cargo pants, boots, and a wet weather jacket emblazoned with the team-building company's logo on the left breast, he looked every bit the outdoorsy physical trainer. A lot like Knox, actually. *Oh. My. God. Enough with Knox.* The poor man was her employee, not some fantasy obsession. She forced herself to turn her attention back to the trainer—what was his name, Gus? The man pointed to a table near the terrace balcony.

"Over there you'll find your kits—they'll contain maps, compasses, bottles of water and trip guides. You'll be assigned a partner, and we'll bus you out to the drop-off point. You'll need to follow your team instructions in order to get to the next stop and collect your flag. First team back wins a hamper generously provided by the Eagle Express management."

The group made enthusiastic noises, and Gus held up his hand. "Ah, but this isn't a follow-the-leader kind of activity. Each team gets a different course, and you're going to have to work closely with each other to get to the next point." He held up a clipboard. "Okay, so when I call your name, pair up, and get your kit and head down those stairs and across the parking lot to the waiting shuttle. We'll give you some orientation on how to read a compass and your maps, and then we'll get going."

Gus started calling out names, and halfway through the list she found she was teamed up with … Knox. She planted her feet solidly on the ground to prevent herself from doing a little jig. *Down, girl.* Knox started to walk over to the table, but Luis frowned in protest.

"Hey, I thought we were supposed to team up with someone we didn't work with?" He indicated his partner, Camilla, a woman from customer service whom Mic had had occasion to work with sporadically.

"I'm fine with this," Knox said, his tone light.

"Of course, you guys have an unfair advantage. You already know each other, work with each other. You'll go faster together."

Mic bit back a sigh. She didn't know if Luis was incredibly competitive, or just plain combative when it came to anything she did or was involved with, at present.

Doug nodded as he stepped forward. "Luis is right. I think there's been a mistake. We're supposed to pair up with someone outside of our department."

Gus glanced at his list and shook his head. "Nope, those are the names I've got here."

Doug made a face. "Okay, well, let me have a look at that." He crossed to the man's side and quickly scanned the list.

"Uh, again, I'm fine with this," Knox said, gesturing toward Mic. "I don't mind teaming up with my boss."

Doug smiled as he shook his head. "No, the purpose of these activities is to get to know people you may not normally have the chance to work with," he said. He pointed to a name on the list. "Why don't we swap partners? George, you're supposed to be with me. Why don't you go with Mic, and I'll team up with Knox?"

Mic glanced over at George. He was in the IT department, right? Just the fact that she found it hard to place the man in the company highlighted the need for Doug's approach. She smiled as Knox opened his mouth. "That's fine by me," she said, interrupting whatever it was he was going to say. She really should talk with more of the staff. She didn't want to think about the tiny flare of disappointment at the realization that she wouldn't be spending the afternoon with Knox, hiking through the wilderness. And it was that very same flare that showed her she needed to put some distance between the two of them. The man was taking up way too much real estate in her mind.

George looked uncertainly around the remaining group, then shrugged and stepped forward. "Okay."

She nodded at him and smiled. "Hey, George. I hope you know how to work a compass."

~*~

Knox forced a smile at Eagle Express's CEO. *Damn it.* Fitz eyed him briefly, then continued with assigning partners. Knox held back while the others collected their kits, and knelt down to tie his bootlace.

"Well, that didn't go as planned," Fitz muttered. He held out his hand and Knox grasped it, accepting his colleague's help as he rose to his feet, and surreptitiously shoving the satellite trackers Fitz had palmed him into the pocket of his jeans.

"No kidding."

"Sparrow's itinerary and map are pre-loaded onto that device, and I've attached a tracker to her kit. Here's another one for you to attach to her when you get the chance. I'll have to get Smithy to load it all onto a second device, so we can track her back here." Fitz shook his head. "Save me from well-intentioned bosses."

"Yeah, well, I'm more worried about Montenegro. Please tell me our guide gets me close to the package," Knox said as he started to walk in the direction of the parking lot.

Fitz nodded. "There's an intersecting point on your third flag. If you can race through the first two, you can make that as a rendezvous."

Knox sighed. "I don't like this."

"Look, the guy who was bothering her is dead. In reality, the only danger she's in is from insect bites as she wanders through the forest. Besides, what were we supposed to do? Go against the boss's clear orders?" Fitz shook his head. "What could you or I say in front of everyone? Actually, sir, this guy is her secret bodyguard that she doesn't know about, and has to dog her every move?"

"I still don't like it."

"Neither do I, but let's be realistic—this is a two-and-a-half hour orienteering activity. She'll be taking a nice walk through the countryside, you'll catch up with her in less than thirty minutes—I don't see anything happening between now and then, especially after last night's developments. Her stalker is dead. I'll be waiting at the end of the course like a good little team builder, tracking her every move. None of the operations staff have seen these guides, and nobody else knows the routes. You'll be close by. She'll be fine."

~*~

Mic peered over George's shoulder. "Okay, which direction do you think we should head?" She was purposely letting George guide their actions, although it was hard not to just take the lead. She bit her lip as George looked left, then right, then behind.

"Uh …"

Uh-oh.

"I think maybe this way?" he suggested tentatively, pointing to the right.

She checked the directions they'd been given against the compass. Nope. Not that way. That guy, Gus, had been very thorough with his instructions on how to read both map and compass. How was it that both she and George could attend the same orientation session, and come away with such a different understanding of how a compass worked? Thank God the trainer would be at the rendezvous point, waiting for them, and able to send out reinforcements. At this rate, she and George wouldn't make it back until after midnight.

"Um, let's see. It says here we should head west, yeah?" She looked him in the eye, and he nodded. Slowly. "Where is the sun?" she muttered, looking about, hoping he'd take the hint. It hurt to talk, especially after her presentation this morning, and she just wanted to go sit somewhere and suck down some tea, preferably with honey.

"There," George said, pointing to his left.

"Oh, so it is," she said brightly, although her voice still sounded like a phone sex operator, and patted him on the shoulder. "Good job. Yeah, so if it's the afternoon, then …"

she glanced in the direction of the sun, then looked over her shoulder to the right, hoping again he'd take the hint.

"Sun sets in the west," George stated, and this time his voice held a little more confidence. He gestured to the left. "We should go that way."

"Oh, good," she said, and exhaled with relief. They'd been at this for forty-five minutes, and still only had one darn flag. She hadn't realized George couldn't read the compass until just a little while ago, and didn't want to embarrass him by taking charge. She could gently steer him, though.

She strode around a tree fern, then climbed over a fallen tree trunk. It took her a little while to realize she'd left him behind, and she sat down on a boulder as she waited for him to catch up, unzipping her jacket to let herself cool down from the hike. She inhaled—the scent of moss, dirt and detritus was strong—and gazed about her for a moment. It was quiet, apart from George's panting as he hurried toward her. The dappled light countered the deep shade where she sat, and there was a tranquil hush that relaxed her better than a warm bath and a scented candle ever could. A weird crack, followed by a pip, echoed through the woods, and she glanced about. Was that a deer stepping on a branch? Another one of the teams? She zipped up her jacket to hide her bruises as George approached.

George paused in front of her and tugged his bottle of water out of the drawstring bag in the field kit he'd wrapped around his wrist.

"This place gives me the creeps," he muttered.

She smiled. "I was just thinking how serene it was." She kept her voice low, almost whisper soft, not just because the tranquility of the surroundings seemed to encourage it, but because that was the optimum mode of speaking for her at the moment where she could still be heard—mostly—without straining her voice or throat.

She looked over her shoulder when she heard another soft crack—but again, it sounded weird, followed by the pip.

Or was it a pop? Low, but reverberating, as though from a great distance. She wasn't quite sure how far away it was, or what direction. Maybe a really big, heavy deer stepping on a branch? Were there deer in the California wilderness? She had no idea.

"What was that?" George asked, spinning around and almost tripping over a clump of soil.

Mic shook her head. "No idea."

"You don't think it was a bear, do you?" George whispered, wide-eyed.

She shot him an exasperated look. "No, George, I don't think it was a bear. There are no bears around here." At least, she didn't think there were. "It could have been one of the other teams," she suggested.

"Hello?" George called out, his expression worried.

Mic listened, but there was no response. She sighed as she rose to her feet. "We should probably get moving, otherwise we'll still be here at sunset."

It was as though she'd used magic words, because George instantly galvanized into action.

"Whoa, George, this way," she called out, pointing in the general direction they should be going, as opposed to the completely random turn George had taken. George changed direction and hustled to catch up with her.

"So, George, I know you work in IT, but I don't know exactly what you do …" Mic said in the hope of generating a casual conversation with the man. This was the point of the whole weekend, right, to get to know your fellow workers better?

"Uh, I'm a systems administrator." George paused to look at the compass, and Mic pointed him in the right direction.

"Oh? What does that entail, exactly?"

She trooped on, clambering up a small rock formation.

"I maintain and analyze the financial systems, and make sure they gather data from the operational systems for billing,"

George muttered, shaking a clump of something dark and stinky off his shoe.

Mic paused on top of the rock. "Really? Like, getting the weight from consignment notes and scanners to charge the right amount to the account holder?" She tried not to sound too interested, despite the warning lightbulb flashing in her brain.

George nodded as he started to climb up toward her. "Yep."

"Oh."

She'd been trying to figure out how the weights on the drug shipments had been entered incorrectly. Most had registered below significant weights, and yet she knew from personal experience someone had fudged those records.

"Interesting." Maybe George could help her figure that out. She turned to climb down the other side, but a flash of color in her peripheral vision caught her attention. She craned her neck. Red. She was pretty sure she'd seen red—there.

It was a shoe—a sneaker, to be exact. With a white tick on the side. She frowned. And it was still attached to a leg— a leg that suggested its owner was lying down and very, very still.

"Oh, my God," she whispered, and jumped down the rock, ran down and across the gully, and up to the pine tree and rocks that hid the rest of the person from view.

"Where are you going?" George called out, trotting behind her.

She clambered over a boulder, then halted. *Oh. My. God.*

A middle-aged man lay on the ground where he'd fallen, his unzipped blue jacket revealing a white T-shirt that was red and wet with blood. What the hell? Chills crept over Mic's arms and shoulders.

"Wayne!" George exclaimed, stumbling to a halt next to Mic.

She crossed over to the man. He was familiar, but she couldn't quite place him.

"You know him?" she asked hoarsely as she knelt beside him. She leaned over to find his pulse. Nothing.

She pressed her fingers to various points around his neck, and then grasped his limp wrist, her heart pounding as she fought off panic.

"Wayne Caulder, he's in accounts—I work with him on some of the systems," George choked out, then raced over to a small bush and threw up.

Mic blinked as her vision blurred. *Oh, God. Oh, God.* She raised her shaking hands over his bloodied chest, but stopped short of touching him. The man was dead. She couldn't give him first aid, couldn't stop the bleeding—that had happened on its own when his heart had stopped beating.

She folded her arms, hugging herself tight. He was dead. Wayne Caulder from accounts was dead.

# Chapter 7

"I—I don't understand," she whispered, glancing up at George, who now straightened and wiped the spittle from his lips with a shaky hand. "What happened?" She glanced down at Wayne—she squeezed her eyes shut. Wayne Caulder, who maybe had a wife, children, siblings, parents … She took a deep breath, held it, then exhaled. Get your crap together.

"I thought you said there were no bears," George screamed. Mic's eyes flew open at his panic, just in time to see him stomp his foot uncontrollably.

She glanced down at Wayne. Blood. So much blood. She reached with shaking fingers, and grimaced as she touched his shirt, smoothing it down and trying not to puke herself. A round hole, singed around the edges caught her eye.

"I don't think this was a bear, George," Mic said in a low voice. She glanced about, even more alarmed. That looked like a bullet hole. Hell, had some hunter mistaken Wayne for a deer? Was it hunting season? She had no idea. She wiped her hands on Wayne's jacket, and rose to her feet.

"What else could it be?" George exclaimed in a high-pitched mini-scream. "A cougar? A wolf?" He glanced wildly about.

Mic held up her hands. "Calm down, George," she said in a low, even tone. She hurried toward him. "This wasn't a wild animal."

George whirled to face her, his face twisted in anguish and fear. "Then what the hell wa—"

Something blasted into his chest, throwing him back off his feet and tumbling him over the rocks to the small gully below.

"George!" Mic screamed hoarsely as she vaulted over the rock, hissing as she skidded down the hill toward where George now lay on his stomach.

She raced to his side, kneeling by a smaller boulder. George's blue jacket had a dark purple stain spreading across the back. "Stop shooting," she screamed, scanning about, hoping whoever was hunting would realize they were people, not prey.

"George, George, are you okay?" Mic half-sobbed as she reached for him. The young man groaned, and his foot moved, just a little.

"It's okay, George," she soothed, patting his shoulder gently. "I'm here, it's going to be fine." She couldn't see the initial injury. She reached for him, then hesitated. What if he had a spinal injury? George groaned again, a soft little sound of intense pain, and he moved his arms just a little. Okay, that was good, right? She needed to give him first aid, needed to turn him over …

She grimaced as she rolled him over very carefully, then choked on a horrified gasp when she got her first look at him. His chest was bloodied, and she could see the dark ring on his jacket. George coughed, and blood spurted out of his lips, his eyes wide with shock. George was not going to be fine.

"Oh, my God," he whined, his eyes all shiny with tears.

She shrugged out of her jacket and bundled it up to press against the wound on his chest.

"It's okay," she crooned, her hands shaking, tears streaming down her face. It so wasn't okay.

His face was gray, and tears rolled down his temples and into his hairline as he met her gaze.

"I'm sorry," he wheezed, and coughed up some more blood.

She shook her head as she tried to staunch the flow of blood dampening her jacket. "Don't talk, George," she whispered, and fished her cell phone out of her pocket. "I'm going to get us some help. You just hang in there."

George grimaced, his teeth red with his blood. "It wasn't supposed to happen like this," he sobbed.

"Shh." She unlocked her screen and typed in 9-1-1 and got a 'No Service' message on her screen. "No," she wailed, holding the phone up in a number of directions, trying to get a signal.

"You need to—" George gritted his teeth and groaned against a wave of pain, then panted.

"Stop talking, George," she told him through her tears, her heart thudding in her chest. "You need to conserve your—"

George grasped one of her wrists. "No, you need to listen," he said with enough force to shut Mic up. "I'm sorry, Michaela. You weren't supposed to get hurt."

She frowned, confused. "What? What are you—"

A haze of red splattered over her, and George jolted, his head rolling to the side. His hand dropped from her wrist, and she stared in horror at the hole in the side of his head.

Wha—? Wha—she blanched, shaking her head in denial. No, no—it couldn't— He was— She fell backwards, and the dirt exploded near her knee. Oh, God. Her phone snapped in her hand, and she dropped it, momentarily stunned at the cracked screen with a hole in it.

She recoiled, tumbling further down into the ravine as tufts of grass and dirt flew around her. No. It couldn't be. This didn't seem like some stupid, blind hunter mistaking them for animals. This person *wanted* to shoot them.

"Help!" she screamed past her tight throat as she scuttled along the gully floor, diving behind some rocks. "Someone— anyone, *help!*"

~*~

Knox halted on the trail. "Did you hear that?" He glanced about.

Danvers paused for a moment, listening, then shook his head. "No." The man kept moving down the trail. Knox frowned, then started to walk behind. He was in a short vale and wasn't sure what direction the cry had come from. He glanced at the tracker he held unobtrusively in his hand. He'd managed to attach the second tracker to the sleeve of Mic's jacket as the Eagle Express staff had been transported by bus to the drop-off point. Danvers didn't realize it, but he'd been surreptitiously guiding the man in Mic's general direction.

Mic was on the other side of the low ridge. If she and that IT dude kept walking in a southerly direction, he and Danvers should bump into them in that valley at the bottom. A faint crack-and-pop sound made his muscles tense. He knew that noise. Long-range rifle with a suppressor. It was followed by another sound, like a faint cry, and the hairs on his arms rose. Then he heard the screams.

It was coming from over the ridge. Knox took off, leaping from boulder to boulder as he made his way up the rocky ridge toward the crest. Danvers cried out to him in surprise, but Knox didn't stop. Mic was in trouble.

~*~

Mic scrambled behind the rocks, ducking to avoid the bullets, her heart hammering. She ran down the incline, her pulse thudding in her ears, her breath coming in short, uneven pants. *So close, so close to the trees …* She raced across the patch of grass that led down toward the tree line, darting left to right and back again, and feeling the sting of dirt as bullets hit the ground as she ran. She dived over a log and rolled until another tree trunk stopped her, then crawled around so that the trunk gave her some cover.

Oh. My. GOD. Someone was shooting at her. Eyes wide, she glanced about. She'd made it into the forest, and here it was cooler, darker, quieter. Her chest rose and fell with her pants, and she gulped, her throat dry. Where could she go? What could she do? What *should* she do? She took a deep breath, held it, then slowly peeked above the trunk.

A chip of bark flew off near her head, and she reared back again. *Son of a bitch.* She felt like a sitting duck. There was sporadic cover in front of her. Some boulders, bushes, trees … if she ran further into the forest, she'd have more cover, and would be further away from whatever psycho hunter had decided to use her for target practice. She couldn't stay here, though. All this guy had to do was move, and she'd probably be exposed. A cloud of dirt showered over her hand, and she snatched it closer toward her, swearing. She clenched her hands into fists.

Mic jolted as a clump of dirt sprayed up over her shoes, and she rolled away in reaction. *Oh, my God. Too close.* She kept rolling, grimacing as small stones dug into her hips and shoulders, until she had rolled down the small dip that gave her enough cover to commando crawl along, out of the line of fire. She didn't think, she just did, moving swiftly.

She gritted her teeth. This move looked so easy on TV and in the movies, but crawling along on your forearms and legs felt about as coordinated as a whale bucking along on land. Heart hammering, she dragged herself along the ground. The dip deepened, and she sighed in relief when she could scurry along on her knees. She ignored the pain from the small rocks and bark bits digging into her knees and palms. She saw a flash of something light-colored ahead, and dropped to the ground, eyes wide, breath held. *Oh, God.*

Her shoulders sagged when she recognized Andy Rickerson, one of the couriers, in his pale mustard windcheater, walking away from her along the gully. She rose to her feet and scurried toward him. *Thank God.*

~*~

Knox skidded to a halt, swearing. One man, obviously dead, lay on the leeward side of the ridge. He eyed the bullet hole in the man's chest, then glanced about. *MIC. Where was Mic?* He fought against the panic, the dread of what he might find. He glanced at the tracker. She was just down in the gully, from the looks of things. It looked like she was stationary, for the moment. He bent down low and used the rocky terrain as cover, scurrying and leaping down the small decline, then halted again when he found the guy who'd been Mic's partner.

Knox dropped to one knee, his elbow resting on his other knee. He swore again. The guy was dead. A wadded-up jacket he recognized as Mic's sat on his chest, and he lifted the blood-soaked garment gingerly. A bullet in the chest, and one to the side of his head. He pulled gently at the guy's shoulder to lift him a little. His back was worse than his front. Knox laid him back down, then uttered a soft expletive when he saw the field kit. Mic didn't have the tracker, her partner did, and she'd left her jacket behind. He gazed around the area. *But where was Mic?* There was a mild sense of relief that she wasn't also lying on the ground, her body riddled with bullets, but that sense of relief was quickly countered with apprehension. Where the hell was she? Was she safe? He couldn't help it. Memories of Kayleigh, confused and frightened, resurfaced. She'd been under his protection, too … that last moment haunted his vision as he peered around frantically, and that same sick helplessness rose within him. *No.* It took a conscious effort to push them aside, to relegate them to the past, and focus on the current situation. *Mic.*

He turned and eyed the ground. He could see the sections where the dirt had been disturbed. It looked like she'd somehow dragged herself further down into the gully, and then followed its course. There was no blood, something he noticed immediately. *Thank God.* He glanced up and around.

From the looks of the wounds—smaller on entry, larger on exit—and with his experience in Afghanistan, his initial suspicions were confirmed. Someone was out there with them, using a rifle with a muzzle on it. In this terrain, though, the noise bounced about, making it difficult to pinpoint origin. Where the hell was Sparrow? She'd somehow managed to dodge a bullet—or maybe more than one. He gained his feet and started to run down the gully. He needed to find Mic, ASAP.

~*~

"Andy. Andy," Mic hissed.

The courier turned around, his blue eyes widening when he saw her. He was older than her, with a stocky, muscular build from years of handling parcels. She almost cried in relief when she saw him. She wasn't alone, anymore. She had help. Andy glanced around, then frowned.

"Mic? What are you—?" He stopped talking when she held her finger to her lips.

"I am so glad to see you," she said in a low voice as she approached him. Her hands were shaking when she reached out to him, and she took a deep, shuddering breath. "We need to get help. Fast. Do you have your phone on you?" She wanted to scream, wanted to collapse and sob hysterically, but her heart still hammered in her chest, her muscles were still tense, and she couldn't quite relax.

Andy nodded, although his expression was guarded. "Why?"

"We need to call for help. Someone—" she had to take another breath. She couldn't fill her lungs properly, now that she had company. Someone shot George—and Wayne. This time, she couldn't stop the tears rolling down her cheeks. She leaned over and braced her hands on her knees, as her body shook. Oh, God. George and Wayne were dead. She lifted her chin to look up at Andy. *Get it together.* Andy and—she glanced around. "Who's your partner?"

They were all supposed to have partners in this stupid, crappy little activity.

"My partner?" Andy stilled.

She nodded, trying to swallow past what had to be a lump of sand in her throat, it was so dry. "Yeah." She straightened and glanced about the forest. Oh, God. Had the shooter got someone else? Or was Andy as lost as she was?

Andy sighed, his lips tightening. "I don't want to do this," he muttered, stepping toward her.

She nodded. "You and me, both. I hate this—oof." Andy's fist hit her in the stomach, and she doubled over as her breath rushed out, wincing at the sharp burn of pain. He grasped the fabric of her navy sweater with one hand. "You should have kept your mouth shut, Mic," he rasped, rearing back with a clenched fist.

"What?" Mic rasped as she raised her arm to block Andy's strike, but the force of the hit still made her lose her balance, and she fell. She felt the material of her top give, just a little. "What the—"

Andy followed her down, still grasping her sweater. "You ruined it for all of us," Andy growled as she struggled beneath him.

"Andy, stop," she gasped, trying to push him off her.

"It didn't have to be like this," Andy said, rearing back to strike again.

Memories of the night before, of the heavy body straddling hers, choking her, flashed through her mind's eye. Rage, hot and intense, burst through her. She reached up and jabbed him in the eyes. Andy reared back, yelling in rage and clutching his face. She shoved him off her and rolled over to scramble away, grunting at what she knew was going to be a hell of a bruise on her abdomen.

A hand grabbed her ankle, and she tripped. She landed roughly, her palm hitting a fallen branch, and she grasped it as she rolled back to face her courier-gone-rogue. She swung the branch—hard. Andy's head jerked to the side as the branch hit him on his temple, and he slumped down, dazed.

Mic shuffled backwards, pulling her ankle out of his now-loose grip. "You son. Of. A. Bitch," she panted at him, and rolled to her feet as he groaned. He raised his hand to his head, and Mic took off running. Her feet thudded through the soft dirt, arms pistoning by her sides as she bolted through the underbrush.

What the—? Why did—? How—? She couldn't spare the energy to follow any thoughts to a logical conclusion. Fear was like holding connected jumper cables, shocking her body into motion. *Get the hell out of here.* Footsteps were thudding behind her. *Damn you, Andy.* Her fists clenched as she ran. The ground was uneven and rough, but she leapt over branches, logs, boulders and bushes.

She didn't look over her shoulder, but could hear the thud of footsteps gaining on her. She lowered her chin and pumped her legs harder. Each thud on the ground set up an answering throb in her gut. There were so many hazards here: branches, uneven ground, rocks … she ran as fast as she could, leaping, stumbling, skidding, sprinting. Still, she could hear the footsteps behind her.

Keep going, keep moving.

There was that familiar crack-and-pop, and she darted around a tree trunk, but didn't stop. She raised her shoulders, expecting to feel the burn of a bullet in her back, like George.

But until she did, she was going to keep moving.

Her breath was coming in deep, regular pants. A large boulder loomed up in her path, and she took a deep breath, planted her palms on the surface, and vaulted over it. Her left foot hit the ground on the other side a little awkwardly, and she hissed, faltering a little. She started running again.

Keep going, keep mov—a hand whipped out as she ran past a tree trunk and clapped over her mouth, and her feet left the ground as another arm snaked around her waist and lifted her back against a hard body.

# Chapter 8

Knox's hold on Mic tightened as she bucked and kicked, her screams muffled beneath his hand. "Shh," he whispered into her ear, but it had no effect on her attempts to hurt him, to escape. He could hear the thudding footsteps coming closer. He whirled, stepping around the tree and carrying the struggling woman along with him. In a smooth movement he slid to the ground and hooked his leg over both of hers, his thigh muscles tensing as he rolled them under a tree fern frond.

"Shh." This time he lost all pretense of soothing as he clamped his body around hers to still her struggles and quiet her. The footsteps ran past their spot, and he caught a brief glimpse of Nike sneakers and jeans, and a flash of color he could only describe as baby diarrhea.

Mic stiffened in his arms, and he realized she was holding her breath as they listened. Knox kept his gaze on the sneakers, watching as they skidded to a halt, twisted to face one way, then another, then took off running again.

He remained still, breathing calmly until he couldn't hear those sneakers anymore. And then he waited some more. Mic started breathing again, faint puffs of air blowing across the top of his fingers. His arm was braced across her body, trapping her arms, and he could feel her heart thudding in her chest. She was still tense, still ready to bolt.

"I'm going to remove my hand from your mouth," he whispered in her ear. "Don't scream. Nod if you understand."

He eased up the pressure across her mouth, and Mic nodded, small movements that he might have missed if he wasn't holding her.

"Okay." He gently lifted his cupped hand from her mouth and held it poised, just in case she freaked.

"Let me go," she whispered. He couldn't see her face, didn't know what was going through her mind. She seemed calm, though.

He let go of her slowly, relaxing his grip, and sliding his leg off—

She jackknifed up to her hands and knees, and he grabbed her before she could bolt. He yanked her back again, pulling her around to face him and managed to cover her mouth before she screamed. He winced as she bit down on his hand, and he pulled her in toward him.

"Shh," he cautioned.

Her eyes widened when she saw him. She said something, and it was muffled by his hand. "Shh." He looked over his shoulder. He didn't want the guy with the Nikes to double back and find them tussling on the ground. He glared at her as she bit harder. "Stop it." The words came out low and terse.

Her eyes narrowed with suspicion, with anger, and damned if she didn't chomp down even harder.

His lips tightened, and he shot her an exasperated glare. "I'm going to remove my hand again," he whispered, leaning forward until their noses almost touched. "Don't run, don't scream, otherwise that guy is coming back."

The press of teeth against his fingers immediately lessened, and she blinked, her gaze uncertain as she glanced beyond him, then back at him. He lifted his hand off her mouth, and then raised both hands in a placatory gesture, palms facing her as he drew back. "Easy, now."

Her eyes glistened, and she swallowed. "What the hell is going on?" she whispered fiercely as she sat back on her heels.

He noticed she kept her hands fisted, and her expression was borderline suspicious. Of him?

He shook his head. "I don't know," he told her. She shuffled back a little. She didn't believe him.

"I heard you screaming, and came running. I saw—" he hesitated, then, "I saw what happened to the others."

This time a tear rolled down her cheek, and she brushed it away with the back of her hand. He jerked his thumb over his shoulder. "Who was that?"

Her expression became wary as she glanced in the direction the guy had taken. "Andy Rickerson, one of the couriers."

"What happened? Is he armed?"

She opened her mouth, but hesitated, and slowly rose to her feet, glancing from him to the area around him, her gaze constantly moving. She folded her arms across her body, leaning forward slightly. "I don't think so. He didn't--," she paused, then took a shaky breath, "he didn't reach for a gun." She winced. "We need to get help."

Knox frowned as he rose to his feet. She was skittish. Of him. Just the thought pained him. He didn't want Mic to fear him. Ever. He wished he could tell her to relax, that she was safe with him, that his job as her bodyguard was to ensure her safety, but one of the conditions of this job as stipulated by her father was that she couldn't know he'd hired bodyguards for her. And yet she'd still been in danger, damn it. Mic shifted one foot away from him, poised for flight.

"I'm here to help, Mic. I won't hurt you," he said quietly. Earnestly. Hoping she'd believe him. He'd never hurt her, never harm her. He made sure to keep his stance relaxed, to not reach for her, even though every instinct in him cried out to hold her, make sure she was safe, unhurt. "Are you okay?"

"I don't know who to trust, here," she told him frankly, her chin lifting.

His eyebrows rose. "Oka-ay," he said slowly, digesting that. She'd seen two colleagues murdered, and was hiding from another. Caution was good. "I don't even know where to begin with that, but—" he held up a hand, "I saved you last night from an attacker, and I'm here to help you, not Rickerson," he said, jerking his thumb over his shoulder in the direction Rickerson had taken. "Do you want to tell me what the hell happened back there? Why are you running from Rickerson?"

Mic's lower lip trembled, and his gaze was drawn to her mouth when she pressed her lips together.

"Someone's shooting at us," she said in a low voice. "George and I found Wayne, and then George was shot. I managed to get away." Her voice was still a little raspy, and he could clearly see those bruises on her neck. She looked battered, bruised, and scared, but also a little angry.

Knox took a deep breath. Holy crap. If it weren't for Mic's resilience, they wouldn't be having this conversation. Yeah, he deserved whatever his dead father would have dished out, damn it. Anger, hard and hot, started to boil in his gut, and he clenched his fists.

"And Rickerson?" Why was she hiding from him? What had that bastard done to her that made her doubt his own intentions?

"He attacked me when I approached him."

Knox closed his eyes briefly. *Damn, damn, damn.* He flicked his eyes open and looked at her carefully. She hugged herself, leaning over. Could be a comfort thing, could be a pain thing.

"Did he hurt you?" He had to push the question past the lump of fury he was trying to contain. He reached for her, turning her arm over gently. She had some light grazes on her hand, her sweater was torn at the neck, and she still clutched her middle. "What did he do to you?"

"I'm fine," she said, trying to brush him away, and he didn't miss the tight clench of her jaw at the movement.

"Where are you hurt?"

She shook her head, but he wasn't buying it. From what he'd observed of her over the last few weeks, Mic would limp around on a broken leg and tell folks she was just peachy before admitting that she was in pain, or in trouble. He gently tugged at her sweater, and she sucked in a breath. His gaze met hers. "Where?" His voice was low, firm, and she must have seen the determination in his face because she sighed and gestured to her stomach.

"The bastard punched me in the gut," she muttered. "It's fine—"

He ignored her efforts to brush him away as he gently lifted up her sweater, and he sucked in his breath at the red mark on her abdomen. Another bruise in the making. He raised her arm to test for mobility, and to test for any broken ribs. He pressed against the skin gently. She hissed. "Does it hurt to breathe?"

She shook her head. "No, just when I move."

He moved around her, gently touching her bared midriff. "I don't think anything is broken—"

"No … just bruised."

"But it looks like it hurts." He sighed as he pulled her into his arms, gently embracing her. "I'm so sorry," he whispered. "That shouldn't have happened to you."

For a moment she held herself stiff and still, and then relaxed, dipping her forehead to rest on his shoulder. "It's not your fault, Knox," she said quietly with that slight rasp.

He closed his eyes briefly as he held her against him. Yes, it was his fault. She'd been alone and unprotected on their watch. This new bruise, this new nightmare she'd found herself in, was because he and his team worked on the assumption they'd gotten the guy last night, despite his own misgivings—but she had more than one threat working against her.

"Still, it shouldn't have happened," he muttered, rubbing her back. He stepped back. "Come on, let's get to the rendezvous point." He gestured for her to walk with him, keeping close to her side. His gaze swept the area, looking for something, anything, that shouldn't have been there.

Rickerson was nowhere in sight—which was good for Rickerson, at least. When he caught up with that bastard—

"I don't suppose you have a phone, do you?" she asked hopefully as they walked.

He shook his head. "Nope. Not one that gets cell service here."

She paused, and he gently grasped her arm to urge her to keep walking. They'd already spent enough time here, they needed to get a move on.

"Wait, what about Doug?" she asked, her eyes wide with worry.

Damn. He'd forgotten all about the Eagle Express CEO. But Doug Danvers wasn't his package, Mic was. "I'm sure he's fine, and he'll be trying to get to the rendezvous point, too." At least, he hoped he was, for the CEO's sake.

"We need to find him," she said, turning about. Knox's grasp firmed, and he kept them walking in the same direction.

"No, we need to get to the rendezvous point," he corrected. Fitz would be there, and he'd have a satellite phone on him. They'd be able to call law enforcement.

"But he's in danger—they're all in danger," Mic protested.

Knox spared her a brief glance. "You're in danger, too, Mic. I need to get you to safety."

She tried to dig her heels in. "But, Knox—"

He kept walking, and tugged her along. "But Mic, those guys back there were *shot*," he hissed. "There is someone out there with a long-range rifle who is determined to kill people."

She frowned. "How do you know it was a long-range rifle? It didn't sound like a normal gunshot to me."

He shrugged. "I've been around hunting guns for most of my adult life," he said, and it was kind of the truth. He'd joined the marines straight out of school, and they … hunted. "I'm not sure where the shooter was, but I heard the shots. He's using a suppressor, which is why it sounds a little weird."

"Which is why we should look for Doug—and the rest of our staff out here," she insisted.

"And risk another Rickerson incident? You didn't even know if you could trust me, how do you know you can trust the others?" He had to admit, he enjoyed that brief moment when Mic's mouth opened and closed, and nothing came out. "Let's just get to the rendezvous point."

This time Mic did manage to halt him, with a little effort—and her heels in the dirt and her knees locked. "Knox, we can't just leave everyone here."

He frowned as he faced her. "What if the next person you go to help isn't just a jerk, like Rickerson, but is an armed jerk? We don't know who is involved in this."

"I'm not even sure what *this* is," she protested.

He shot her a dubious look. "You don't know why anyone might want you dead?" It was the topic du jour in the lunchroom. Constantly.

"Of course, I do—I'm supposed to testify at a trial in a little while, but why kill Wayne? And George?"

Knox's lips tightened. She was right. This was pretty extreme. "I don't know. Maybe they were just in the wrong place at the wrong time…"

Mic's gaze flicked away, and she shook her head. "I don't think so … Not George, anyway."

His eyes narrowed. "What do you mean?"

Mic would have stopped completely if he hadn't pulled her along. "George tried to tell me something before the second bullet—" she swallowed, "before he died."

"What did he say?" Knox lowered his voice as he scanned the forest.

"He—he apologized, and said I wasn't supposed to get hurt."

Knox halted, frowning as he turned to face her fully. "What?" That sounded like dear old George knew something was planned for today … damn it.

Mic shrugged. "He said he was sorry, and that I wasn't supposed to get hurt. And then that bastard shot him in the head." Her lips tightened.

"Did you see or hear anything else? Did you glimpse the shooter?" Damn it, she'd been so damn close to George when he'd been shot. So close, so at risk … Anger, cold and lethal, rose in him.

"No."

Knox started walking again, ushering her alongside him. "We need to get you out of here." He needed to get her the hell out of this forest, get her back to safety. He kept his gaze on the terrain, watching for anything that moved. They'd thought last night's attack would be the end of it—her attacker died, for Pete's sake. To be able to marshal this kind of action within twelve or so hours—no, this was planned. And others in the company had known something about it. Damn. It looked like this drug-trafficking case was not a couple of mules in a freight company pushing stuff through, but a well-organized, well-funded operation with deep pockets and violent killers-for-hire.

"Don't you see, Knox? Someone is killing my co-workers because of me." She shook his hand off her arm. "You're not even safe." Her gaze darted about, peering through the shadows and trees. She stepped away from him. "We should separate."

Knox frowned. "What?"

"If they're coming after me because of the trial, anyone I'm with is in danger. I was wrong, I shouldn't be anywhere near the other staff out here. We should split up."

Did she— How would she— That was so— "That is the most cockamamie thing I've ever heard." He couldn't begin to form a rational position for that.

"No, you should head that way, and I'll head this way," she said, stepping off to his right.

He leaned over and grasped her arm, pulling her back toward him. "No. We're sticking together."

"No," she argued, trying to jerk her arm out of his grasp. He tugged her closer, turning until he could back her up against a nearby tree. Her worried gaze met his, and he could see she was already primed for flight. He moved until his body pressed against hers, trapping her against the tree trunk to prevent her from trying to take off again.

"We are in this together. I'm not leaving you." He made sure his words were clear, succinct. No way was he about to abandon her to some sniper psycho.

She shook her head. "No, if someone is after me, then let him come after me, Knox. You weren't even at the company when this crapshoot went down. I don't want you hurt."

Knox's mouth opened for a moment, and he struggled to process her argument. "You—you want to separate so *I* don't get hurt?" *Really?* She was trying to protect *him?*

Mic nodded, her expression pleading. "If anything were to happen to you—", she swallowed, and he was pretty sure her hazel eyes shone a little bit. As though the thought of him getting hurt … upset her. Something warm unfurled deep in his chest. Uh, wow. That was … making him feel stuff.

She blinked rapidly. "I don't want you to get hurt," she said in a whisper, putting voice to the faintest of hopes he didn't dare follow. Just those words, though—it was as though he'd fallen in altitude, that little air pop in the ears that made everything else seem so muted and distant, sharpening his focus on what was in front of him.

There was something in her voice, an interest, a level of intimacy that went beyond an ordinary concern for another's wellbeing. His gaze dropped to where her torn sweater gaped at the neckline. The pulse in that little dent in her collarbone picked up in speed. He tried to tell himself it was because she was being sweet—but no matter how much he tried to convince himself, it didn't stop his body from responding to the tender concern in her eyes, or the curves pressed against his frame. She cared—and she was trying to keep him safe.

Wow. He was floored. "But that's my job," he blurted, then could have kicked himself. He was just so surprised that she was trying to look out for him. She, the package, was trying to protect him, the bodyguard. The fact that she didn't know he was her bodyguard just made him a little more humble. She was looking out for her staff, putting his safety above hers. And yet, when her gaze dropped to his mouth, and her lips softened, and her breath shuddered, it struck him that maybe it went beyond the professional to the very, very personal. And then she inhaled, and he didn't move back.

Her breasts brushed, ever so lightly, against his chest, and their gazes collided. Something beyond concern flared inside her hazel-gold eyes, something that kicked up an answering heat in his own stare, and an answering throb further south. *Uh-oh.*

She blinked, then frowned and shook her head. "No, Knox, it isn't your job. You should be able to go to work with the full expectation of going home again, safe and sound— and not in a body bag. I've lost two men already." She grasped the lapels of his jacket. "I don't want to lose you, too."

Did she just mean to bring him closer? Because all of a sudden, he was struggling to keep his attention on the conversation. Be professional. Just be damn professional. *She's the package.* His hands grasped her waist. He so intended to put some space between them.

His gaze drifted over her face, taking in her worried expression, the luminosity of her eyes, her concern. His fingers grasped the belt loops of her jeans at the side of her waist. "You won't lose me, Mic. We're going to make it out of here just fine." He'd tried to sound reassuring, but his words came out low and husky.

"Go to the rendezvous point, and get help," she told him, her voice firm. Surely there was phone coverage there. If not, there'd be a vehicle that could be used to go and raise the alarm. "I'll—"

"Stay with me," he interrupted smoothly. She shook her head, her eyebrows drawn into a fierce little frown that he had to admit was kind of cute. Everything, her eyes, that tight little purse of her lips, the dip in her eyebrows as they drew together, and her need to make sure others' safety came before her own—made him seriously drawn to this woman.

"I'm your boss, Knox, and I'm ordering you to make your way to the rendezvous point while I—"

Knox leaned in closer, his gaze intent on hers. "Forgive me, *Boss*, but I'm feeling a little rebellious. For the last time, sweetness, I'm not leaving you."

Her gaze dropped to his lips for a moment, and then her frown deepened. "But Knox—"

"But Mic," he interrupted with a ghost of a smile, and then leaned in to kiss her.

# Chapter 9

His lips pressed against hers, and Mic's eyes widened at the contact, then drifted closed as she opened her mouth to his kiss. *This is so wro—*

Knox's tongue slid against hers, and she sighed. *Oh. Wow.* She relaxed against his body, raising her hands to rest against—*oh, my, those biceps* … Knox angled his head, and darned if the kiss didn't get even better. For just a moment, Mic put aside all the troubles, the inner voice that said this was *sooooo* unprofessional, he's a member of your *staff!* and just let herself be swept away on a hot, sexy kiss with this gorgeous man.

She smiled against his lips when he pulled her hips against his, but things got all serious when she felt his hard length against her lower stomach, and his hand slid up her back, pressing her closer. He was so much bigger than her, so much stronger, but she wasn't scared, wasn't threatened.

No, she was horny. Her tongue parried with his, and her breasts swelled against her bra, jutting forward as she arched her back.

She ran her hands up his arms, loving the feel of his strength beneath her fingertips. This man had caught her eye every time she'd stepped into the warehouse. For five weeks, she'd fought the temptation, but now … she was ready to handle temptation.

She sighed, her arms entwining around his neck, and he wrapped one arm around her back, lifting her slightly as he deepened his kiss. *Holy mother of—*

"Whoa," he rasped, pulling back.

Whoa, indeed.

He set her back down on her feet, and he looked about, blinking. "Uh—"

"Uh…" Yeah. *Uh.* She took a deep breath, then flicked her gaze up to meet his when her nipples brushed against that soft T-shirt material. Knox swallowed.

"I'm sorry," he said, and tried to step back.

It took her a moment to realize he couldn't because she was still clinging to his neck like a monkey clinging to its mother. She let go, and stepped back, right up against the tree trunk.

"Ow," she muttered, rubbing the back of her head where it had met the bark with a low thud.

Knox dragged his hand over his face. "I'm so sorry, Mic—"

"No." She shook her head, then had to step forward again to pull her tousled ponytail away from the tree trunk. She was sure she'd left some strands embedded in the bark, but she kept her face composed … she hoped.

"No, Knox, I'm the one who should be apologizing …" She wiped her hands down her jeans. Okay, this was … mortifying. He was sorry they'd done that. "I shouldn't have …" she gestured between them.

"You didn't. I did."

"I should have stopped it," she said, making a slicing X motion with her forearms. "I shouldn't have …" *Stuck my tongue in your mouth.* She closed her eyes as an inferno started a party in her cheeks. "It was really, uh … not—I'm your boss, and uh …" She took a deep breath, and then finally opened her eyes to meet his. "It was highly inappropriate of me, and I apologize."

Knox nodded, his gaze skidding away from hers. "Yeah, it was … unprofessional."

Her heart crushed in on itself, just a little, at his words. Oh, God, now he felt … what? Embarrassed? Oh, God, *harassed?* She was his boss, and she'd kissed an employee. Yes, he started it, but she so should have ended it. Actually, she should have shut it down before it got anywhere near getting started. She looked away. But she hadn't. He had.

"Michaela?" A woman's voice echoed through the forest, and Mic whipped around to trace the source, happy to be thrown a rope to save her from further humiliation. She caught sight of two shadowy figures walking toward them from a distance.

"Kelly?" She squinted. It looked like—

She was suddenly looking at the back of Knox's broad shoulders, and had to crane her neck to see beyond him, trying to figure out how—and why—he'd stepped so quickly in front of her.

"Oh, my God, Michaela," Kelly gasped as she broke into a run. "We're so glad we found you." Her data entry team leader looked relieved as she approached them. "We heard shots."

Aidan Cleary, the junior freight handler, followed closely behind. His jeans had dark wet patches, and his shoes squelched as he walked. "Do you know what's going on?" His tone was on the high side of curious, and his eyes were wide as he kept glancing about the forest.

Gosh, how old was he? Twenty? Twenty-one? He looked scared, and his demeanor, his efforts to keep his panic under control, again brought home the gravity of their situation.

And here she was, playing nookie with Knox while some wacked-out shooter was taking potshots. So wrong, so embarrassing, so …oh, she could just *die.*

Aidan put his hands on his waist, and straightened, shoulders back. The move puffed up his chest, and he reminded Mic of a bird trying to look bigger than it is … like when it feels threatened. He was the youngest person on her team, and the poor guy was scared—for good reason. His unease, along with Kelly's concern, brought home the fact that she was their boss, and they were looking to her for guidance.

"We're not exactly sure," she said, keeping her voice low and calm. She was responsible for the safety of these people. "You did hear shots—" she glanced up at Knox, then tried to nudge him out of her way. He didn't budge. She dodged around him.

"Do either of you have cell reception on your phones?" she asked them. Kelly and Aidan fished their phones out of their pockets and checked. Kelly shook her head, and Aidan swore, tapping his screen.

"Okay, uh, where is your map? We don't currently have one," Mic said, gesturing between her and Knox.

Kelly turned to Aidan. "Do you want to tell them, or will I?"

Aidan's cheeks bloomed with heat, and he looked away for a moment, then finally met Mic's gaze. "We had to cross a creek—"

"Did we really?" Kelly interrupted, folding her arms.

"It was a shortcut," he argued, then he shrugged as he looked away, "but it didn't work out so well."

Kelly turned to Mic. "Aidan fell into the water, and we lost our kit—with the map, our water bottles…"

"And I'm *sorry*," Aidan exclaimed. It looked like it was a continuation of a conversation they'd had before.

"Okay," Mic said quickly, to prevent the two from arguing. "So, we have no maps, no phones …" and someone out there with a long-range rifle and a suppressor was trying to pick them off. "It's going to be fine," she said calmly. "We just need to figure out which direction to go—"

"This way," Knox said, pointing to her left. "If we head in this direction, we'll eventually hit that stream that Aidan fell into, and we can follow that down to the rendezvous point."

Mic blinked. "How—how do you know that?"

"I looked at the map while we were on the bus, to get an idea of where we were going."

Her eyebrows rose. "You *memorized* the map?"

He lifted his hand, palm horizontal, and waved it side to side. "Meh, sort of. We each had to follow the hunt, and when we got to a point, we'd find out the next point, but I wanted to see what kind of terrain we were dealing with." Knox seemed to notice she was staring at him. "What? You mean you didn't?"

Mic blinked again as she shook her head. "Uh, no, I—that sounds very Boy Scoutish of you."

He gave her the three-fingered salute. "Always be prepared."

"Right." She looked about the forest. Shadows were lengthening, and her concern was growing. Sure, it meant they'd have some cover, but so would the shooter. They needed to get to someplace safe, and call the sheriff. "We should get a move on, then."

It wasn't lost on her that a short while ago she was prepared to split away from Knox, to fumble about on her own in order to protect him from being collateral damage walking alongside her. Now, instinctively, she wanted to look after Kelly and Aidan, wanted to pull them in tight under her wings and make sure they didn't stumble into the scope of a shooter.

Maybe it was because Knox seemed more than capable of looking after himself, and she'd felt like a liability with him. Maybe it was because she saw Kelly and Aidan as her staff, her responsibility, and Knox was something … different. More. Or maybe it was because she was finding it really hard not to be fascinated and drawn to the man beside her, and after her experience with Sebastien, her own self-protective instincts were telling her to back away from the man, or risk more than her physical safety …

Or maybe it was because he'd called her sweetness, and she'd never been called something like that before, and it had made her feel soft, and feminine, and cherished, and that just wasn't who she was. She was strong, and capable, and didn't need a man to call her soft words that made her want to curl up on his lap and do things slow and tenderly.

Okay, let's not go there. That was way too deep and personal, and required all sorts of psychoanalysis; she didn't have the time or the brain space to make up mental avoidance strategies that would allow her to keep her head buried in the nothing-to-see-here sand.

Kelly frowned. "Wait—where are your partners? You got Doug, didn't you?" She looked up at Knox. "Where is he now? Why isn't he here?" She turned to Mic. "And where's George?"

Knox pursed his lips, then looked at Mic. Behind his calm expression she could see the question in his eyes. *Should we tell them?*

She caught her bottom lip between her teeth. If she told them the truth, that would really freak them out, and she wanted to keep them calm, and get them moving on. But— could she really *not* tell them someone out there had shot dead two of their co-workers, and another out there was quite happy to go on the attack? Could she let them walk through this maze of trees, shadows and threats, and have them completely oblivious to the danger they were all in? Especially as she was the cause of the danger?

No.

"Uh, George is—" *Oh, heck, this is hard.* Just mentioning his name brought back those last images of him and bile rose in her throat. "George is dead," she said in a low voice, and had to blink back the tears those words spawned.

Kelly frowned. "What?"

Mic felt a tremble start low in her knees, and her throat was dry—like, Mojave dry. Kelly was looking at her as though she'd grown two heads, and Aidan's mouth reminded her of a dying fish.

"George was shot," Mic said, and the tremble seemed to have expanded from her knees all the way up to her larynx. Knox grasped her hand, and she squeezed his, as though trying to draw in some of that strength. It must have worked, because she took a breath—a little shuddery, but still bolstering—and got control of her shakes. She couldn't lose it, not in front of Kelly and Aidan. Why she felt she could lose it front of Knox was another thing to be buried deep in that nothing-to-see-here sand. *Be calm. Keep it together.*

She dipped her chin, and met Kelly's gaze straight on. "Those shots you heard—someone with a rifle shot George— and Wayne too, from accounts. They're both dead."

"Oh, my God!" Kelly gasped, her eyes welling up with tears. "Are you serious?"

"I am."

"Oh, my God," Kelly said, then repeated it over and over as she turned to bury her face in Aidan's shirt. Aidan's expression was shocked, and then it turned to surprise as Kelly clung to him. He wrapped his arms around their colleague, but Mic could see he was struggling to process what had happened.

"I know it's a shock," Knox said, raising his hand in an almost soothing gesture, his palm out. "But we really can't stay here any longer, we need to get moving."

"Is he—is he still out there?" Aidan asked nervously, then swallowed.

Mic shrugged. "I don't know. I haven't heard any shots for a while now—"

"But we're not going to make any assumptions," Knox said, using his arms to herd them into motion, and Mic realized she still held his hand in a white-knuckle grip. She let go. "The sooner we get to the rendezvous point, the sooner we can be safe."

Mic nodded, then started to walk, her arm going around Kelly's shoulders as the woman sobbed. Aidan stumbled along behind, glancing all about the forest. Mic was doing the same, watching for any movement. Sadly, though, she now knew how fast a bullet could hit, and they wouldn't see it or hear it until it was too late. Her lips tightened, and she increased her pace, gently spurring Kelly and Aidan along as they followed Knox through the lengthening shadows.

~*~

Knox glanced behind at his motley troupe. They'd been walking for forty minutes and, from what he could recall of the map, they still had a way to go.

He paused and held up his hand. Kelly, Aidan, and Mic paused as well, silent, listening. *There*. Running water. Blessed, gurgling, tumbling water. "Come on," he said, and hurried up the low incline. He paused when he crested the top. The creek. Well, stream was more like it. It was too wide to jump across, and the water was flowing over rocks, and every now and then he could glimpse the reflective silver of a fish darting about in the shallows.

He skidded down the small hill to the water, and leaned down to test it. Sweet, sweet water. His shoulders sagged in relief. Just because it was moving water, didn't mean it was clean water, but they could drink a little of it. At least it would be enough to quench their thirst.

He glanced up cautiously. So far, so good. They hadn't encountered any gun-toting psychos, nor couriers who liked to beat up women. He gritted his teeth at the thought. He wanted a word with Rickerson. And by 'word', he meant beat the crap out of the man for what he'd done to Mic.

He turned toward her. She'd been holding her side, and he'd noticed she now had a slight limp. He wasn't sure if she'd done something to her leg, or if it was just a ripple effect from having a bruised and battered core. At one point he'd had to walk through a section of Afghani desert with two broken ribs, and he remembered trying to favor that side of his body, just to alleviate the pull on muscle and tendon and broken bone.

Her face was a little pale, but she'd pulled her compressed lips into a smile, and was quietly encouraging to Kelly and Aidan, who remained oblivious to her injury.

"We need to drink," he told them. They'd been walking for a while, and before that Mic and he had been running. He didn't want any of them getting dehydrated, they had other issues to worry about. He strode back up the hill. "We should rest here for a bit, and then follow the gully downstream."

Kelly and Aidan shuffled and skidded a little as they went down the hill, and Knox held his hand out to Mic. "Let me help you."

She paused as she looked at his hand, and his eyebrows arched at her reluctance to touch him. She hadn't been reluctant before, when they'd been alone. He prided himself on being focused, disciplined … a professional. But as they'd walked through the forest, it had taken effort to focus on the here and now, to resist the undisciplined compulsion to pull Michaela Robson in for another kiss and to finish what they'd started, in the most unprofessional but totally pleasurable way.

Kissing her had been unplanned, and he blamed her eyes. Those big, beautiful hazel-gold eyes that swallowed him up in a warm blanket of worry and protectiveness and a care he couldn't remember being directed at him before. He was a soldier, a former marine, and you signed up knowing the danger you were getting yourself into; you accepted that, as did everyone around you. You had a job to do, and your job was in one of the most dangerous environments on earth. Everybody faced the same danger. Your superiors tasked you with missions with a high fatal risk factor, and he was used to being put into situations that were life and death. Everyone accepted that because it was part of the job, and what you vowed you would do in the name of protecting your country.

But Mic—Mic had put his safety before hers. Tried to, anyway. He wasn't having any of that, but he couldn't believe she was prepared to risk her safety for his own.

And then her mouth had ordered him to leave while her eyes had begged him to stay. That kiss … well, he'd had to come up for air because somewhere in his caveman brain he'd realized he was about to give himself up to the moment—and he never gave himself up to the damn moment, especially while on a job. *And* they were in danger, for Pete's sake. He should have had his bodyguard credentials revoked in a spectacular lightning strike. And now she was looking at his hand, as though he'd spat in it or squished a bug or something before he'd offered it to her.

"Let me help you down there," he said, then jerked his chin in the direction of her midriff. "I know you're hurting, and you're going to hurt more if you slide or fall."

She eyed the distance between them and the stream. Mic was nothing if not pragmatic, he'd seen that with her at work, and her pragmatism won out here. "Fine," she said brusquely.

His brow dipped as he helped her down the incline. Since they'd met up with Kelly and Aidan, she'd been polite, but distant, focused on her staff. Just like the elevator ride that morning, as though she was trying to put him back in the mental box she liked to store him in. *Employee.*

He should let her. If that's what worked, and kept them from giving each other the steamy eye, then he should let her set the level of connection. All he had to do was get her back to the resort safe and sound.

"You didn't mind me touching you before …," he commented quietly, and his hold on her hand tightened when she slid a little down the hill. So, letting her set the parameters hadn't lasted long. Sheesh.

Her glance shot to Kelly and Aidan, who were already hunkered down at the stream, slurping water through their fingers, and paying them no attention whatsoever.

"I thought we agreed that it was unprofessional," she muttered. "Again, I apologize. It won't happen again." She looked up at him briefly, and her gaze fell on his lips. The look in her eyes heated, and a pretty flush covered her cheeks.

That made his gaze drop to her mouth. Her cute, sexy little mouth.

"You're right, it shouldn't," he said, and he wasn't sure if he was telling her, or himself.

"It won't," she reiterated, and let go of his hand as they reached the stream. She bent down to scoop up some water, and it took him a moment to realize he was staring at her butt, shapely in those jeans. He blinked, then looked away. Okay, maybe he looked back to check her out again, but no, he was just making sure the package was safe and not in any … real … danger. Damn, she was gorgeous.

"Hey! Hey, guys!"

Knox whipped around at the sound, his fists clenched. Damn it, she was too distracting.

Doug Danvers staggered over toward them on the other side of the stream, a bruise covering his jaw that extended up toward a darkening, swollen eye, and blood trailed from a gash on his cheekbone. "God, I'm so glad I found you!"

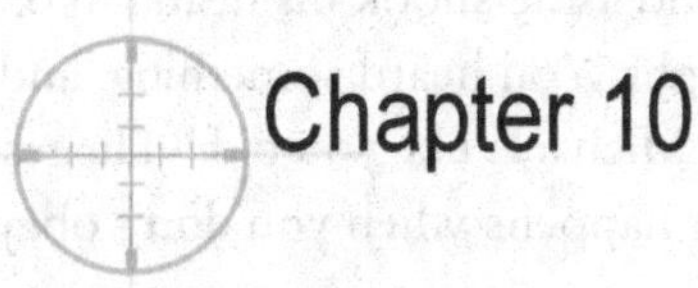# Chapter 10

"Oh, my God, Doug!" Mic cried out in relief, then splashed across the shallow stream, wincing at the slight pull of muscles in her stomach when her foot slid on a slippery stone beneath the cold water. She reached the other bank and held her hand out to the CEO as he skidded down the small hill toward the water. "I'm so glad to see you. Are you alright?"

Doug nodded and smiled, then winced as the movement pulled at the bruised area around his eye. "I'm okay. Damn, I'm so relieved to find you guys." He grasped her hand and pulled her in for a hug.

She heard splashing, and turned to see Knox wading out toward them. His hips swung from side to side as he twisted against the force of the water, making his progress look both graceful and effortless.

She turned back to Doug. "What happened to you?" She guided him down to the water, and helped him sit down on a boulder. She scooped up water in her palm, and tried to ignore the dull pain in her side at the movement. She used the water to wash the blood from his face, repeating the process until she could see the wound clearly. "You look like you've gone ten rounds with Mike Tyson."

Doug chuckled wearily, then hissed when Mic gently touched the bruise on his eye. "I feel it."

"Let me see," Knox said as he reached them, and gently tilted the CEO's face. He touched the swollen area, his expression grim. "You might have a slight fracture," he surmised, wincing as he surveyed the damage. He turned

Doug's face on an angle, and stared at his eyes. "Maybe even a concussion." For a moment, Mic saw regret on his face. "I'm sorry I left you like that."

Doug waved a hand as he shook his head. "No, don't be. Your instincts were right. You heard something, and I'm glad you went running for Michaela like you did." He gestured to his face. "This is what happens when you don't obey those instincts."

Mic frowned. "So, what exactly did happen?" she asked quietly. Kelly and Aidan remained on the other side of the stream, watching anxiously but out of immediate earshot.

Doug shrugged. "I'm not exactly sure. I tried to keep up with Knox, but I think I took a wrong turn somewhere—" Doug paused to look up at Knox, "You move fast, for a big guy, you know that?"

Knox inclined his head, just once, and Mic wasn't sure if it was in agreement, or just merely an acknowledgment of fact. Either way, she had seen Knox in action, and had to agree with Doug. The man could move.

"Anyway, I must have been walking for a bit, and I heard this noise behind me, but when I turned, something just hit me in the face, and it was lights out. I'm not exactly sure what it was, it happened so fast." Doug shrugged. "I don't know how long I was out, but when I came to, I couldn't see or hear anyone, so I started walking."

If at all possible, Knox's face became grimmer. "It looks like a rifle butt," he said, pointing to a slightly darker outline within the bruise.

Doug's face slackened with shock. "A what? Who the hell has a rifle out here?"

"You're lucky, you only got hit with the gun," Knox said as he straightened.

Confusion darkened Doug's eyes, and Mic took a deep breath. "It gets worse, Doug." She told him quickly about what had happened with George and Wayne, and she rubbed him on the shoulder as he blinked back tears at the news of two of his staff being brutally shot to death. His grief dissipated when she told him about Andy Rickerson.

He looked up at Knox. "You saw him do this?"

"I didn't see the attack, and I didn't see his face, but I could see Mic was running from a guy. My priority was Mic, though."

Doug nodded. "Of course, of course." He covered his mouth with a shaking hand for a moment, and Mic could see his gaze jerking from one object to another as he rapidly processed the information.

"I just—I'm in shock," he admitted finally, shaking his head.

"So are we, but Doug—we have a dozen staff out here who are at risk. None of us have phone reception, we can't call for help. We need to get to that rendezvous point—I'm figuring we can call for help there." Mic glanced up at Knox, and he nodded.

"Up here, it'll get darker earlier. We need to get moving," he said, his tone terse.

"What about the others?" Doug queried.

"We'll keep an eye out for them as we go," Mic told him, holding out her hand to him. "But the best thing would be to get those we have with us at the moment to safety, and call for help for the others."

Doug accepted her hand, and Knox shifted in to help him to his feet. They crossed the stream carefully, and Doug greeted Kelly and Aidan warmly. Mic noticed her boss's wariness as he glanced about, and the smile he put on his face when he spoke with the others. It was a relief to have someone else there with her, someone to shoulder the responsibility for the staff. Even though Knox seemed to do that instinctively, the Eagle Express management still had a duty of care for their staff, and it felt like a load was lifted off her shoulders just by having Doug with them.

She took another sip from the stream before they all scaled that small hill to the more even ground at the top. She glanced about. Knox was right. It was getting darker. She glanced at her watch, then growled softly. The watch face was cracked, and no matter how much she pressed the pushy buttons on the rim, she couldn't get the screen to light up and display the time. She wasn't quite sure when she'd broken it, but not knowing the time was damned annoying … maybe it was having some sense of awareness about something, as opposed to wondering if and when the shooter would strike next.

Doug stumbled, and both she and Knox caught him. They exchanged looks. Doug had taken a hit to the head, and he was a little unsteady on his feet. She hoped the man didn't have a concussion—for his sake. But Knox was keeping an eye on him, and she was again grateful she wasn't alone.

Kelly and Aidan were ahead of them, and Aidan paused. "Is that Roger? Hey, Roger!"

Mic heard Knox swear under his breath, and he increased his pace. Mic stayed with Doug, but craned her neck to keep her eye on Knox as he jogged through the underbrush toward Roger Brown and John Slazinger. Roger worked in the operations section in the imports division, and John was a phone operator in customer service. She was relieved to see them safe and uninjured. Still, she couldn't quite relax, not after what Andy had done to her.

Both men seemed surprised and somewhat happy to see them. Knox spoke with them quietly, and she could see their expressions fall into more serious lines. He was bringing them up to speed on what was going on.

She glanced about. That brought their party to seven. Out of the twenty staff that had set out, two were dead, one had gone rogue, so that left ten others … somewhere. She eyed the forest. It really was getting darker, the air cooler. The sun had already passed over the crest of one of the mountains, and the ravine they were in seemed to be settling into its gloom. She bit her lip. None of them had flashlights. She turned hopefully toward Roger and John. With their map and water bottles—John shook his head at Knox as he raised what was left of their kit. There was a large tear in the bag, and it looked like they'd lost the contents. She cast her gaze skyward, cursing inwardly. Come *on*. Surely, they could catch a break, *somehow*? What else could go wrong?

Knox patted John on the shoulder, then strode over to where she stood with Dave. "They stumbled a little on some rocks and tore their bag. Lost everything except one bottle of water."

"We're going to die out here, aren't we?" Kelly said, approaching them, her face anxious.

"No, we're not going to die," Mic said, reaching to place her hand on the woman's arm. "We're going to get through this."

"How? We've got one bottle of water between all of us, we're lost, and some shooter prick is out there gunning for us." Kelly's jawline was tense as she lifted her chin toward Mic.

"We have one bottle, but a stream right there," Mic pointed out quietly, keeping her voice calm. "We won't die of thirst, and we're not as lost as you think, we know the direction we need to head in—and we haven't heard any shots for ages … this guy may have lost interest, may have gone home, hell, may have even turned the gun on himself …" She hesitated. That wasn't a scenario she really believed, but it could have happened, right? That could be the reason why a shot hadn't been fired in nearly two hours, right? "We just need to keep calm, and keep going."

Kelly's lips tightened, and it looked like she wanted to say something else, but finally decided against it. She looked downstream. "Fine."

"We should get moving, then," Knox said quietly. "It's going to get real dark, real quick, and it's more dangerous if we try walking at night, without seeing where we're putting our feet."

Doug nodded wearily. "I agree, we should keep moving."

Knox rounded the others up, and they started to walk on through the underbrush, the sound of water tumbling over rocks and birdcalls as the gloom spread an almost tranquil soundtrack.

It's a hike. We're just on a hike, enjoying nature. Mic wondered if she repeated that often enough whether she'd really start to believe it. Her gaze darted through the forest, trying to track any movement, looking for … what? A rifle barrel poking out of a bush? A dark figure taking aim?

She took a deep breath, trying to stop that hoppity-thump of her heart kicking up in gear.

"I can't believe this is happening," Doug said quietly beside her, and she glanced at him briefly before returning her attention to making sure she didn't sprain an ankle on a tree root or trip over a rock.

"Me neither," she responded.

"In all the years we've held the retreat, this …" he gestured to the group, the forest surrounding them, and shook his head. "We've never lost an employee."

Again, visions of George apologizing, his tears, the regret and fear in his face, slapped at her mind, and she squeezed her eyes shut to try and block it out—unsuccessfully. His last gasps, then his head—she stumbled a little as she stepped on a rock, and opened her eyes reluctantly to focus on where she walked.

"How did—how did you survive?" Doug asked, and she saw the curiosity, his incredulity, in his eyes.

She shrugged. "I guess God doesn't want me walking through those pearly gates just yet." She eyed her fellow hikers. "I don't know how, or why, but … he missed me." She held up a hand. "Not for lack of trying, though, let me tell you." That scramble through the ravine, with bullets flying and tufts of dirt and rock exploding around her—that heart-hammering fear was right there, ready to surface whenever she wanted to walk down that particular memory lane.

"I just—I don't understand *why*?" Dave said, clenching his hands into fists and giving them a little shake.

She frowned, and turned to him. He halted, so she did the same, letting the others walk on ahead. "It's the case, Doug. The trial."

His eyebrows rose, and he gave the tiniest of head shakes. She nodded. "Yes, Doug. That guy in my room last night—he wasn't a random thief."

Her boss opened his mouth to argue, and she lifted a hand to forestall him. "No, you can't believe that the two incidents are unrelated. A guy tried to kill me in my room," she hissed, stepping closer so none of the others would hear. She didn't want to scare them any more than they were already.

"Someone tried to kill me last night, and failed. Today, we have some sharpshooter hiding like a skunk in the hills, picking off staff. George was involved, Doug, and now he's dead. I think Wayne was involved, too. George and Wayne worked together on a few things, were good friends …"

Doug tripped a little over his feet, and braced himself against a tree trunk. He frowned. "What makes you think George was involved?"

"He said something to me before he died, about how he was sorry, and that I wasn't meant to get hurt. That means he knew something … I believe he was involved, he and Wayne together."

"But—but if they were involved with the drug trafficking, why would whoever they're working for want them killed?"

That stopped her for a moment. Doug had a point. "It does sound a little chop-your-nose-off-to-spite-your-face, doesn't it?" She shrugged. "Maybe whoever is behind this is cleaning house."

"I don't know, Michaela. This is all supposition, and if it is the guys behind the drug trafficking—and we don't know that it is—I just don't see how it could benefit them."

"Well, apart from getting rid of anyone in a position to testify …" Mic said, giving him a meaningful look. She straightened, placing her hands on her hips. She took a deep breath. Oh, that felt good. Slightly painful, but good, releasing some of the strain on her core muscles and filling her lungs. She looked her boss in the eye.

"Either way, they've made a huge mistake."

"How so?"

"If they thought killing our staff would scare me off testifying, they're wrong. I will make damn sure everyone involved with this whole operation gets what's coming to them. They kill George and Wayne, then come after us, put these guys—Kelly, Aidan, the others, at risk, attack you, attack me—I won't stop until I lay waste to their whole operation, until all that is left is a pile of ashes." The resolve burned in her, fueling her muscles, giving her strength and purpose. She was going to bring these bastards down.

Doug blinked, then nodded. "Okay, then."

She turned and started to walk on. She could hear Doug follow on behind her, the sound of his feet shuffling through the brush. "We have to go through everything. I know the FBI are searching, but if they're coming after us, it suggests there's something—or someone—that is still to be found."

Which meant she was back to suspecting the bejeebus out of everyone. Damn it. She paused. George had known something. George had been involved, and he'd been shot. The only reason she'd been paired with George was because Luis Montenegro had protested her teaming up with Knox. But how had he known she'd end up with George? She guessed it wasn't too much of a stretch to realize the other executive involved in the activity would volunteer to swap. Had Luis orchestrated the situation to set her up with George intentionally? Kill two birds with one bullet, so to speak.

No, seriously? Sure, he'd been acting like a pain in her proverbial ever since his three colleagues had been arrested, but did she really think Luis could be involved? Was he somehow involved with the man who'd attacked her?

"Hey, was Luis still in the bar last night when you got the call about my attack?"

Doug didn't comment, so she shrugged. "I know, I'm grasping at straws. It's ridiculous, right?" She turned to where she thought Doug would be, but … he wasn't. She frowned, scanning the forest behind her.

Doug was back near the tree, collapsed on the ground.

"Doug!" Heart hammering, she started to run toward him. She hadn't heard a shot—not even a suppressor could completely silence a bullet, right?

"Doug! Knox! Help!" She skidded to a stop next to Doug, and reached for him gently. There were no marks on his back, no bullet wounds bloodying his clothes. Footsteps thudded toward her, and she looked up. Knox was moving through the group with startling speed. He halted when he reached her, and dropped to his knees.

"What happened?"

"I don't know. One minute we were talking, and I thought he was right behind me, the next I turn around and he's on the ground, out cold."

Knox touched Doug's neck, and was quiet for a moment. "He's still got a pulse. Help me move him—be careful, though." Knox positioned himself at Doug's head and shoulders, and counted Mic into the turn. They carefully rolled the unconscious CEO onto his back, and Knox gently pushed back the eyelids. Doug's eyelashes fluttered, and he coughed, his hands coming up to ineffectively swat at Knox's hands.

"What are you doing? What happened?"

"You passed out," Knox told him. He sat back on his haunches, then gazed about the area. "I think you may have a concussion."

"He needs medical attention," Mic said, and she could feel the strain pulling at her shoulders.

Knox nodded, then forced a smile on to his face as he turned to her. "He needs rest. We can at least give him that." He glanced about. "Okay, folks. Change of plans. I'd hoped we'd get a little further before nightfall, but this looks like as good a place as any to set up camp. We'll stop here for the night."

Damn it. He should have thought to grab Mic's bloodstained jacket, along with the tracker he'd embedded, when he'd found George's body, but he'd been so worried about finding Mic alive and pulling her out of danger that it hadn't occurred to him. Right now, Fitz would be searching that area. He would have no idea how far they'd run off-course, or where the hell they were, currently. With the fading light, Fitz wouldn't be able to mount a proper search party until dawn. He eyed the terrain. No cell reception, heavily wooded … he'd almost consider giving Dan his cousin's phone number in exchange for a satellite phone, right about now.

"What?" Kelly frowned, stepping forward. "What about the shooter?"

Knox grimaced. "He hasn't fired another shot for ages, now. If we continue walking in the dark, we're more likely to get injured from that than from a shooter who may or may not still be around. Besides, Doug needs a break."

"No, I can keep—" Doug tried to rise, and Knox had to catch him as he fell back again. "Oh, wow."

"Okay, let's at least take a break." Knox said, glancing up at Mic, and she nodded in agreement. Doug looked pale, and while she didn't want to spend the night in the forest, short of them carrying Doug in the darkness and putting them at risk of more injury, this seemed the most sensible course of action.

"By this stage, they should have noticed our absence at the rendezvous point, and will be marshalling search parties," she said, crossing her fingers behind her back. She hoped that was the case—it seemed logical—but she had no way of knowing unless some park ranger walked up to them with a torch and a map and food … "We'll set up camp, and trek out at first light." *God willing.*

~*~

Knox knelt by the fire he'd started, gently putting more kindling onto it so it got a good hold. Sure, there was a risk it could act like a beacon for their hunter, but this group was hungry, exhausted, sporting various injuries and they were exposed to the elements. To limit further injuries or sickness, a little warmth and light was a calculated risk. Mic had gathered some firewood, with the help of Aidan and John, while he'd cleared the area for the fire. Kelly was sitting with Doug, keeping an eye on him, keeping him talking, and Roger was taking first 'watch'. The man was perched up on higher ground, his back against a tree, as he gazed out over their campsite and immediate surrounds.

"Wow, I can't believe you managed to start that from scratch," Mic commented as she dropped another armload of branches on the pile nearby.

He sat back on his heels, and raised three fingers. She smiled and nodded. "Always be prepared. I'm beginning to take that to heart." She glanced in Doug's direction, and sobered. "How is he doing?"

Knox spared the man a quick glance. Kelly looked like she was in an animated discussion with the man. "He's going to be fine. If it is a concussion, it's mild. Otherwise, he's probably just got a headache the size of Texas going on inside his skull, and he's a little dehydrated. We're probably looking at maybe a two-hour hike tomorrow, and he'll be able to manage that after a night's rest."

Mic sighed as she stared at her boss, and Knox could see the worry, the tension, in the lines that bracketed her mouth, the shadows beneath her eyes … and then there were the bruises around her neck. He reached for more kindling and tossed it on the fire.

"I don't like this," she said in a low voice, and he glanced up. She was now glancing about the group, and further, into the darkening forest. He wondered if she was talking to him, or just thinking aloud. Her gaze flicked to his, and he realized she did want him to hear her, that she was talking to him, and him alone, about her fears.

He nodded as he rose. "I don't either," he told her quietly. Hell, he hated this. Andy Rickerson was still out there, somewhere, and he didn't really think the shooter had just packed up and gone home. He wanted her back at the resort, hell, back in her home would be even better, with nobody from Eagle Express within reach of her. "But it is what it is. Doug needs rest, and we're likely to hurt ourselves if we wander round in the dark. We'll all take turns during the night as lookout …" But yeah, he didn't like this, and the fact Mic wasn't falling into complacency showed her survival instincts were finally trumping those self-sacrificing tendencies of hers. Or maybe it was just her protective instinct coming to the fore. As soon as Kelly and Aidan had appeared, he noticed her talk of separating had stopped … as though she recognized the best way to protect her staff was to deliver them to safety herself.

He touched her briefly on her upper arm. "You'll be safe, Mic. Don't worry. I won't let anything happen to you."

She looked down at the point where his hand rested on her arm, then looked up at him, her smile bittersweet. "I'm the one who should be looking after you, Knox." She tilted her head. "What did you do, before you started working with us?"

He blinked. "It's on my résumé. I was a storeman at a seafood distributor." Smithy had thought that hysterical when he'd created his background.

Mic shook her head, and jerked her chin toward the fire. "No, the way you handled yourself when the shooting started, finding me instead of taking cover, the way you fought off that guy last night, the way you started the fire—"

"I told you, I used to be a—"

"I think this goes beyond being a Boy Scout. I know you're ex-military, but what branch?"

His eyes narrowed. "How do you—"

Shouts broke out in the camp, and they both turned to see Luis Montenegro stagger out from the underbrush, half-dragging, half-carrying a woman who was clutching her side, blood streaming from between her fingers and down her leg.

"Oh, my God, Camilla," Mic breathed, and Knox joined her as she ran toward the couple.

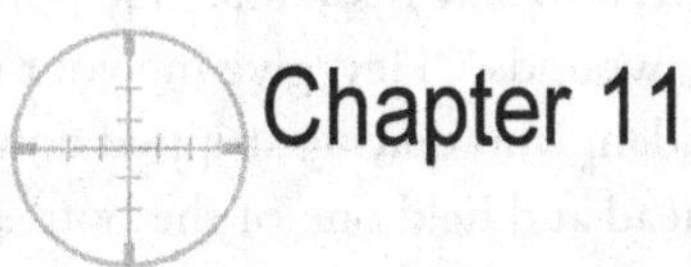# Chapter 11

"Camilla!" Mic called as she ran. Knox overtook her, reaching the couple just before she did.

"What happened?" Knox asked.

"Some asshole shot at us," Luis muttered. He nodded at Knox, relinquishing his hold on the woman, and Knox scooped her up and carried her over toward the fire. Mic followed closely behind, and beckoned John over with the one bottle of water.

Camilla was shivering, her lips blue, and Knox spoke to her in a low, calm voice as he lifted up her shirt. Mic blanched at the sight of the wound. A small, ragged hole had torn into the woman's stomach. Knox gently rolled her over, and Mic swallowed her gasp when she saw the larger hole in her back.

"Okay, it's a through-and-though," Knox said, settling the woman on her side. "You're going to be okay, Camilla," he told her in a low soothing voice. He shrugged out of his jacket, and then tugged at the sleeves of his shirt until the fabric tore at the shoulder seams. "I need water—oh, thanks," he said in surprise as Mic handed it to him. Mic looked up at Luis.

"Do you still have your water bottles, your map?"

Luis glared at her for a moment, before finally nodding, his lips tight.

"Good. Get the bottles out." She turned to John. "These are the only things we've got to hold water at the moment. I'm going to give you empty bottles, and I need you to run to the stream to refill."

Camilla whimpered as Knox poured the water over her wounds, then used his sleeves to clean the area in order to get a good look. "Give her something to drink. She's lost a lot of blood, she's going to need to stay hydrated." He poured more water, flushing out the wounds. "Hey, give me your shirts," he called to Roger and Aidan, who quickly stripped down.

Luis cradled her head and held one of the bottles to her lips. Camilla drank, her throat muscles working hard to swallow. Mic knelt behind her. "What can I do to help?"

Knox inspected first the entry wound, then the exit wound. "We need to stop the bleeding." He dragged his shirt over his head, sank his teeth into the hem, and then started tearing the garment into strips, his muscles flexing as he pulled at the fabric. He started knotting some of the ends together.

He folded up one of the shirts into a thick, wadded mass, then held out the fabric to Mic. "Press that against the wound on her back. Firmly."

She did as instructed, grimacing as Camilla flinched and gasped.

"It's okay, Camilla, you're going to be fine." She smoothed the woman's hair back from her forehead, and for a moment her gaze met the young woman's. Camilla was in the track and trace department, and they'd worked together to locate a number of lost parcels. The woman was smart, able to handle stress, and had a good sense of humor. Mic got along well with her, respected her. Mic's stomach muscles clenched at the fear, the pain she saw in the younger woman's eyes. "You're going to be fine," she repeated in a murmur, and a tear rolled down Camilla's cheek.

Knox nodded as he pressed the other shirt to the wound in front. "This is going to hurt, Camilla," he said, and Camilla's gaze switched to meet Knox's. "But it will help slow down, maybe even stop the bleeding, and that's what we need to do with you at the moment, okay?"

Camilla's head moved in a semblance of a nod, and Knox glanced briefly at Luis. "I need you to press this against her entry wound."

Luis leaned forward and pressed the bunched material to Camilla's abdomen, his hand already streaked with her blood, and Knox looked over Camilla's body at Mic. "Keep it firm. We're going to ease her up, just a little, and I'm going to wrap these cloths around her body, okay?"

Mic nodded, applying pressure as the three of them helped lift Camilla's shoulders slightly off the ground. Camilla sobbed, her head lolling back at the pain. Knox worked rapidly, wrapping the makeshift bandage tightly around her body. Mic held the wadded shirt in place, as did Luis. Knox pulled the last bit firmly, and knotted it off.

"Okay, let's ease her back down. You're doing great, Cam—whoa, there she goes," Knox said. Mic felt Camilla slump, and realized the woman had passed out.

Mic sat back on her haunches, fighting her own trembling. She clenched her hands into fists. Camilla had been shot. Badly injured. She glanced down at her hands, and uncurled them, staring in horror at the blood that now stained them. Her vision blurred as tears formed, and she rose to stalk back toward the stream, occasionally stumbling over a stone or a tuft of grass as she left the faint light of the fire and stepped into the night's gloom. Her breath shuddered past her lips.

Camilla didn't deserve this. There was no way she was involved in the drug case. Mic wouldn't believe it. She knew Camilla. Sure, she thought she'd known the others, as well, but—Camilla worked so damn hard, she always put in one hundred percent effort in finding other peoples' shipments, she invested so much damn care in her work, Mic couldn't see her being a part of this. No way.

She dropped to her knee on the muddy bank, ignoring the squelch, the smell, and the damp sensation oozing through her jeans, and leaned forward to wash her hands. So much blood. *Too much.*

Her hands shook, causing bubbles and waves in the water. Images—of Wayne's body, of George, of the blood and gore, flooded her mind, and the shaking spread through her arms and body, and something hot trailed down her cheek.

She could hear the crackle of the fire up the bank behind her, could hear the hum of quiet conversation. She brought her hands up to cover her face.

Oh, my God. This was just—this was *hell.* Camilla. George. Wayne. Doug, too. She heard Aidan's voice, not quite as deep as the others, and she took a deep, shuddering breath. These people needed her to be calm, to help them. She couldn't just dissolve into a puddle of hysterical tears, here. And quite frankly, Camilla was the one whose sides had been torn apart by a bullet. If anyone deserved to cry here, it was Camilla.

She took several deep breaths, forcing herself to pull at an elusive calm and drag it over her like a blanket, covering the turmoil and the holy-crap panic that was itching to get out. She splashed her face with the cold water, then dragged her sleeve across her lips. She didn't have the luxury of giving in to the hysteria. Her boss had a mild concussion and was weak. Camilla was hopefully not bleeding out on the forest floor, and the others—well, they needed direction. They had to get out of here, no more injuries, no more deaths. Her mind started scrambling over their options, and this time the calm felt a little more real as she did what she did best—considered the logistics, and what they needed to do to make things happen.

She rose from the stream and turned, mentally making a list of things as she walked back to the camp. She stopped at the clearing and looked about. Kelly was now quiet, and Doug lay comfortably on the ground, using his jacket as a pillow. Aidan sat near the fire, holding a branch and tipping the end into the flames. John and Roger sat close by, staring morosely into the fire. Luis was sitting near Camilla, and it looked like her head was resting on his jacket, Camilla's own blood-stained jacket carefully draped across her for warmth. He held a twig in his hand, turning it over and over as he stared unseeingly at the fire. Knox sat just a little further away, his arms resting on his knees. He'd donned his jacket but was shirtless, his bare chest a burnished gold in the firelight. She skittered her gaze away from his body, and she turned to address the group on the other side of the fire.

"Camilla's not going to be able to walk out of here tomorrow morning," she said in a low voice. "As soon as it's light, we'll have to build a stretcher for her, and help carry her out. It's too dark to make it now, and you'll need your coats through the night. I suggest we all huddle up for warmth. The later it gets, the colder it will be. We're going to have to look out for each other, but we are getting out of here."

"And wouldn't that be peachy," Kelly muttered.

Mic frowned. "What do you mean?"

The data entry team leader rose to her feet, her eyes flashing. "This is all your fault," the woman hissed.

"Kelly," Knox said, rising to his feet, his voice low in warning.

"No, she should hear this." Kelly flung her arms out, encompassing the basic campsite. "We're all here because of you. Wayne, George, Camilla—they were all shot because of you." The woman turned, finger pointing at Mic's chest. "We are all in danger because of *you*, and here you are giving us pep talks on how we're all getting out of here."

"Kelly—" Mic said, but startled when Luis launched to his feet, his expression twisted.

"She's right. You're the one who started this," he said, advancing toward her, finger pointing in accusation. "Camilla is lying there in a pool of blood, and that's on you."

Knox quickly inserted himself in front of Luis, his hands up to ward him off. "Stop."

"No, man," Luis argued, although he was forced to halt because Knox was too big and stubborn to walk over. "This is all her fault. Adam, Jerry, Vito—none of this would have happened if she hadn't ratted on them. Now Wayne and George are dead, and Camilla probably won't make it through the night."

Hurt, hot and vicious, sparked inside her as the barb cut deep. In reaction, anger, like a pure stream of molten mercury, coursed through her, tinged with the guilt, dismay and the remorse she'd felt since she'd found Wayne's body. And it was that remorse that made her anger flare hotter. Her eyes narrowed as she stepped closer to Luis.

"Let's get something straight. The reason Adam, Jerry and Vito were arrested is because *they* screwed up, not me. Your so-called friends were using the company that pays you, so you can feed your family and keep a roof over your kids' heads, to run *drugs*," she hissed. "And yes, I found out, and yes, I reported it—because why the hell wouldn't I? Why wouldn't *you*?" Luis's eyes narrowed, and Mic indicated Camilla, still passed out on the ground. "Do you think I'd want her hurt? Or Wayne and George killed? Seriously? Why don't we put the responsibility for this on the people who did the act? Those people you hold in such high esteem; Adam, and Jerry and Vito—they're who you're loyal to here? They're the ones who started this, not me. I'm not the one trekking through the damn hills with a rifle—no, it's someone acting on *their* behalf, not yours, and sure as hell not mine."

She shook her head in disbelief at the sheer injustice of it. "I can't help but wonder, seeing as you're so eager to pin this on me, are you involved in this whole mess, too?"

Luis's eyebrows rose, and his lips curled back as he reached for her. "You bitch!" Knox pushed him back, and kept pushing, despite Luis's attempts to get her. Luis was jumping and swearing, but Knox still put considerable distance between them, batting away Luis's arms.

"Stop it," Knox growled, Luis's eyes darted between her and Knox, but something in Knox's eyes, or maybe it was the implacable tone he'd used, or the fact that Luis looked like a fly swatting at a mountain as he tried to wrestle with the larger, stronger, more formidable man, either way, he stopped trying to get past Knox.

Knox glanced over his shoulder, frowning at Mic. Yeah, she read his message loud and clear. The shush look. He wanted her to keep her mouth shut, too, just when she'd finally found her voice against all this rubbish. She glared at the others gathered around the camp. Kelly's gaze dropped to the ground. Doug's eyes met hers, his expression unreadable.

"I'm going to get some more firewood," she snapped, and trudged off into the darkness. She didn't care where she went, but she needed space. Before she did something stupid like punch that snarl right off Luis's face.

~*~

Knox watched as Mic stomped away, then shoved Luis just hard enough to land him on his backside and glared down at him. "You idiot." He shook his head. "She has a point, you know. You're protecting drug runners, guys who used you, duped you. And you stick up for them, and then blame her because she was smarter than all of you and figured out what they were doing." His tone was full of disgust.

Luis shot him a surly look. "You don't know anything."

"I know you're acting like a dick," Knox pointed out. He looked over at Kelly. "You both are." He swore, then took a deep breath. "We need the bottles of water re-filled—"

"I'll do it," Aidan offered, rising to his feet. The younger man shot both Kelly and Luis a hard look before scooping up the bottles and walking down toward the stream.

"Great. Roger, finish first watch. Who volunteers for second?" Knox asked, and nodded as John raised his hand.

"Then you, then you, then Aidan," he said, pointing to Luis and Kelly in turn.

"What about me?" Doug asked.

Knox eyed the CEO. The bruising had darkened up the side of his face, his eye almost fully closed due to the swelling. He'd been quiet during the exchange between Luis and Mic, something Knox hadn't quite expected from the boss, and could only assume he was still feeling the effects of the hit to the head. His face looked as if it hurt like the blazes.

"You'll need your rest before tomorrow's hike out. I'll take watch after Aidan, and then Mic can go last." If he could find her and get her back to camp without throttling anyone. He couldn't blame her, and it was good to see her hit back at the poor and unfair treatment from her staff—but Luis had been aggressive, and the whole temperature of the situation needed to be chilled out. Even now, though, he was getting a little antsy that she wasn't within his line of sight, but he could tell she needed some space to take a breather. That should be long enough, though. He didn't like not being able to see her, to reassure himself she was safe.

"I'm going to find Mic," he muttered, and turned to walk past Luis in the direction Mic had taken, but paused when he reached the man. He leaned over. "If you ever raise your hand against a woman again, I will deck you myself." He met Luis's gaze with a steely one of his own, until the other man finally looked away, the muscle in his jaw flexing. Knox hurried off into the darkness, squinting to see where his package had stomped off to.

Night had well and truly fallen, and he paused, listening. There. Heavy footsteps, uneven, as though the walker was pausing just to pound her foot into the dirt before she took off again, muttering under her breath. He jogged in that direction, and then he heard it, that soft little sob that caught at him, tugging at strings that were already wrapping around his heart.

"Hey, Mic," he called softly into the darkness, not wanting to frighten her by his approach. "Mic."

The footsteps stopped, and there was a little sniff. "Go away."

He shook his head. "I can't do that, Mic." A darker mass materialized out of the gloom, and he slowed until he reached her.

"I'll be fine, seriously. I'm just going to pick up some sticks and come back—"

"You didn't have to run this far for sticks."

"I'm not running away." The words were uttered low and fierce, and he sighed.

"I know. He was being a di—"

"He wanted me to keep my mouth shut, you wanted me to keep my mouth shut—" she turned and started to stomp again. "I'm so damn sick and tired of people wanting me to shut up and disappear."

He reached for her arm, halting her retreat. "Whoa, that's not—"

She whirled on him, her eyes bright in the darkness. There was scattered cloud cover, and the moon seemed to be an almost useless sliver, but even so, the low wattage of the stars revealed the streaks of silver on her face from the tears she brushed furiously away. "Really? You didn't give me the shush look?" He didn't need the light of the stars to be able to feel the accusation, the anger thrumming through her, trembling in her voice.

He opened his mouth to argue, but then growled in frustration. "Fine, you're right, I did give you the—" he hesitated, frowning, "the shush look?" He'd never heard it called that before.

"You know, when you want someone to just shut the hell up." She jerked her arm out of his grasp. "I'm so angry right now, damn it." She kicked at something on the ground.

"I know, and you've got every right to be. He was being a jerk. But I think he could have been even more of a jerk, and

things would have escalated, and we all need to calm down
and work together. But I'm sorry for giving you the shush
look."

He pursed his lips. Maybe he should have just let her at
Luis. The guy definitely deserved it. Really, he could have held
the schmuck down for her.

She growled softly. "No, you were right, damn it, and that
just makes me angrier." She kicked at something else, and he
folded his arms as he stepped back. She needed to blow off
some steam. Justifiably.

"It just—I'm not the bad one, here, you know?"

"I know."

"Hollison, Pavlovich, Garcia—they're the bad ones. And
this shooter prick, he's a bad one."

"A very bad one."

"And I am getting the blame for every stupid, evil, bad,
bad thing they've done, and it's. Not. Fair. Damn it." She
pounded a tree trunk with the base of her fist to punctuate her
words.

"No, it's not."

"But it shouldn't matter, because I'm his boss. I shouldn't
engage like that, and at the moment he's being a dick
because ..." her voice trailed off, and her shoulders slumped.

"Because?" Knox leaned forward, curious to hear what
she had to say.

"Because he's stressed and scared and ..."

"And ...?"

"And he's right."

Knox blinked. "What?"

Mic tilted her forehead to rest against the bark of the
trunk. "Because he's right." The words were so low, almost a
whisper, he had to step forward to make sure he heard her
properly. "Me reporting the drug trafficking started off a chain
of events," she said, and he could hear the tremor in her
voice. "If I had kept my mouth shut, then Wayne and George

would still be alive, and Camilla wouldn't be fighting for her life."

Knox was too stunned to do anything but let the silence stretch between them for a moment.

"I didn't know Wayne very well at all, but George—even though it sounds like George was involved, he didn't deserve … that." The word emerged on a croak, as though the memory was stripping everything back to pure essence. She shook her head, and her ponytail swung across her back, like dark coils stretching down. "I didn't pull the trigger, but I was the reason he got shot."

Ah, hell. Knox shook his head in denial, then reached for her, resting his hand against her shoulder. "That's not true."

"It is," she argued softly, and shuffled around to face him. He let his hand remain on her shoulder. "I started this, Knox. I—I keep seeing Wayne, lying on the ground, and then George …" she wrapped her arms around her waist, hunching over, and he could feel the vibrations of agony emanating from her, could see the silvery gleam of tears tracking down her face.

"George—he was in so much pain, and he was scared, Knox. He was afraid to die, afraid of the pain …" Her hand was a pale flutter in the night as she covered her mouth. "Luis and Kelly are right. I *am* responsible for all of this." Her voice was so raw, so hoarse with pain, with recrimination, with grief-stricken misery.

He couldn't stand it, couldn't stand seeing her, hearing her, tear herself apart like this. He pulled her close, wrapping his arms around her. "No, this isn't on you, Mic. You caught them, but if you didn't, somebody else would have … that's the nature of these sorts of operations. So many people … sooner or later, someone does something, says something, and somebody else notices. This time, you noticed. That's all." She sagged against him, as though drained. He rubbed his hands up and down her back, folding her close. "This isn't your fault, sweetness."

She rested her cheek against his chest, and they stood like that for a while. Eventually he realized he could feel the flutter of her eyelashes brush against his skin each time she blinked.

And it was like a tiny electric shock to his libido. His skin became so sensitized to the sweep of an eyelash. Her heart thumped, steady and regular, against his chest, and her stomach rested against …

He cast his eyes up to the cloudy night sky. *For Pete's sake, get control of yourself.* Mic sucked in a deep breath, and he closed his eyes against the swell of her breasts pressing against him. And then she exhaled, and her breath gusted across his nipple.

Knox clenched his jaw. Swallowed. Counted to ten. Recited the alphabet backwards. He had got to T when he felt that slow, sweep of long eyelash, and lost his place. He brought his hand up to her head and stroked her hair. He tried to keep it soothing. Friendly. Platonic. Stroke. Stroke … *Count the stars, damn it.* Her hair was long enough to hang on to, and he absently coiled the tangled length of her ponytail around his hand before he realized what he was doing. He shook his hand as though he'd slammed it in a car door.

"Oh, crap," he muttered.

"Ow," Mic gasped, her hand reaching for her ponytail, and she stepped back.

He sucked in a breath at the distance, at the space—thank God, because in another millisecond he would have kissed her.

"Sorry," he said. *Great. This is … awkward.*

"No, that's all right. I should be the one apologizing." She glanced up at the sky, then back in the direction of the camp. From their viewpoint they could see the glow of the fire, but not the fire itself. "I shouldn't be blubbering all over you, especially about your colleagues." She smoothed her hands over her cheeks, and her gaze met his briefly. In that moment, he saw her need, her vulnerability, her … desire. She blinked, then rubbed her sleeve across her nose. "Uh, why don't you go back to the fire, and I'll be along shortly."

"Uh …" he looked about, frowned. "I'd rather not." For the life of him he couldn't find an excuse to stick around her without saying something like … *I'm your bodyguard and I need to protect you*, or … *I really want to kiss you and show you how special you are.* Besides, he didn't trust Luis. The guy was too eager to blame Mic, and to get physical with her. He had no idea whether the air ops supervisor—or any of the others in their group—could also be part of this drug fiasco. "I think it's best—under the circumstances—that I stay with you. You know, because of the shooter."

"Yeah, the shooter." She folded her arms and scanned the darkness.

"But if you don't want to head back just yet, I'm happy to hang here with you …?" he gestured to a patch of grass beneath the tree. They'd started the fire for necessity, but it was a bit of a beacon in the night, particularly for a random shooter intent on killing anyone involved in the illicit operations at Eagle Express. Unless the guy had a night scope—and Knox had no way of knowing—he wasn't expecting an attack overnight. But if he could separate Mic from those who could potentially do her harm, then he would work with that.

Mic folded her arms, glanced back toward the camp, then at him again. She nodded. "Okay."

She dropped to the ground, scooting up so that her back was against the tree trunk. "So, tell me, who are you, Knox Jones—really?"

Chapter 12

Knox paused, just for a moment, then sat down on the grass next to her, his movements slow. Mic saw him blink, and then glance out into the forest surrounding them before finally meeting her eyes.

"What do you mean?" His tone was confused, but his eyes were wary. "I'm Knox Jones."

Mic's lips curved at his insistence. "I know that, I mean where did you come from? What did you do before Eagle Express? Your résumé mentioned courier jobs, a bit of warehouse packing … but the way you've handled yourself the last couple of days makes me think there is a little more to you than that."

Knox drew his legs up and rested his arms across his knees. His jacket was parted, and she tried really hard to keep her gaze on his face, and not his chest, but her gaze would dip, every now and then, to look at him, the firm pectoral muscles, the corded strength of his abdomen. *And back to his eyes, Mic.* She forced herself to meet his gaze.

Knox shrugged. "What you see is what you get, Mic."

Well, she could see plenty, and wanted to see more, but it didn't distract her from the fact that Knox was handling this situation like a pro. She shook her head.

"No, I don't think so. I mean, take the way you fought off that guy last night in my room." This time it was Mic who drew her legs up, hugging her knees at the memory. "I couldn't fight him off, he was fast, he was strong, and then you came in and went all Jackie Chan on him."

Knox snorted. "I'd hardly call me that," he said, shaking his head, but he shrugged again. "I know a little martial arts, that's all. Not much."

"Enough, though." She tilted her head as she looked at him. He kept his gaze on the grass at his feet. "What kind of martial arts? My older brother, Matt, did karate when he was a teenager."

Knox shook his head. "Uh, it's more of a mish-mash. I studied a little Taekwondo when I was younger, but then learned some rough hand-to-hand combat stuff."

She opened her mouth to ask him more, but he beat her to it. "So, you've got a brother, huh?"

"Two, actually. Both are older than me. You? Do you have any brothers or sisters?"

"No," Knox said, shaking his head again. He shot her a dry smile. "I'm an only child."

"Where did you grow up?"

Knox glanced back at the grass. "Uh, lots of places …" She raised an eyebrow at his vague answer, and he chuckled. "I'm an army brat. We moved around a lot."

"Ah … did you end up joining, yourself?"

That wary look came back in his eyes. "For a little while."

Ah. The hand-to-hand combat stuff.

"Huh. That wasn't on your résumé." That was odd … it wasn't something to be ashamed of. In fact, she would welcome anyone who served to protect their country. She knew the discipline and sacrifice that went with the job, and respected it, valued it. "What branch? My youngest brother, Rick, is a Ranger. Well, he's older than I am, but the younger of my brothers."

"Marine."

Again, his response was clipped, limited. Normally she'd just drop it, recognizing that it was a subject he obviously didn't want to talk about, but this wasn't a normal situation. "So that's where you learned to take on would-be hitmen and treat bullet wounds, huh?"

He nodded. "Yeah. I saw a fair bit—saw too many men die. Men and women." His gaze was clear, direct. "I know what it's like, Mic, to lose people you work with in a violent way, and to feel that if you'd just done something more, or not done something else, that they'd still be there with you."

Her jaw relaxed, surprised by the intensity of his words. He'd pretty much voiced the thoughts she'd been attacking herself with since George was killed in front of her. She looked away. She wondered if George would have died if Knox had been there, or if Knox would have reacted in a way that would have saved him … like he'd saved her the night before. She felt useless, powerless, against what had happened, what was *still* happening, to them.

"It took me a while to learn that shoulda, woulda, coulda doesn't change did." He shrugged. "This situation—it is what it is. If you keep taking on the responsibility, the guilt for what happened to your coworkers, it will wreck you just as effectively as a bullet ever could." His words were so matter-of-fact, so deliberate, they hit her in a way his previous placations hadn't.

She sat quietly for a moment, letting his words sink in, feeling the weight, the gravity of them. She couldn't begin to imagine how he'd learned that life lesson, but suspected it had been a very hard, painful lesson.

She looked at him again, and this time there was a shared understanding in his eyes, a compassion brought about by his own pain, that was both humbling and relatable. An unexpected connection that went deeper than anything she'd experienced before, and that she felt ill-equipped to completely understand.

He smiled, as though he saw her awareness, but also recognized her struggle to process it. He braced one hand on the grass next to his hip and leaned in her direction. "So, tell me. What about you? Why are you in logistics, for example?" He waved a hand casually back in the direction of the campsite. "Why Eagle Express?"

She thought about it for a moment. She could blow him off with a general answer … the type of thing you'd say to a new employee, but under these circumstances, and with what he'd already shared with her, she felt they'd gone beyond the normal employer–employee status. She considered him more than that, which was rare, after Sebastien. Did she consider him a trusted friend? Possibly, if she'd stop perving at his chest. But she could at least be honest with him.

"I've grown up with freight," she said simply. "My family have worked in the industry for decades … it just seemed natural to move into it."

Knox frowned. "But your brother, the ranger, didn't. What does your older brother do?"

She smiled. "Oh, he's in freight. He works with my father."

"Robson Global." He wasn't asking a question, and it didn't sound like much of a revelation. She supposed it was pretty easy to put the pieces together. She didn't go around bragging about the fact that her father's company was one of the biggest logistics companies in the world … but she never hid from it.

"Yeah."

Knox shifted, as though a little uncomfortable in that position, and she scooted over so that he could also lean back against the tree trunk. He accepted her unspoken offer, shuffling a little closer. He rested his back against the bark, their shoulders touching. He turned slightly to give her a perplexed look.

"Why are you working for Eagle Express, and not your family's company? I mean, surely that has more opportunities? You could work anywhere in the world, in whatever department you chose …"

Mic grimaced. "That's exactly why. I love logistics, I love getting stuff from one end of the earth to the other, and overcoming any challenge doing it. I want people to know that any success I make in this career is my own, and not because Daddy gave it to me. Eventually, I do want to work at the company, but as an equal, having earned my spot at the director's table through hard work, and not nepotism."

"Your brother?"

"Oh, he's definitely earned it. He worked in naval logistics for a few years before commissioning out to join my Dad—and he's a guy." She shrugged. "No matter which way you cut it, it's different for a woman, especially in such a male-dominated industry—or in my family."

"So, this is your version of earning your stripes, huh?"

She nodded, then sighed. "My father was dead-set against me taking this job," she said in a low voice.

"Why?"

She pulled at a blade of grass. "He didn't think I was the right 'man' for the job."

"I'm sure he didn't—"

"Oh, he did." That argument with her father was one she wasn't about to forget any time soon. "Eagle Express was 'not the right fit for me', and it would demand more than I'm capable of giving. His words." She tore the blade of grass into tiny pieces. "Up until this weekend, I believed I could prove him wrong." She sighed. "Sometimes I feel that unless I'm right there, under his supervision, he doesn't trust me to look after myself, or do my job."

Knox was silent for a moment, and Mic grimaced. "Ugh, I sound like such a princess with Daddy issues. Tell me about your family. What are your parents like?"

"Uh, well, they're both dead," he said.

She covered her face with her hands. "Oh, my God, I'm so sorry." She was the worst, peeling back all that pain for him. First his experience in the service, now his dead parents. She should just keep her mouth shut.

He chuckled as he dragged her hands back down to her legs. "It's okay, Mic. Dad died when I was a kid, and Mom died about six years ago. Cancer."

Oh, now that made it even worse. All that suffering … "I can't even begin to imagine what your mother went through, what *you've* been through …"

He made a face. "I've got good memories of Dad, and the stories I've heard since he passed …" He sighed. "But Mom loved him until the day he died. He was gone twenty-two years, and she never remarried, never wanted to." He pulled his legs up tighter against his chest. "I was devastated when she died, but she was happy to go. I mean, the suffering notwithstanding, she was finally going to see her Jack again."

Mic pressed her hand against her chest. "That is … wow. That's beautiful. And sad," she said quickly, not wanting him to think she was romanticizing his mother's death.

Knox nodded. "Yeah, it was beautiful. She was so peaceful, so … ready." He blinked rapidly for a moment, then drew in a breath. "Phew. I haven't talked about Mom in … years."

"Do you still have family around? Cousins, aunts, uncles?"

"Yeah. I try and catch up with them each Christmas, if I'm around."

She nodded, and had to fight off a giant feral curiosity cat. She couldn't deny it, Knox fascinated her, and she had so many questions about his life, his experience, his family. She didn't want to open up old wounds, though.

"Did you join the marines because of your father?"

Knox smiled, and there was something so bittersweet, so sadly charming, about it, that it caught and held her attention. "Yeah. He was a marine. A war hero, killed in action."

"I'm so sorry, Knox."

He shrugged. "It is what it is." He shifted to face her a little more fully, tilting his head to the side until his temple rested against the tree. "I've grown up with the stories about his service, his sacrifice …" he swallowed, and Mic's gaze dropped to the strong column of his throat, before returning to his intent gaze.

"How did he die?" she asked quietly.

"He was killed in a small Iraqi village, protecting women and children. They survived. He didn't."

She caught herself from saying 'I'm sorry' once again. It was such a deep, painful insight for him to share with her, anything sounded trite in response, so she remained silent.

"I've spent my life trying to make him proud," Knox admitted in a hoarse voice, his green eyes almost silver in the starlight. "You know, he wasn't around a lot, when he was alive, but … I do remember I felt loved by him. I admired him." He chuckled softly. "Hell, I worshipped him."

She twisted around to give him her full attention.

"I said goodbye to him when he deployed, but I never really got to say *goodbye*." Knox grimaced. "I have grown up trying to make him proud, and I wonder … would he be proud of the man I've become?" His voice grew raspy with emotion. "And there is a little part of me that fears maybe he wouldn't."

She placed her hand over the one resting on his knee, and Knox smiled, although the smile didn't quite reach his eyes. "So, you see, Mic, you're not the only one with Daddy issues."

Mic stared at him for a moment, her eyes taking in his forehead, the way his hair curled over it, those troubled green eyes, the shape of his lips. She found it incredible that he doubted whether his father would be proud of him. She squeezed his hand.

"Knox, I don't know what your father would think, but I think you're incredible."

Warmth suffused her cheeks. Okay, she hadn't quite planned on saying *that* to him. "I mean, I was in real trouble last night, and you came to my rescue—at considerable risk to your own safety," she said quickly. "And then today, with Andy, and everything else that's happened—the way you're so calm, so practical under extreme circumstances, the way you helped Camilla … yeah, incredible," she said, nodding. It fit.

Knox eyed her for a moment. "You're not doing too bad yourself, you know," he said quietly. "I know some guys who wouldn't have held up so well under the strain, particularly after what you experienced this morning."

She didn't want to see those images of George and Wayne again, or remember the look in Andy's eyes as he'd attacked her. There was so much death and violence—she didn't want to think about it anymore. Didn't want to have to deal with it.

Her gaze dropped to his chest, a fascinating play of darker shadows between ridges of muscle. There was so much strength there, so much formidable power, and it covered a core of pain and vulnerability that she'd never have guessed existed. He was beautiful. Intelligent. Honorable ... so damn gorgeous. She took a slow, calm breath in. Faint traces of his aftershave teased at her. Her gaze drifted up to meet his. His green eyes held admiration, along with a glimmer of curiosity and ... desire.

It was the desire that caught her. The warmth she saw there, the hint of awareness, the intensity, sparked something inside her.

"You're a very good man, Mr. Jones," she whispered. *Decent. Sexy. Sexy decent? Decently sexy?*

His gaze dropped to her mouth, and he blinked. "Who?"

Her lips curved. He sounded so distracted, so confused. "You." She lifted her hand to his cheek. The beginnings of a beard scratched at her, awakening her skin to a new level of sensitivity. She caught her bottom lip between her teeth, and the desire in his eyes heated. He raised his thumb to her lips, teasing out that bottom lip to caress it.

It was the lightest of pressure, that stroke against her lip, but it made her heart thump just that little bit harder, that little bit faster, in her chest. He stared at her with a fierce focus, at the movement of his thumb gliding across her lip, his own mouth slightly agape. He leaned closer.

She swallowed, and there was a sexy little tilt to his lips as he watched her throat.

A faint line appeared between his brows, and he dragged his gaze back to her eyes, blinking.

"Mic, I need to tell you—"

She didn't want to talk anymore, didn't want to get lost in the drama again, in the dark seriousness of everything. For just a brief moment, she wanted to leave all that gritty horror, that overwhelming weight, and feel light, carefree … "Later," she said, reaching for the lapels of his jacket.

Arousal flared in his eyes. He blinked, shook his head, as though she was distracting him. Like she had that kind of power over him. That thought filled her with a confidence, her own feminine power that made her heart thud, her breath shorten—and his breathing matched hers.

His gaze focused on her lips. "But—"

"Are you married?"

"No—"

"Girlfriend? Fiancée?"

"No—"

"Boyfriend?"

He frowned. "No—"

"STD?"

"Ew, no—"

"Then we've covered the important things. Everything else can wait." She smiled, pulling him closer.

~*~

Knox's eyes widened as Mic pressed her lips against his, and then his eyelids fluttered closed. He should tell her. He wanted to tell her. She needed to know. She deserved to know. Her lips were light and supple against his. Sweet. Seductive. She caressed his lips with her own, brushing against him, that same soft skin he'd touched with his thumb now trailing against his lips. He hesitated, his conscience pricking at him. Her tongue flicked at his lip. God, she was hot. He really should tell her.

Mic's tongue touched his lips again, caressing them, and then between them, to slide against his own. It was shy but sexy, delicate but tantalizing, and it tipped any attempt to do the right thing into the decency-be-damned basket. He quickly kicked his conscience to the curb, squeezing out everything but them. Here. Now.

He flicked his tongue in response, and she sighed, a sexy sound of surrender that zinged straight to his groin. He slid his hands into her hair, twisting her head, anchoring her lips to his so that she couldn't, wouldn't leave him.

Not that he had to hold her. She rolled over to her knees, her arms sliding around his neck, and then it was him being held secure.

He grinned against her lips, then growled softly when she slid her hands inside his jacket, over his shoulders. *Hell, yeah.* He let go of her just long enough to shuck out of his jacket, then slipped his hands underneath the hem of her sweater.

She moaned against his lips, pressing her breasts against his chest as he lightly raked his fingers up and down her back. Her skin was soft, smooth, warm, and he pressed his palms against her.

Mic straddled his lap, and he snugged her hips tight against his. She arched against him, and he sucked at her tongue, shuddering as she clenched his hair in her hands, their mouths moving with the sole purpose of driving each other crazy.

He caressed her beneath her top, his hands travelling from her back to her chest. She tilted her head back when he cupped her breasts over the lace of her bra, and she gasped into the night sky. He looked up at her.

The stars and speck of a moon bathed her skin in a silvery glow, her throat arching as he smoothed his thumbs over the taut peaks he could feel beneath the delicious abrasion of lace. Too much. No, not enough. Not enough skin. He bunched up the material, and she helped pull the sweater up over her head.

His lips were already on the upper swells of her breasts as his hands got busy getting rid of that frustrating piece of lace that did what he wanted to. He unclasped the garment with one hand, and slid his other over her breasts, removing the scrap as he went.

He followed with his mouth, kissing, licking. She gave a low, guttural moan as he cupped her breasts, lifting them, weighing them, loving them. He loved the feel of them, with just enough weight to fill his palms. He loved the way her skin was cast in silver, and the pebbly sensitivity of her areolae, and those stiff peaks that cried out for his touch, his tongue. Her hips rubbed against his, and he could feel the liquid heat emanating from her. He was so damn hard for her, ready to thrust, ready to explode, and he had to battle against the instinct to take his pleasure in order to draw out hers.

Her fingers tightened against his scalp, delicious pinpricks of pain that expertly counterbalanced the blissful torture. He dropped one hand down her back, past the waistline of her jeans and the lace cotton of her panties, to cup the silken skin of her butt. As though in retaliation she trailed her hands down his chest, flicking at his nipples. He bucked a little. She was driving him crazy, pushing him to the precipice. Well, he had no intention of going over without her.

He caressed her midriff, then paused when he remembered what Rickerson had done to her. He was going to make sure Rickerson paid for hurting Mic. Dearly. With the silver and shadows, it was difficult to see the extent of her bruising. She leaned back, just a little, to meet his gaze with a questioning one of her own.

"I don't want to hurt you," he murmured to her. Ever.

She shook her head. "You won't, now shut up and kiss me."

She leaned down, and he took her mouth in a ravenous kiss, smiling against her lips when she made an approving sound. He grasped her ponytail, angling his head to deepen the kiss. Scorching heat licked at his scalp, the back of his neck, his shoulders, wherever she dragged those tantalizing nails of hers, activating a slow-building but insatiable hunger inside him.

It must have done something similar for Mic, because she drew back, panting. Her gaze never leaving his, she reached for his fly, unbuttoning it. Each time a stud slid through the hole, there was a torturous release of tension. He smiled when he saw her eyes widen when she felt him. She slid her hand beneath the waistband of his boxers, and he sucked in a breath when she clasped him. He raised his hips a little, and helped her pull his jeans and boxer shorts down, just enough to give her full access to him.

She stroked him, her gaze meeting his. She was a fascinating temptress, shy and yet wickedly confident, a seductive mix that equally intrigued and delighted him. He would never have guessed she could be such a vixen, and he was captivated. He watched her watching him, but when she caught her lip in that come-kiss-me way, he had to, well, kiss her. Knox raised himself up, capturing her mouth in a hot, slick kiss. He reached for her shin that rested against his leg. She tumbled against him, a breathless chuckle escaping her lips as he tugged at her shoe, then the other, pulling them off her feet. He then dealt with the button and zip fly of her jeans, delving beneath her panties.

Her breath hitched as he touched her, slick and wet, and he slid his finger inside her heat. He hissed at the sensation, and she smiled at him. He wanted to take his time, savor her, play with her, tease her wild … but she was so hot, so ready, and he was past ready. He grasped her hips and rolled her over onto his discarded jacket, his gaze never leaving hers as he slid her jeans and panties down her legs. She helped, drawing her legs out of the garments, then pushed his own clothing down his legs.

Shoes. *Damn it.*

He got one shoe off, freed one leg, but that took way too much time, especially when she pulled his head down for another kiss. He trailed his hands down her form, and her body, bathed in silver, undulated with the movement. He fumbled in his pocket for his wallet, and she helped him open the packet and roll the condom on. He paused, rock hard and ready, but wanting to make sure *she* was ready, that *she* wanted this as much as he did.

"Are you sure you want this?"

Chapter 13

Mic stared up at him for a moment. He looked like a silver Adonis, flanked by dark shadows and stars, equal parts hidden and revealed. His face was drawn taut with arousal, his arms braced on either side of her, biceps and forearms bulging with strength, but his eyes … there was so much heat, yet she could see tenderness, too. His abdomen rippled with each harsh breath he took, his chest a bumpy, tight playground for her.

Good grief, the man was the definition of sex.

She grasped his shoulders and rolled him over, straddling him. "Yeah, I'm sure," she said, her voice husky. "I want you inside me, now."

He chuckled at her insistence, until she knelt down and whispered what else she wanted from him."

"So, demanding," he commented. She gave him a slow smile, one that was full of feminine seduction, that reached inside him and ratcheted up his desire.

"You have no idea." The husky promise almost undid him. She slid down on him, his length filling her, and she trembled at the heat that rose inside. He moaned, his head lifting off the ground as he pushed against her hips. She pushed back, and they slid against each other, the heat building between them. She leaned down to kiss him, her tongue caressing his in tandem to the movement of their hips. His thumb found its way between them, and he did something weird and cool and so damn perfect she shuddered, bliss rolling over her in waves. He rolled them over again, one arm beneath her back, arching her into him as he kept up the rhythm, his other hand caressing the thigh she pressed against his side, and he tipped her over the edge once again, capturing her cry in a kiss as he, too, lost himself to pleasure.

~*~

Knox stared up at the stars, waiting for his heart rate to calm down to a pseudo-normal state. Hole. E. Crap. He blinked. That was … It was … They'd …

She'd wrecked him for anyone else.

He snugged Mic to his side, the move instinctive, possessive, and tender, and she sighed against his chest. Once again, he felt desire flicking at his body. Yep, wrecked.

What they'd just done had been intimate. Not just sex. *Intimate.* He'd never really talked about his family. Well, sure, he'd talked in general terms with Fitz and Dan … not so much Smithy, but Smithy wasn't the type to talk about his past, ever. Mic, on the other hand—it was like he had verbal diarrhea with her, spilling his guts about stuff he normally kept locked inside.

All this time of watching over her … he thought he'd gotten to know her, but he realized now there was so much left to discover with her—and he had every intention of doing that. For the first time in—well, that he could recall—he'd shared more of himself with a woman than pleasantries and a sexy interlude.

All that stuff about his mom and dad … he hadn't lied to her, not about that. Not about how important it was for him to feel like he made his father proud, to live up to the heroic legacy he'd left behind … and how he always felt like he was failing at it. Nor did he lie about how desperately, completely and irrevocably his mother had loved his father … until the day she died.

He hadn't told her that he hoped to experience that. Not the dying part, of course. Well, that came to all of them. But if he could have just a fraction of the kind of love his parents had shared, then he'd be a happy man. But in his line of work, with the grab-and-go nature of the job, the secrecy, the very real danger … he'd stopped looking, and he hadn't realized he'd done that until just now. When he found it with Mic. She was the kind of woman he'd like to come home to. He'd told her last night, in the hall outside her room, that they'd be very good together. He was wrong. They were *great*.

He dragged his thumb along her bare arm, enjoying the sensation of her soft curves against his body, her warmth, that delicate little shiver against him. "Are you cold?" He pulled her even closer.

"No way," she said, her voice a low purr as she snuggled up to him. He dragged her thigh across his hips, hooking her to him. He knew they both needed to rest, but darned if he wasn't feeling the stirring of arousal again. Along with a lot of other stuff, like … possessive. Fierce. Happy. No, happy was too tame. Exuberant—but that sounded like a romcom, and he didn't do romcom.

All he knew was that with Mic, he was feeling way too Neanderthal Ned, ready to beat his chest and roar his claim over her to the world. Or was that Tarzan? Either way, it felt instinctive, natural, and something any strong, independent woman would give him a roasting over—and Mic was the definition of a strong, independent woman. Which is why he found her so damn sexy. With her being so strong and independent, if he even looked like he was about to get possessive over her, she'd probably put his balls in a vice.

But damn it, he would be by her side for as long as she'd let him.

Which might not be long, once she found out why he was working at Eagle Express, and who had hired him. His mouth turned down at the corners. The way she'd talked about her father hinted at a strained relationship. How would she feel when she found out her old man had hired SafeKeepers Inc to protect her? Maybe … maybe she'd find it thoughtful and loving … Or maybe not.

Regardless, he was more determined than ever to keep her safe … He glanced about. "We should head back to camp," he murmured. While he didn't trust any of the Eagle Express staff as far as he could throw them, out here they were alone … Yes, there were benefits to that, but it also made them vulnerable.

Mic sighed, then stretched against him. He relished the feel of her skin against his, of that dark, heated core of hers that made his body throb again.

"You're right. We should check on Camilla," Mic said, and sat up.

The faint starlight caressed her silhouette with a pearly glow, revealing the peaks of her breasts, with the contrast of dark shadow across her ribs, her silver-cast thighs … *Camp schmamp*. He sat up, slid his hand beneath her tangled ponytail, and drew her in for a kiss.

~*~

Mic trudged carefully through the undergrowth until the glow of the firelight finally reached her, and she could see where she was putting her feet. She carried a bundle of branches and twigs, as did Knox, and she set them down next to the depleted pile off to the side of the fire.

She crossed over to Camilla to check on her, ignoring the dark glare Luis gave her. "Has she come to, at all?"

"What the hell would you care?" Luis whispered harshly. Mic finally met his gaze, reminding herself that he had seen a co-worker shot, just like she had, and was scared, out of his comfort zone, and under considerable stress, and that he hadn't always been a king-sized douche.

"We're better than this, Luis," she reminded him gently. "I care. Of course, I care. I care about all of you, and I want to know, has Camilla regained consciousness?"

Luis dropped his gaze, and either it was a trick of the firelight, or there was a little color rising on his cheeks. He finally nodded.

"Yeah, for a little bit."

Mic nodded. Good. That was a good sign, right? Well, her experience with dealing with bullet-wounded patients in the wild was … zilch.

"Call me if there are any changes. I'll check on her during my watch."

A muscle in Luis's jaw twitched, but he eventually dipped his head to acknowledge her words.

And that was about as good as it was going to get, Mic figured.

She crossed over to Doug. His eyes opened to slits as she approached, and she held up a hand to forestall him rising. "How are you?" she asked quietly, squatting down next to him.

He gave her a self-deprecating smile. "I feel like I walked into a truck."

She eyed his injuries. His eye was swollen shut, and she could see the lighter shape surrounded by dark bruising. He'd been hit hard, but at least he was conscious, and would recover. He indicated the firewood.

"I thought you'd forgotten," he said.

She battled the blush, but failed. "I needed to clear my head, calm down." Not that there was anything 'calm' about what she and Knox had done. In fact, it had been very exciting. And oh, my God, Doug was her *boss*, and here she was getting all hot and bothered over one of their staff.

"Uh, I should go catch some Zs …" she said, gesturing casually to … somewhere. He nodded, but his gaze was shrewd as he watched her stand.

Ugh. He knew. Her boss knew. Well, he'd guessed. She kept her gaze on the ground as she walked past a now-sleeping Roger, and found a spot where she could feel the warmth of the fire, but not be smoked out.

Within seconds of settling herself on the ground, using her bent arm as a pillow, she sensed someone lying down next to her. Knox. She looked at him over her shoulder. He lay on his back, his hands clasped behind his head. Barely an inch separated them. "Do you think that's a good—"

"I'll always have your back, sweetness," he whispered as he tilted his head back and closed his eyes.

Apparently, that was the end of the discussion.

Mic turned back to the fire. She didn't know how that would look to the rest of the group, but for the first time since she'd started working at Eagle Express, she couldn't care less what others thought. She was grateful for his presence, for his comfort and warmth, his protective support. It was a surprise—no, a shock, really, to realize she'd not only made love with the man, but she'd talked to a guy about her career aspirations, her family, and he wasn't running in the opposite direction. She sighed, a small smile playing with her lips. She trusted Knox. It was a revelation, especially after Sebastien. She didn't think she could feel so close to a guy ever again. Maybe unicorns were real, after all.

~*~

A hand touched his shoulder, and Knox turned. Mic stared down at him, her hazel eyes almost golden in the pre-dawn light. Beautiful.

"Hey, I thought you were asleep," Mic said, surprised. "I was just coming to wake you up."

Knox yawned. "I just woke up," he lied. It had been Mic's turn to take the last night watch, and she may have watched over the camp, but he'd watched over her. He rose to his feet and brushed off his jeans.

"How are you?" he asked, and smiled when Mic's cheeks heated.

"Uh, fine, thanks. You?" She clasped her hands behind her back, and rocked a little on the heels of her feet.

He eyed her. No. She was retreating again, just like she had at the elevator, and again after he'd kissed her. After what they'd shared, he wasn't about to let her hide behind a polite aloofness.

"So polite," he murmured, dipping his head so only she could hear his words. "Such a contrast to your demands last night …" his tone was low and suggestive. He hadn't stopped wanting her since their interlude the night before. Didn't think he'd ever stop wanting her.

"Knox," she gasped, glancing about.

"Mic," he mimicked. His gaze flicked about. Most of the others were still asleep. Kelly was awake, but already stumbling away from camp, probably to relieve herself. He tugged her close, leaned down and pressed his lips against Mic's in a quick, hard kiss before relinquishing his hold and heading off in the direction of the stream.

By the time he got back to the camp, Mic had marshalled everyone into constructing a makeshift stretcher for Camilla, using two strong branches and all available jackets. He nodded in approval. The woman was smart, and efficient. It wasn't too much longer after that they were ready to break camp.

He lifted Camilla onto the stretcher, and smiled grimly when the woman sucked in her breath in obvious pain. Camilla had woken, and was lucid, but she needed immediate attention. He wasn't going to say anything, but he knew Mic had noticed the beads of perspiration that gave the woman a slick appearance. Camilla's face was pale from loss of blood, and her body felt like a furnace. The woman had a fever. Once he got her settled on the stretcher, Knox checked the strength of the knots of fabric around the stretcher's supports. He nodded, satisfied that they'd hold Camilla's weight.

Mic smoothed back Camilla's hair from her forehead and gave her an encouraging smile. "We're getting you out of here, Cami," she told her in a calm voice. She held out a bottle of water to the woman. "Drink as much as you can, we want to keep your fluids up. We can always refill the bottle, okay?"

Camilla nodded weakly, and her smile looked more like a spasmodic twitch of the lips, but she seemed comfortable. Aidan and Roger took each end of the stretcher, and John and Luis each took one side, giving as much support as they could to the thick branches and fabric. Knox made sure the fire was out, then took stock. If they went overland, they could reach the rendezvous point a little quicker, but with Camilla on a stretcher, it would be a difficult trek for them all. Following the stream might take a little longer, but it was an easier walk out, with a ready supply of much-needed drinking water.

"Let's get a move on," he said, indicating the trail alongside the stream. It looked like at least the deer and other forest creatures used the same path. Mic slid in behind Luis, grasping hold of the branch, and Kelly did the same on the other side. Knox led them along the stream, making sure he was within reach of Doug, in case the man faltered. Knox glanced at him briefly, and Doug caught his gaze with his one open eye.

"Does it look as bad as it feels?"

Knox grinned. "Nah, just a scratch."

"Liar," Doug said with a chuckle, then winced at the pain of smiling.

Knox shook his head, then eyed their surrounds. It was still early, but he knew Fitz would have organized a search party for first light. Even now he could hear the far-off drone of a helicopter. He pressed his lips together. They were in a lightly wooded area, the ground uneven. A chopper couldn't land here, but they'd at least be able to get word of their location back to searchers on foot. They just had to be found.

He glanced back at the group behind him. Roger's face was drawn with exhaustion, but his gaze was fixed on the ground ahead as he plodded along. At the opposite end of the stretcher, Aidan's features were tight. Maybe exhaustion, maybe pain, maybe stress. Still, the young man was doing well, under the circumstances.

Kelly and Luis wore almost identical stony expressions, and he didn't know if Mic just chose to ignore their occasional glares, or whether she was truly oblivious. She walked with a smile on her face, her shoulders back, and exchanged casual chatter with John and Aidan. She even made Camilla laugh, before the woman clutched her side in pain and Mic apologized.

Knox faced forward, and had to scoot to catch up with Doug. He lightly grasped Doug's elbow as the older man stumbled over a tuft of grass.

"Sorry," Doug muttered.

Knox dropped his hand when he was sure the man had regained his footing. "Don't be. You've only got one eye working properly. Bound to happen." The man's depth perception would be screwed. He gave him a reassuring pat, and deliberately slowed his pace. He wanted to be next to Mic. Needed to be next to her—and yes, that made good bodyguard practice—and Doug wasn't his package—but it was more than that. Since their interlude the night before, he'd craved her presence, her nearness. He wanted to reassure himself she was safe, but it went beyond something that was part of his job. No, this was coming from somewhere else, this desire to be able to reach her, touch her, listen to her, whenever he could.

He glanced up. So far, so good. It was mild weather, the sun was shining, and they had a water source at their side. The helicopter was sounding louder, and he could see the dark shape as it crested a hill in the distance. He could almost pretend he was on a normal mountain hike, taking in the fresh air. He inhaled. They were walking out. He had full confidence in his SafeKeepers colleagues, he knew they'd be found today. Mic was almost at his side when he heard her gasp. He turned. She'd stopped, her eyes fixed on something off to the side, and then her eyes widened.

"Gun!" Mic yelled, just as a shot cracked loudly in the serene morning.

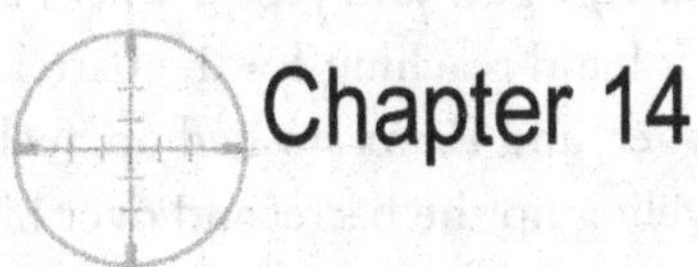# Chapter 14

"Get down!" Knox yelled, pushing Doug to the ground. He whirled back toward Mic.

Camilla cried out when the stretcher hit the ground. Kelly screamed, and John pulled her down with him.

Knox started running back to Mic, his gaze scanning the forest. There. The rifle barrel was pushing through the branches of a bush. He turned back to Mic, and everything seemed to slow down. Images of a different woman's face, of her horror, her realization as the bullets hit, kept superimposing themselves in his vision, and his gut churned. No matter how fast he tried to move, he was stuck in slow motion, pushing through thick dread.

Luis stood, his jaw slack in shock, eyes wide. Mic yelled—what, Knox couldn't hear over the thunderous beat of his heart—and she turned to Luis.

He saw the realization in her eyes, the split-second decision, the intention as her muscles bunched.

"Nooooo!" he roared, but Mic moved fast, launching herself at Luis as the rifle fired again.

Mic tackled Luis, and there was a splash as the bullet hit the water behind him. Mic crashed on top of him, covering his body with hers. Everything flipped from slow-mo to super-fast, and Knox turned. He was closer to the rifle than Mic. He could hear the slide as a bullet was chambered. He bolted up the slight incline. The rifle barrel wavered. Mic, or him. He let loose a roar. He wanted the shooter to realize he was the bigger risk. It worked. The rifle barrel swung in his direction.

Mic screamed. Knox dived behind the bush. He had a brief glimpse of camouflage gear and yellow lenses before he tackled the shooter, his hand reaching for the barrel. The shooter pulled the trigger, and Knox pushed up, feeling the burn of the bullet traveling up the barrel and over his head. He punched the guy in the face, and knocked the rifle out of his hand.

The shooter snarled, and hit back, his fist connecting with Knox's cheek. Knox grabbed the man's collar as he fell backwards, dragging him down the small hill that flanked the stream.

They tumbled down, and Knox kept punching, white hot rage filling him. This guy had tried to kill Mic. He could hear screams, yells, but didn't turn, his attention on the man he was trying to throttle. Knox wheezed as the man's fist connected with his side, knocking the breath out of him. The shooter shoved him, and Knox fell on his back.

The shooter stood, his face harsh with anger as he unsheathed a dagger from his boot. Knox's eyes narrowed as he braced his hands on the ground above his shoulders, arched his back and flipped up to his feet. Hands out, Knox nodded at the man. *Bring it on.*

As though recognizing a fellow combatant, the shooter nodded. He flicked the knife from a tip-up grip to an icepick grip. Knox bent his knees slightly, shifting one foot so he stood side-facing, minimizing the strike zone. The shooter took a step forward, his arm moving constantly from down low to shoulder height. Knox danced a little on his feet, and slid closer, reading the guy's muscle shifts to gauge where he was going to thrust. The shooter lunged.

A shot rang out. The shooter jerked, a red bloom spreading across his chest as he was flung backwards.

Knox whipped around. Doug stood at the top of the hill, holding the rifle. Mic appeared by his side, her expression changing from anxious to relieved when she spotted him.

"Oh, thank God," she said, and skidded down the incline toward him. Knox glanced back at the shooter. The man lay on his back, staring sightlessly up at the sky. He leaned forward, anyway, to check for a pulse. Definitely dead. A bulge in the man's breast pocket caught his eye, and he shifted, using his body as a shield as he palmed the phone he found there.

Mic reached him as he rose, and he caught her to him, sliding the phone into the back pocket of his jeans. She was trembling. "Sh, hey, it's okay." He wrapped both arms around her and looked at the dead man, then back up to the CEO who lowered the rifle, his shoulders sagging. "It's over."

~*~

Mic clutched the blanket around her shoulders as she sat in the waiting room of the hospital. She didn't want to leave until she heard how Camilla was doing. She glanced around the waiting room. Doug was in emergency, getting checked over for a concussion, and to stitch up the gash on his temple. Kelly was also in emergency, being treated for shock, and Aidan, Roger, Luis and John had just been given the all clear, just as she and Knox had. He was now talking with the trainer who'd organized the orientation exercise, as well as raised the alarm when they hadn't gotten back to the rendezvous point. They'd been joined by … the bartender? She narrowed her eyes as she looked at the handsome, dark-haired man. Yeah, she was pretty sure he was the bartender from the resort. Huh. Strange.

Mic tilted her head back against the wall. They'd each given their statements, multiple times. Andy Rickerson had been found. Dead. She didn't know how he'd died. Mic closed her eyes briefly. She didn't know how she felt about that.

Happy that she wouldn't have to face him again, but still … she hadn't necessarily wanted him dead.

She yawned. She just wanted to go home and sleep for a week. The county sheriff was letting them all go home, but they were warned that there would be further questioning, further statements, until the matter was finalized.

The matter. Three Eagle Express staff dead, two more injured, one quite seriously. Several others traumatized. It was going to take time before the staff recovered, before the company recovered. She blinked slowly, her gaze fixed on the sliding doors on the other side of the waiting room. She was phasing out. She'd blink, and realize long minutes had ticked by.

Knox walked over and took the seat next to her, watching her intently. "How are you doing?"

Mic yawned again. "I'm so tired," she murmured, blinking drowsily.

He nodded. "That's a normal reaction, after an adrenaline rush."

She eyed him. "Oh. How are you feeling?" He didn't look like she felt, as though he was about to slide off the chair and take a nap in a puddle.

"Much better, knowing you're not about to be shot." He leaned closer, his expression grim. "Don't ever do that to me again."

"Me?" Her eyebrows rose. "You're the one who ran *toward* the man with a gun." She shook her head. Who *does* that? "You nearly gave me a heart attack." This time she leaned toward him. "Don't do that again." She didn't think she'd ever get rid of that image, of that dread, that terror, when he'd dived at the shooter. She didn't want to think about it, about what it might signify. She was too … exhausted to think. Deal. Whatever.

His lips quirked. "Touché."

She tilted her head against the wall again. "I'm just so glad it's over." Her gaze drifted over the group sitting in the waiting room, looking a little shell-shocked. The doors beyond slid open, and her father walked into the waiting room.

It took a moment for her brain to notice that detail. Gerard Robson. She blinked. *What? Dad? No.* She frowned. That really did look like—

"Michaela, thank God," her father breathed as he hurried over to her. She rose to her feet, stunned.

"Dad? How did you—"

Her father pulled her into a gentle but strong embrace. "We were worried sick."

"But how did you know?" Mic tilted her head back to see her father's face.

"I got a call."

"A call? A call from who?" She'd been missing less than twenty-four hours … for folks to have contacted all the families of those involved … she glanced about the group—nobody else had family joining them. No. Only her family.

Her father glanced to the side, and let go of her. "You must be the bodyguard. Thank you." He reached for Knox's hand.

Mic looked away. Her father must be kidding, right? Bodyguard, indeed. Well, admittedly Knox had saved her life what, twice? Three times?

Gerard turned back to her. "Are you all right? Really?"

"Yeah, Dad, I'm fine. Really," she reassured him when he clutched her shoulders to survey her from the top of her head to the tips of her muddied, steel-toed boots. Okay, she knew she was punch-drunk tired, and maybe a little spaced out, a little woozy. Was she dehydrated? She blinked. No. She vaguely remembered a drip in her arm as she gave a statement to … someone. She shook her head in bafflement, still trying to process the fact her father was standing in front of her. "How did you—why are you here?" She glanced over his shoulder, and saw the trainer from the team-building company head over toward them.

"I got a call and got a jump seat on one of our flights to LAX," her father said in a tone that implied the answer was obvious. He turned to Knox. "What happened out there?"

"Oh, uh—" Knox wore an uncomfortable expression as his gaze darted to meet hers. He rose to his feet.

Mic blinked, calculating flight times, then frowned. "Wait—when did you hear?" Damn, she felt so slow, like her brain was only working at half-speed. She tried to mentally kick up a gear. She knew the schedule for her father's freight planes—had grown up knowing them by heart. Any way she figured it, he would have left on one of the flights this morning—before they'd been found, before a proper search party could start out, before anyone pretty much knew anything. "Who called you?"

The trainer halted, his eyebrows raised, and then did an about-face and walked back to the bartender from the resort.

Her father's hands slid from her shoulders, and he lifted his chin. "Someone at the resort. I received a call last night, and got on the first plane out this morning."

She nodded. "Oh, okay." Still, that was really fast. "Well, thanks for being here." It was a surprise, especially after their last conversation—fight, whatever. His coming there for her … well, it was touching.

"I still don't understand what happened," he said, turning to Knox. Mic sighed. It was so like her father, to ask the closest guy as opposed to his own daughter about the facts.

"Some guy started shooting at us out on a hike," she told him. Her father nodded, then turned back to Knox, giving him an expectant look.

"There was an active shooter in the hills, sir," Knox responded. "He killed two people, possibly a third—we're still waiting to hear how that employee died. A woman was shot, but is undergoing surgery, Danvers is being treated, but Michaela was unhurt."

"What about the shooter?"

Mic chewed the inside of her cheek. She may as well be invisible, here.

"He was killed, sir."

Gerard nodded, his lips pursed. "Good."

"I should add that I didn't kill the man, sir. Doug Danvers did."

Her father's eyebrows rose. "Danvers?" He eyed Mic. "Really?"

"Really. I had engaged the shooter in hand-to-hand combat, and Danvers shot him. Unfortunately, the man died at the scene and couldn't be questioned."

She almost didn't recognize Knox, standing beside her, his feet planted shoulder-width apart, chin up, his words uttered in a clipped, matter-of-fact and slightly officious manner. He almost sounded like he was rattling off a report to a senior officer.

And her father was relying on the information from one of her staff, a staff member he had never met, while she was right there—his *daughter*—who had experienced all of this, yet he wasn't asking her. She folded up the blanket and placed it on the seat, then started walking toward the sliding doors.

"Michaela, where are you going?" her father turned, frowning. She waved her hand over her shoulder.

"You don't need me for this," she said brusquely, then halted when she felt a hand clasp her elbow. She turned in surprise. Knox. He'd snuck up on her again, damn it.

"You need to stay here with us," he told her gently.

She shook her head as she tried to disengage his hand from her arm—unsuccessfully. "No, I think you and Dad are getting along fine without me, and don't need me to contribute to this conversation." She glared at her father as he approached.

Gerard shot her an exasperated look. "Of course, I want to talk to you, Michaela, but I need to hear from your bodyguard, first."

Mic halted. That was the second time her father had called Knox her bodyguard. She frowned. "What are you talking about? Knox works for me, Dad. He's not my bodyguard."

Her father hesitated, his gaze switching from her, to Knox, then back again. "Oh. You didn't tell her."

Knox shot her father a resigned look. "You asked us not to."

"Tell me what?" A headache started to thump, right between her eyes.

"Oh, I would have thought, under the circumstances—"

"Maybe we should take this chat somewhere private," Knox suggested, ducking his head to look through the glass panel of a nearby door, then opening it to step inside, dragging Mic along with him. Her father stepped in behind them and closed the door. There was a single unmade bed in the room, a couple of tiered trolleys bearing first aid supplies, and a stand to hang a drip from.

"What chat?" The muscles in her stomach tensed, as though getting ready to revolt. Suspicion, sickening and disconcerting, had her backing up against the small exam room wall. Her gaze darted between her father, looking calm, and Knox, looking … resigned. Grim. So unlike the Knox of the night before, all smoking hot and sexy silver … "What chat?" she repeated, her voice low.

"I hired a security detail for you," her father stated. He lifted a hand in Knox's direction. "This man is your bodyguard."

Mic blinked. Oh, God. Her gut heaved. She placed a hand over her stomach. She looked at Knox. He wasn't denying it, wasn't laughing at the really bad joke her father just made, wasn't doing anything but looking at her with an expression that mixed regret with the resolute.

"What?" Yeah. She needed that repeated.

"He's your bodyguard. There are more—"

"There are *more*?" She looked at the door, then at Knox. They'd—she squeezed her eyes shut. Just like Sebastien. No. She couldn't go there. She opened her eyes again, but kept her gaze on the floor. "The bartender? The trainer?"

There was a pause. She looked up. He nodded. She hadn't understood why the two men were waiting with them at the hospital, but it was beginning to make sense. "Any more?" Just how far did this secretive campaign of her father's extend?

Knox hesitated, then nodded. "Yes, we have an IT guy back at the resort."

An IT guy. Why did that sound so understated? And what would they need an IT guy for? She could figure out what the bartender was doing, maybe even the trainer, and hell, she knew what Knox had done, but the IT guy …? Her cheeks cooled as the color drained. So many thoughts. They'd made—*oh, God*. She shut down that train of thought again. Had they bugged her phone? Her laptop? Any illusion of privacy went up in smoke as her outrage heated. What had she said on the phone? Who had she spoken to? What could they have overheard? Oh, God, what had she done on her laptop that they could have seen? Apart from looking at vacation locations and kittens …? "What did he do?" Her voice was low and raspy as the violation, the sense of vulnerability, of being spied on, slithered up over her. And yet again, a guy was with her purely because of her connection with her father. She swallowed. *Oh, God.* Her hand clenched into a fist against her stomach. How could her father do this to her? How could *Knox*?

"He was able to get into the resort security, reservations, and so on to ensure I had a room next to yours," Knox said quietly. He flicked a gaze at her father, then back to her. "He's the reason I was able to get into your room and stop the intruder from killing you."

She braced a hand against the bed. "The door." She sucked in a deep breath as realization blazed through her. The

door she, along with everyone else in the room at the time—
her boss, the deputies, the resort staff—thought she'd left
unlatched, like some stupid, vapid, careless klutz. She lifted
her gaze to glare at the man she thought she'd grown to know
so darn well. "Do you know all the names I called myself, for
doing something so stupid? Do you know how I beat myself
up over that? Or what the others now think of me?"

His expression was implacable. "We couldn't tell you or
the others how we gained access. We didn't want to tip off
anyone that you had a security detail."

She lifted her chin. "Oh. Of course. That's *perfectly*
reasonable." Okay, so that was sarcastic, but damn it, she
wanted to hit something. Or someone. She'd slept with the
bodyguard. A guy who'd been paid to hang around her, act …
like he'd acted. She still couldn't quite go there.

She looked over at her father. "Why did you do this?" she
blinked away the blurry vision. If she burst into tears, it would
just reiterate to her father she was some emotional, vulnerable
wreck who couldn't make her own decisions, couldn't stand
up for herself … Couldn't stand on her own two feet without
Daddy's help. She locked her knees straight and let go of the
bed.

Her father made a scoffing sound. "Because I love you,
Michaela," he exclaimed.

Mic forced a bitter smile to her lips. "Wow. It's amazing
how misused that phrase can be."

Gerard frowned, confused. "What do you mean?"

She started to pace slowly. "When I took the job at Eagle
Express, you said I wasn't up for the job. The company wasn't
the right fit for me. I wasn't suitable … but you were only
telling me that because you 'love me'."

He opened his mouth to protest, but she wagged a finger
at him to forestall his words. No, she was just getting on a
roll, a cold, calm, blistering roll. "Then, when I discovered the
drug smuggling ring, you wanted me to quit. Because you love
me. I told you I wanted to see things through, that I wanted to

stick it out, change it for the better, for the staff, and you said it was a bigger job than me—but you were telling me that because you love me." She paused in front of him. "And then you hire men—*without telling me*—to watch me, follow me, *spy on me*—because you love me. You do realize that you *loving* me is just another way to say you don't trust me, right?"

Her father folded his arms and frowned at her, impatient. Unrelenting. Unashamed.

She met her father's gaze head-on. "Tell me the truth … if it had been Matt or Rick in this position, would you have hired bodyguards? Secretly?"

Her father sighed, clearly exasperated at her bringing her brothers into the conversation. "Of course not, they can take care of them—" his voice trailed off, belatedly realizing what he was saying.

"My point, exactly." She turned to Knox, a chill creeping through her veins. "Your services are no longer required. You and the rest of your team are terminated."

She started walking toward the door. A hand snaked past her to press against the door, preventing her from opening it. She tried not to look at the hand, or the attached arm, the corded strength of the forearm, the rounded bicep … or feel the warmth of the strong body behind her. She fought against the instinct to relax back against him—God, how could she still want to do that, after what he'd done—after what *they'd* done. She lifted her gaze as he shifted slightly around to her side. Knox's green eyes were stormy, but he kept any anger, any frustration, out of the smile that curved his lips.

"I hate to break it to you, sweetness, but you can't fire me. Your father hired me, not you, and only your father can 'terminate' me," he said, adding an inflection to the word she'd used.

She glanced back at her father. "Dad?"

Knox twisted to look at the man over his shoulder. "The men we've dealt with so far are hired guns."

She narrowed her eyes. "What is that supposed to mean?" She was sick of Knox and her father talking as though she wasn't there, as though she didn't matter, didn't have a say in what went on in her life. Damn it, she'd had enough.

"It means that someone hired them, and that someone is still out there. You're still in danger."

"He's right, Michaela. You might not like it, but these guys are keeping you alive. They stay."

Crushing hurt, anger, rage, they all swept over her like a tsunami, buffering her about. She glared at Knox. They'd made *love*, damn it. She'd told him things, things she hadn't shared with another guy, not even Sebastien, things that had seemed so easy to say, in the dark … to him.

The man who was paid to be with her. Who was paid to act like he … no. Following that thought would make her feel even more pathetic. She switched her glare to her father. If her father only knew … "You're hiring guys to—" she bit the words off. *Sleep with me.* Knox shifted, as though knowing what she was about to say, and preparing himself for the consequences.

"What? Protect you? Keep you safe? Keep you *alive*?" her father prompted.

She opened her mouth, but she couldn't quite find the words to tell her father she'd made love with the man he'd hired to be her protector. Friend. Confidant. Lover. The humiliation, the hurt was just too deep, too raw, to reveal to her father, the man who didn't think she was capable enough of managing her own life. Just like she'd never really disclosed why she and Sebastien had broken up. It was just too soul-destroying.

"Is this how it's going to be?" she asked, her voice sounding rusty as she pushed it past the sandpaper lining her throat. "No matter what I want, no matter how much it hurts, or ticks me off, you're going to do what *you* want, and whatever *I* want be damned?"

"Michaela, it doesn't have to be like that," her father said as he took a step toward her. "This is for—"

She held up her hand. "I swear, if you pull the 'it's for your own good' card, I will show you what my bad looks like," she said, pushing the words between clenched teeth. His eyebrows rose.

"I'm not going to apologize for trying to keep you safe," he said, lifting his chin.

"No, because then you'd have to admit the way you've done it sucks," she argued. She folded her arms. "Does Mom know?"

His hesitation was answer enough.

She nodded. "Right. Well, good luck with that conversation. I'm done."

She turned back to the door, and glared at Knox's hand. He didn't move.

"These men will take you home, and will be with you until the court case concludes," her father told her. Michaela's back stiffened. She could hear her father's tone, the stubborn determination—like so many conversations she'd had growing up. She knew when to push the boundary, and when to save her breath. He wasn't going to budge on this.

She forced a smile. "Fine. It's your dime." She turned to Knox. She wanted to scream at him, hit him, make him hurt as much as she did. But she was a Robson, and Robsons didn't lose their crap in front of their father. "I might not be able to fire you from your bodyguard duties, but I can fire you from Eagle Express. You can hand in your uniform on Monday."

The muscles in his jaw clenched, and for the briefest of moments, she felt triumph and satisfaction, knowing it was petty but enjoying it anyway. And then she realized he would no longer be at work. No more smiles and nods, or intimate conversations, or knee-weakening kisses, or much-wanted embraces, or smoking hot sex, or feeling like she'd maybe found Mr. Right.

Damn it, she should have known. Mr. Right was about as real as a rainbow-sprinkled unicorn.

"I won't leave you," he said in a low voice. "I will protect you."

She leaned closer. "But who will protect me from you?" she asked in the softest of whispers. Knox flinched, letting go of the door long enough for her to open it and stalk out.

Chapter 15

Knox preceded Mic up the front path to her home, his gaze sweeping the front yard, side passage and windows. He glanced over his shoulder, and Mic swept past him, her expression stony. Dan was scanning one end of the street, Fitz, the other. Smithy remained in the second car, either bored or sleeping, with his head tilted back against the headrest of the front passenger seat.

Knox caught up with Mic when she reached the door, and leaned against the door jamb. "Keys, please." He held his hand out.

She kept her gaze fixed ahead as she fished them out of her bag. Her jaw set, she dropped them into his palm, then folded her arms. She looked so … cool. Not like before. No, this was … next level.

He hated it, but he couldn't blame her. He felt like a stone had ripped through his gut when her father had dropped the B word. He turned to unlock the door, then had to pull her back gently before she entered. "Let me check." He glanced over his shoulder, and Dan nodded, striding up the path to stand by Mic's side.

He moved past her, feeling her glare boring holes in the middle of his back. Yeah, she was pissed. For good reason. He quickly checked her home, going to every conceivable hiding place before moving out to her back deck and tiny yard. Knox walked back through the house. It was … nice. It was the first time he'd gotten past her front door, and he had to admit, he liked her taste. A pale sand-gray color on the walls, wooden floorboards, and timber and leather furniture. She had a brown leather sofa with big, sandy and sky-blue cushions, and a matching throw over one end. Her coffee table looked like it could double as low seating for a casual get-together. He eyed the mismatched navy armchair. It looked like it had seen better days. No, better *years*. He bet there was a story right there. He sighed when he started back down the hall toward the front door. He didn't think he'd be hearing that story any time soon.

"All clear," he told her, beckoning her inside.

Mic stepped in and turned to hold the door as she gestured for him to leave. "Thank you. You've done your job, now you can leave."

Dan 's eyebrows rose. "Uh, actually, ma'am, no, we can't."

Mic smiled. "Actually, you can. My father doesn't own this property, so I get to say who stays," she said as she tilted her head to the side to look at Knox. "And at the moment, you don't."

"Mic, we need to talk—" Knox started.

"I don't think I want to talk to you ever again," she hissed.

Knox was conscious of Dan's stare, skittering between them like an inquisitive bird. He took a deep breath. "I need to explain—"

"Oh, I think my father pretty much covered everything."

Damn it, he needed to explain things. "Not everything."

"Look, if it's Knox you object to, I'm more than happy to come inside instead," Dan offered.

Knox narrowed his eyes as he glared at his friend. There was a reason why his code name was Casanova. Dan shot him an innocent look.

Mic smiled. "Why, that's—"

"Not happening," Knox growled, and moved Mic away from the door so he could close it in Dan's face.

"Knox," Mic protested as he took hold of her hand and strode down the hall to the living room.

"Mic," he shot right back at her. He turned to face her in the living room, that hideous armchair behind her. She tugged at her hand, and he let go, holding his hands up in a hands-off pose. "I know you're pissed—and you have every right to be," he acknowledged when she opened her mouth. "But please, you have to hear me out."

Her eyes rounded. "I do, do I? You're ready to tell me everything? It's a little late for that." She closed her hand over into a fist, and for a moment it looked like she was going to thump him. She shook it a little. "Argh. You—you *lied* to me."

"No. I did not lie to you," he held up a finger. "There were things I couldn't tell you, and didn't tell you, but I never lied."

She folded her arms and tilted her head to the side. "Oh, really? So, your name is really Knox Jones?"

He hesitated, then winced. *Ouch.* "Okay, that's a fair point."

"Were you ever a Boy Scout?"

Knox dipped his head. "Er, no."

She gaped briefly, then took a step forward, and the spark of anger lightened her eyes to a golden hazel. "I *slept* with you," she growled, "and I didn't even know your *name*."

"Landon."

She blinked. "What?"

"Landon. That's my name. Knox Landon." He shrugged. "It was only a half-lie." He held up his forefinger and thumb in a pincer-like gesture. "Tiny."

Her eyes narrowed. Her lips pursed. "Damn it, I *trusted* you," she said, and the hurt in her voice, that darkness behind the anger, damn near ripped his heart out.

"I know, and I'm so sorry," he said, nodding. "I get it, but I need you to hear me out." He clasped his hands together. "I couldn't tell you," he said quickly, trying to get the words out before she either pelted him with something, or yelled at him, or cried, or threw him out of the house, or anything else she was perfectly entitled to do and he thoroughly deserved, but—he needed her to know the truth, and he'd seen her reaction at the hospital, could only guess at the things that had gone through her head … what she thought of him, of *them*. He needed to set the record straight.

"Your father hired us to protect you, and we weren't permitted to let you know," he told her. Then he met her gaze directly. "I did try to tell you. Before we …"

Her eyes rounded. "Oh, my God. I thought that was something like you don't like cats, or you've got an ex-wife somewhere … not that my father hired you to be with me!"

Crap. He took a deep breath, but damn it, he was going to be honest. She deserved at least that. "I didn't want you to know that I was hired by your father. You were the job. You were supposed to be easy—"

Her eyes rounded, then narrowed, and he realized what he'd said. "No, I don't mean *you're* easy, not like that—" hell, everything he said just made it worse. "The job of watching over you was supposed to be easy—and it was. I could set my watch by your routine."

Her eyelids fluttered. "What—what do you mean by my routine?"

Uh-oh. "Uh, I mean, what time you got up of a morning, what you'd have for breakfast, when you'd head to the gym, when you'd go for your run—"

She pressed her hands to her cheeks. "Oh, my God! You *followed* me? I thought you were just at work!"

He sighed. "We all took turns. I was point man, designated to spend the most time with you—"

"To get close to me," she said, and he winced at the bitterness in her voice.

"In a way. Not that way, though," he told her, gesturing between them. "My job was to watch over you, and I did. But … then it started to change."

She folded her arms, her lips pressed together. "Oh, let's not go there."

"I have to, Mic. You have to know." He brushed his hand through his hair. "I have *never* mixed my work with pleasure. Never. I don't get personally involved with people I work with—I have always been professional. Until you. What happened between us—that wasn't part of the job."

She blinked furiously, and had to brush away a tear. *Ah, hell.* That tore at him. He reached for her, but she shook her head, ducking away from his touch.

"Great. So that was just an added bonus, huh, sleeping with the boss's daughter?"

"The client," he corrected her. Gerard Robson might be calling some of the shots, but he wasn't Knox's boss. "And no, I didn't consider it a bonus."

She glared at him. "Really? So, if it wasn't a bonus, what was it? A value-add? Or will you be billing my father for the extra services?"

Ah, hell. No matter how he answered that, it was going to be wrong. He decided to go with the truth. "I like you, Mic," he told her simply.

"I thought I liked you, too," she told him, then brushed the back of her hand across her nose. "But then, I didn't really know you, did I? I don't know who Knox London is."

"Landon," he corrected her automatically, and she gave him a steely stare.

"You lied to me," she said in a low voice that should have sounded soft, whispery, but hit his ears like ground glass. "And I—I *slept* with you." She hugged herself, and he wanted to reach for her, hold her, contain the pain that looked like it was folding her in half. "It was all a farce—"

"No, that wasn't," he told her quickly. "That's what I'm trying to tell you. What we did—that was honest, that was—" *amazing,* "that was true. Sincere." And he couldn't remember the last time he'd formed such an intimate, earnest connection with a woman. Maybe never.

Mic drew herself up straight, sucking in a deep breath. Held it. Released. "Sadly, I can't trust that. You lied then, you could be lying now to save your skin." Her eyes narrowed. "Do you normally sleep with your clients?"

"You're not a client," he told her roughly.

"Oh, what am I, then? What do you call the person you protect?"

He put his hands on his hips, and looked away for a moment. *Ugh.* "Package. We call them the package."

Her eyebrows rose. "Wow. The package. So personal."

He met her gaze. "We call them the package to create distance. We're not supposed to get emotionally involved with the package."

A line appeared on her forehead, between her brows. "What about physically?"

He tilted his head to the side. "What you and I did—it wasn't just physical, Mic."

"Well, then, you're not very good at your job, are you?"

She turned and walked to the front door. "I want you to leave, now."

"Mic—"

She held up a hand and shook her head. "No. I can't take any more, not tonight." She opened the door and lifted her gaze to meet his. The sadness, the grief he saw there, hit him square in the gut. Her face was drawn, as though the life had been sucked out of her. She was exhausted, physically and emotionally battered. The best thing he could do for her now was to give her some space.

"Are you sure you won't let us in?" he asked quietly. "I wasn't kidding, before. You still need protection, until everyone involved in this case is revealed and dealt with."

This time she let the tear fall. "I never asked for a bodyguard. Never wanted one. My father may think he rules my life, but here, in my home, *I* rule. Please, leave."

"We'll need a spare key, then."

She started to shake her head, but he held up his hand. "If anything were to happen, we need to get to you, fast. It's either a spare key, or we knock the door down. I promise, we would only use it under those circumstances."

Her gaze narrowed, and he raised his hand. "Scout's—"

"Don't."

She glared at him for a moment, then crossed to a dish on a shelf on her bookshelf, and pulled out a key.

Oh. God. She kept her spare key out in plain view. He opened his mouth to lecture her on the importance of home security, but shut it again when he saw her expression. He could leave that conversation until another time.

He accepted the key as he stepped outside. She really wasn't going to budge on letting any of them in. He understood. It hurt, but … he understood. "We'll be right outside, then," he told her, and he hoped it sounded reassuring and not dominating.

Mic smiled bitterly. "I don't care." She closed the door.

Knox's shoulders sagged, and he turned to the path. Dan was there, arms folded, shaking his head.

"What?" Knox asked as he stepped down toward his friend.

"You sly dog."

Knox brushed past him. "I don't know what you're talking about."

"You slept with her." Dan slapped him on the back. "That's impressive. One night, shooter in the hills, and you still managed to get some action. Not that I blame you, she's—"

Knox turned and grasped his friend's jacket by the lapels. "Be very careful what you say next," he growled.

Dan's hands rose. "Hey, I'm just saying, if you're going to risk your career, then she's—"

Knox's eyes narrowed, and Dan sighed. "Worth it."

Knox slowly let go of his jacket, and eyed the front windows. The curtains were drawn. "Yeah, she is."

They turned to walk down to meet Fitz at the car. Smithy climbed out of the second car and yawned as he walked up to meet them. Fitz leaned back against the passenger door. He scrunched up his face. "She's not happy with us, is she?"

"Knox. She's not happy with Knox," Dan corrected.

Realization dawned on Fitz's face, and he looked at Knox. "Seriously? The package? You did it with the package?"

"You—" Smithy dragged his hand over his face, blinking. "Yikes. You are in deep doggy do-do."

"Can we not talk about this?" Knox asked.

"Oh, we are talking about this," Fitz muttered. "What do you propose we tell Walker? That we've compromised the package?"

"Hey, *we* didn't do anything, *I* did." He did this on his own, and he wasn't about to let his colleagues take any of the blame for his mistakes.

But calling what he did with Mic a mistake was … wrong. You were supposed to regret mistakes. He regretted the hurt, but he couldn't regret something so moving, so damn powerful it had shaken him to his core.

"But apparently not very well, because she's not happy. I can give you tips, if you like," Dan offered. Knox shot him a dark glare. "Just offering," Dan said innocently.

"Quantity doesn't mean quality," Smithy pointed out.

"I've had no complaints," Dan responded.

"Or maybe you never stick around long enough to hear 'em," Smithy suggested.

"Oh, trust me, there are no complaints."

Fitz rolled his eyes, then looked at Knox. "So how do you propose we watch Sparrow if she won't let us anywhere near her?" he demanded.

Knox folded his arms. "Same as we did before. You and Dan can take daylight, I'll do nights. Smithy monitors her incoming calls, and both he and you can pull that company apart and find out who the hell is behind this." He looked at Dan. "I'll be back here at two am." He needed some time to sleep after this weekend, if he was going to be any use to Mic, and he was determined that nothing further happened to her.

Fitz pinched the bridge of his nose for a moment, before sighing gustily. "It sucks that she's gone through everything so far, and she still needs to be watched." He eyed Knox. "Did we get anything from the shooter, anything at all that we can use to find out who hired him?"

"Danvers shot him before I could subdue him," Knox said, then grimaced. "I get that he was trying to help me—he had no idea that I could take him, it's just damn inconvenient."

He fished the phone out of his back pocket. "I did manage to get this, though. This was on the shooter when he died." He hadn't given it to the police—SafeKeepers had resources that were faster and better than the sheriff's department when it came to this sort of stuff. Walker would smooth out any issues with law enforcement, and ensure all relevant information was passed on.

Smithy took the phone. "I'll see what I can get from it."

"Let me know as soon as you find anything," Knox said. The shooter had been professional, and Knox wasn't sure if anything could be recovered, but if anyone could do it, Smithy could.

"Okay, so, let's get back to work," he said as he made his way toward the second car, Smithy following him. They'd return to the apartment just down the road that they were renting, and he'd catch some Zs while Smithy did whatever hacker stuff he did on the phone, and then he'd come back and relieve Dan. He eyed Mic's house for a moment before he started the car.

He just hoped that, at some point, he could make up for all the pain he'd caused the woman who'd become so dear to him.

~*~

Mic flinched awake, heart pounding. She stayed where she was, muscles tense, eyes wide, breath halted, until she realized she wasn't being hunted by a man toting a long-range rifle. *Oh, God.* She squeezed her eyes shut, willing her heart to slow down, her breath to fill her lungs.

In. Hold. Out. Slowly, she started to calm. She blinked, peering into the gloom of her bedroom. She was home. She was safe. She rolled over to turn on her bedside lamp, then sat up in bed. It took her a moment to free her legs from the tangle of bedsheets. It was just a dream. A bad, bad dream. She brought her knees up to her chest and wrapped her arms around her legs. She blinked.

George. Wayne. Those images, those memories, were right there, ready to freak her the hell out as soon as she closed her eyes again. She rose from the bed and trotted down the hall to her bathroom, flicking the lights on as she went. She poured herself a glass of water, and lifted it to her lips, her fingers trembling. *It's okay. Home. Safe.* She kept repeating the words to herself as she sipped the water, then set the glass down on the counter with a slight clatter.

She eyed herself in the mirror. Her hair was a sweaty, tangled mess. Dark circles ringed her eyes, and she looked pale. "You need to get a hold of yourself," she whispered to her reflection. Then her reflection started to blur, and her knees shook. She sank to the bathroom floor, scooting back up against the vanity as the tears fell.

There was nobody around. No staff she had to put a brave front on for. No Dad she had to impress, no … Knox. She cried harder. Two men had died—no, four, including Andy Rickerson and the shooter. So much violence. And all because she'd gotten nosy over a shipment, all those months ago. George had had something to do with it, and possibly so had Wayne. Andy, too. They'd all known about 'something' happening, but to her, not them. They must have been so surprised. She sobbed harder, when she remembered George, so scared, so … sincerely apologetic. Whatever he did, he didn't deserve to be hunted and killed like that. Neither did Wayne. These guys—they weren't on her radar at all for this drug stuff. Neither was Andy.

She squeezed her eyes shut. Andy. Andy was one of her couriers. It was still so hard to believe that a guy she knew, whom she worked with, had been prepared to hurt her, kill her. She'd worked side by side with him, helping him sort through parcels for delivery, and had no clue of his darker side, the side that was involved with drug trafficking and was prepared to do harm to a woman.

And then Knox had swept her up in his arms and away from danger. Her nails dug into her forearms. Knox was … amazing.

No, Knox was a lying jerk.

But he'd been there when she didn't even know she needed him.

Because Dad paid for him to be there.

Damn it, she'd been so careful after Sebastien. She'd tried so hard not to expose herself like that again. Don't get sucked into a guy's lies. Don't trust so damn easily. Always look for the ulterior motive. With Knox, though, she'd allowed herself to be completely blindsided. His résumé had checked out, and his approach had been to work at Eagle Express, not to ask her out. She slid her hands into her hair. The fact he'd left out details of his service with the army—why hadn't that rung alarm bells with her?

She'd been so humiliated, so horrified, when she'd learned her first contact with Sebastien hadn't been an accidental, serendipitous event. He'd known exactly who she was, and who she was related to, when he'd literally bumped into her at that charity fundraiser event. Their whole relationship had been carefully constructed so that Sebastien could meet her father and hopefully get him to invest in his GPS app. *Schmuck.* She clenched her hands in her hair. She still remembered those texts she'd read between her supposed boyfriend and his business partner, and how calculated he'd been in 'establishing a connection with the prospect'. She still couldn't admit to her father the only long-term relationship she'd had was with a guy who was more interested in associating with Gerard Robson than her. Fortunately, her father had passed on the investment opportunity without her having to explain why she was suddenly deleting Sebastien from her life.

And then came Knox.

She thought she'd found a unicorn. That one guy who she could talk to, listen to, be attracted to and attractive to … the kind of guy who could hold his own with her, and her family, who respected her and accepted that she had a career of her own, and was genuinely interested in her. The kind of guy she wanted to wake up to … her breath grew ragged.

But Dad paid for him to be there.

She wasn't quite sure what hurt the most, that her father didn't think she could handle herself, and stand by the consequences of her decisions …? That maybe, after this weekend, perhaps her father was right …? Or, just maybe, the man she'd started to feel something for wasn't there for her. Well, not because he wanted to be there for her, but because her father hired him to be there for her. Her stomach twisted.

The bare, pathetic truth of the matter was that she'd fallen for a guy who her father paid to be with her. She covered her mouth with her hand as the realization hit. She didn't just like Knox Jo—no, *Landon*—she loved him. Or at least, she loved the man she thought he was.

How much of what she'd come to know and love was real? She'd worked with the man for five weeks. She'd noticed him, noticed how hard he worked, his sense of humor, his kindness, his intelligence, his … oh, boy, his good looks. His body. His muscles. She clenched her teeth. With everything that had been going on at work, with the way staff had been treating her, he'd been the calm in the storm, that little oasis of acceptance in a desert of animosity. Was that why she was so drawn to him? Because he'd been nice to her when others weren't?

She bowed her head to rest her forehead on her knees. *Oh. Dear. God.* That sounded so pathetic, but in a quiet little place inside, the truth resonated. For once, she'd found a guy who respected her as an employer, a capable, professional woman in her own right, a desirable woman, and she had been mesmerized by the stark contrast he was in comparison to pretty much every other guy she had to deal with, including her own family. He'd said she was the only person he'd ever crossed the line with. Could she believe him? And did it matter? Did it really matter that he normally prided himself on being professional, and had slipped up—with her. She didn't think she could really trust him, did she? How could she make that same damn mistake again?

She took a deep breath. She didn't want to think about Knox anymore. Didn't want to think about how good she'd felt about them, about herself, whenever they'd talked. She didn't want to think about how much she was attracted to the man—still! She didn't want to think about how he could make her forget reason just by looking at her, or how she'd felt in his embrace, how he'd made her feel when they'd made love, or how much she'd started to hope for a shared future … or how hurt she was, discovering that future hope was no longer going to happen, but worse, hadn't been real in the first place, and that the only reason the man had been in her orbit was because her father paid him to be there.

No. She wasn't going to think about Knox anymore. She frowned. She had other things to think about. Like … what was she going to do now with work? Doug had called her before she'd gone to bed. He'd been released from hospital, but had told her and the others on the team to take a few days off. He'd get some temporary staff in to work in operations.

Her shoulders sagged. Just the thought of going back into work was … exhausting. Terrifying. The weight of all those angry stares … being blamed now not only for the arrests of three of their colleagues, but for the murders, too. And in a way, they'd be right. If she hadn't opened that first damn shipment, and then called in the FBI, then George and Wayne would still be alive. Andy, too.

Was there anybody else involved? A fleeting memory burst into her mind. She hitched her breath. The shooter had been aiming for Luis. She stared at the tiles on the floor. Was Luis involved? She shook her head in denial. *No* … He had been furious when his colleagues had been arrested. Men he worked with, and called friends. He blamed her for their arrest, but she'd seen that as misplaced loyalty, and nothing more … lethal. Was Luis so angry because he was also involved in the operation?

She sniffed, and brushed away at the tears. Luis—before everything went down, Luis had been great. Easy to talk to, respectful, cooperative. Since then, he'd been … well, difficult would be putting it mildly. A right royal douchebag, maybe, but she'd always seen that as him being upset over his friends, and making her a convenient scapegoat to avoid dealing with the fact that his friends had also betrayed him …

But what if he was somehow involved, too?

She tilted her head back against the vanity. This was just too … complicated. Not knowing who to trust …

She could trust Knox …

No, he'd lied to her.

But only because he'd had to.

And she was now back to thinking about Knox. Mic sighed. She knew her father hadn't paid him to sleep with her. She didn't know how her father would react if he found out the man he'd hired to protect his daughter had made love with her, but she knew it wouldn't be pretty. She wasn't trying to protect Knox, though. He was big enough to take care of himself; she'd seen him do it. No, she'd done it to protect herself.

Falling in love with a man paid to protect you didn't sound responsible, or professional … mistaking concern and protection for something more, for real care, maybe even love … Well, that just screamed for parental intercession, like a child running with scissors.

Yes, if she told her father, Knox would likely be removed. But then she'd just have some other bodyguard in his place. And a tiny little voice inside her whispered she still wanted Knox around, for some twisted, painful reason …

And if she was honest with herself, looking beyond the hurt, the anger, the humiliation, Knox had kept her safe when she was in very real danger. When that man had tried to strangle her in her room … When Andy had been hunting her down … When the shooter had been so close to her and her co-workers … Mic had to acknowledge that, at least. She had a better chance of survival when Knox was around.

She sighed, then rolled to her feet. She was tired, and she needed sleep, but her brain was whirling, too busy to rest. She had thoughts of Knox, of her father, of Luis, of Doug, even … of work, swishing around like towels in a washing machine. Maybe some warm milk and honey—or better yet, a hot chocolate, would help her catch those elusive Zs. Truthfully, she was a little scared to close her eyes, as those final images of George still clung to her.

She padded into the kitchen and turned the range hood light on. It shed enough light for her to prepare her drink, but wasn't harsh enough to banish all hope of sleep.

She opened the cupboard above the kitchen bench and removed a mug. She placed it on the counter, and then headed for the fridge. She looked briefly through the French doors leading to her backyard. It was still pretty dark outside. The sun wasn't due to make an appearance for another few hours.

A shadow unfolded itself from one of her deck chairs, and Mic screamed.

Chapter 16

Knox flinched at Mic's scream, then held up his hands in a non-threatening pose as he approached her back door. Hell, that woman had a set of lungs on her. And she looked like she really could do damage with the mug she held poised in her hand, ready to pitch.

She reached for a light switch, and he blinked as the back deck was bathed in warm light.

Mic's shoulders sagged when she recognized him, and he saw her lips move in what he figured was a very colorful curse, and he was grateful he couldn't hear her mutter. She stomped over to the door, turned the lock, and whipped the door open.

"What the hell are you doing there?" she hissed. Her hazel eyes glowed like golden fire in the light, her expression fierce. Her hair was a gorgeous, tumbled mess, and her pajamas were … distracting. His gaze skidded past the bruises on her throat that were already beginning to turn green on the edges, and he eyed the long line of her bare legs beneath the black silk boxer shorts bearing the Star Wars logo, and the white tank top that had a storm trooper's face emblazoned across her breasts.

She wasn't wearing a bra.

Knox swallowed, and forced his gaze to meet hers, trying to banish those memories of her breasts in the moonlight, the feel of them, the taste …

She was glaring at him. Waiting for him to respond. Oh, right.

"Uh, I'm working …" he gestured to her.

"On my back deck?"

"Well, yeah. If you won't let us in, we still need to make sure you're safe, so I'm … out here." He rolled his shoulders. What he wouldn't give for a bed. And Mic in it with him.

But he'd totally killed any opportunity for that to happen. He sighed.

"In the dark?" Mic folded her arms.

"Yep. No sense in letting the bad guys know where we are."

At the mention of bad guys, Mic's expression changed from outrage to something that looked borderline worried, and her gaze flicked past him to her backyard. "But don't worry, that's what we're here for."

"We?" She looked beyond him.

Knox waved his hand. "Well, me. I'm taking the night shift." Dan had again offered, but standing here, seeing Mic in the briefest of shorts and a thin tank top he could see the shape of her nipples through … yeah, he was glad he'd declined that offer.

He lifted his gaze to her face, and frowned. She looked like she'd been crying. Ah, hell. "Are you okay?" he asked, stepping inside to smooth back a tangle of dark hair that had fallen over her brow. He noticed she eyed him closely, but didn't step back.

"Uh, yeah. I'm fine."

He tilted his head to the side. That was her automatic response for everything. He closed the door behind him. "Can't sleep?"

Mic sighed, then nodded. He narrowed his eyes. "Bad dream?"

What she'd been through, what she'd seen—it would be normal for her to be traumatized by it all. Hell, he still remembered seeing his first death on that first tour of duty in Afghanistan, and he'd had nightmares for a while after his father had died. And Kayleigh … her death haunted him the most.

Mic bit on her lower lip, and her eyes looked big and haunted. She nodded. Once.

He sighed, then drew her in close to him, enfolding her in his arms. "That's natural," he whispered into her hair. Her hands rose between them, and touched his sides. He thought she was going to push him away, but instead, she slid her arms around his waist, and laid her head on his chest.

He closed his eyes at the contact. They stood there for a moment, holding each other, and then he felt her stiffen in his arms, as though she just realized what she was doing.

"I'm going to make some warm milk," she said as she withdrew. He nodded. Unfortunately, from his experience, warm milk, alcohol … none of it worked when you were trying to evade the visions in your mind.

"If you need to talk …" he offered gently, "it can help." It had helped him. Talking with others in his unit, with guys from SafeKeepers—even his mother after his father's death, it had helped. He'd even spoken with a therapist on his return to the States, and that had been a great help sorting out the messy jumble in his head, and learning about different strategies to cope with his traumatic memories. "After what you've been through, what you've seen, it's normal to feel a little wired, a little tense …"

She looked at him briefly, then stepped back toward the fridge. "I take it you saw some terrible things when you were in the army …?"

"Yeah, I did. We all did." He grimaced. "That's the nature of war, unfortunately." He stepped over to the stool near the kitchen bench, and slid onto it. "I was trained for that stuff, but nothing can quite prepare you for seeing someone die violently in front of you." He met her gaze. "I'm here for you, Mic."

For a moment she was quiet, and then her lips tightened. "Does that form a normal part of your bodyguard duties, or a value-add?" Her movements became jerky, and she placed the saucepan on the stove with a little more force than necessary.

He lifted his chin. "I care for you, Mic." There. He'd said it. It wasn't something he was used to sharing, used to saying, and it was at once both the scariest and the most liberating thing he'd ever told a woman. Now that his secret was out, though, he'd decided he would be nothing but honest with Mic. She deserved no less, and he wanted to build a bridge to her trust again. He'd keep telling her for as long as she'd stay still enough to listen.

She turned to face him. "Really?" She poured milk into the saucepan and lit the stove. "You lied to me before, you could be lying to me now. And I don't know how you can truly care for someone if you're not honest with them." She crossed to the pantry and pulled out a tin of hot chocolate mix.

She lifted her chin. "If there's one thing I really, really hate, it's when a guy is with me for the wrong reasons, and lies to me about it." She spooned hot chocolate into the milk.

His eyes narrowed. That sounded … like something had happened to her before. "What did he do?"

Mic blinked, and she turned back to the stove to stir the hot chocolate in the saucepan. "It doesn't matter. The upshot is, he lied, and it hurt. You lied, and it hurt."

"I wanted to tell you."

"Not enough to actually, you know, tell me." She shook her head, and he watched the movement of her hair against her back.

Oh, no. She wasn't going to dodge that again. "I tried," he reminded her. "Right before we—"

"I know," she interjected hurriedly. She busied herself with making the hot chocolate, and his lips curved when she took a second mug out without asking. She might be angry with him, and hurt, but on a deeper level she cared.

"Would you do it again?"

He paused, sensing the minefield he was about to step into. "What?"

She folded her arms as she turned to face him, and leaned back against the bench. "Would you do it the same way, again? Knowing that we'd ..." she moved her hand briefly between them. "Would you still pretend to be my friend?"

He was determined to prove to her that what happened last night had nothing to do with her father, and everything to do with what was developing between them, whether she'd admit it or not. He rose from the stool, and stepped around the bench. "I never pretended to be your friend, and what we did was more than just friends," he told her. Resolve filled him.

"But let me be clear on this," he said as he stopped in front of her. He placed both hands either side of her on the benchtop and leaned down to meet her gaze squarely. "I will do whatever it takes to make sure you're safe."

He heard her swallow, saw her gaze dip to his chest, the very narrow space between them, before she raised her gaze to his. She inhaled, slow and deep, her breasts lifting beneath that thin top. Mic's eyes were almost gold in the dim light from over the stove and streaming in from the deck. She was beautiful, and the truth he wanted to convey, the realization he wanted her to recognize, to accept, filled him with purpose.

"I will put my body on the line, if it means saving your life." He said in a low voice. His gaze dropped to her legs, her long, bare, sexy legs. She was stunning, beautiful, a woman he wanted to protect, to cherish, to love and to listen to, and not because her father was picking up the bill. And however damn long it took, he would convince her of that truth, of the honest, real connection they shared. But damn it, he wasn't going to apologize for putting her safety, her life, first.

"That's the real crux, here," he said, dipping his head closer, smelling the strawberry scent of the bodywash she'd used in her shower earlier, and the femininity of her just-woken body. He drew those scents in, letting them fill his nose, his chest, and feeling his body's slow throb in response. "If I ever have to lie to you to save your life, then that's exactly what I'll do, because I can live with you being angry at me, and I'll work on earning your forgiveness. But if you die, then that would destroy me." His voice was low and rough with the brutal honesty of his vow. "I can't do that again."

Her brow dipped, and she tilted her head to the side. "Again?"

A cool wash of grief, of self-directed anger, washed over him. He straightened and took a step back. He'd said too much. His gaze shifted to the pot on the stove. "I think your hot chocolate is ready."

She glanced down, then moved quickly to pull the simmering liquid off the stove. He walked back around the bench to the kitchen stool, and watched as she poured the hot chocolate into the waiting mugs.

She slid one of them along the benchtop, and he clasped it, his hands covering hers. Her gaze flicked up to meet his, and he saw the color bloom in her cheeks. He lifted his hands a little, and she withdrew her hand. Her movement was smooth, and so slow, as though there was a reluctance to lose contact.

She blinked, then turned back to the pot. She rinsed it out and left it in the sink to wash later, then picked up her mug. "I'll, uh, leave you to it," she whispered hoarsely as she backed out of the kitchen. She hesitated at the door, then looked back over her shoulder. "Uh, you can sleep on the lounge, if you like."

It was a baby step, but one he was very much going to take. He nodded his thanks and lifted the mug in toast as she left. "Sweet dreams."

~*~

Mic let herself out of the front door quietly, and glanced up and down the street. It was just past nine o'clock in the morning, and it looked like most of her neighbors had left for work already. She pulled down the visor of her blue Seattle Seahawks cap and adjusted the braid she'd slipped through the hole above the snap strap at the back. She slid her sunglasses on. Her zipped jacket had a high neck, and she was confident the bruises on her neck wouldn't catch too many stares. She walked quickly down the path, and started jogging once her feet hit the pavement. She fought back the yawn, but it still snuck through, and she damn near cracked her jaw.

Ugh. She was tired. Exhausted. Had no real enthusiasm to go for a run, but would go stir-crazy if she just stayed in her home to stare at her walls. The hot chocolate had done bupkes. She'd spent most of the night staring at her ceiling, until her circling thoughts had finally exhausted her. And going over and over in her mind was the moment in her kitchen with Knox.

Again. He'd said he couldn't do that *again*, meaning someone dying. She didn't get the impression he was referring to his father, or his mother. Friends he'd lost in service? Or someone she didn't know about … a woman? She frowned. He'd told her he'd have no compunction lying to her, if it meant she was safe. She started to lengthen her stride. What the hell was she supposed to do with that?

The man was frustrating. Confusing. On the one hand he apologized so sincerely, so openly, so fully accepting of his responsibility, and the pain he'd caused her. On the other, he was totally prepared to do it again, if her life was in danger. So darn confusing. She hated it. She loved it. She was hurt by it. She was soothed by it.

She shook her head. She craved the comfort, the familiarity of work, of losing herself in the problems that arose with customer issues, damaged shipments, cancelled flights, inclement weather—anything that kept her from thinking about her life beyond work, and how lonely it was. But no, she wasn't going in to work today.

She couldn't remember the last time she'd had a day off.

She snorted. A day off. Like this was some damn holiday.

She drew in a deep breath, which sparked another yawn. She just wanted to sleep. Seriously, who could relax when there was a hulk of a man sleeping on your sofa? Especially when that hulk of a man made you forget how blisteringly angry you were with him when he sidled up close and vowed to protect your life with his own?

She started to pick up her pace. She had avoided the living room, hadn't wanted to wake Knox up out there on the lounge. Or to have to face that wall of smoking-hot male sincerity. And he was all that. Sincere. Smoking hot. But damn it, she wasn't anywhere near ready to forgive him, and if he kept talking to her like that, kept looking at her like that, she'd do something stupid. Like forget how much he'd hurt her. No. What was that saying? *Fool me once, shame on you. Fool me twice, shame on me.* But if he stepped in close, and tempted her with that low voice, those whispered promises, those hunky muscles—

"Morning," a deep voice said close to her ear, and she shrieked as she turned. She would have stumbled over the fence behind her if a hand hadn't grabbed her to prevent her toppling back.

"Knox," she cried, then thumped him on the chest. Hard.

"Mic," he growled, then stepped back to avoid her next thump. "What the hell are you doing?"

"I was going for my morning run," she growled back. "Geez. Why are you sneaking up on me?"

He let her go, and folded his arms. "Why didn't you come wake me? I'm your bodyguard, for Pete's sake. I'm supposed to come with you. Better yet, we're not even supposed to be out in the open like this." The muscles in his jaw moved as he seemed to clamp down with his teeth. He turned for a moment, scanning the street, then faced her, his lips tight.

"Are you kidding me? I jogged up to you. In the middle of the street. Thumping along, making a normal racket. I didn't sneak up on you." He shook his head, his frown fierce. "How did you not hear me?"

She snapped her mouth closed. She didn't want to tell him she was thoroughly distracted by thoughts of him … standing so close to her, making her go all gooey inside as he pledged his life to keep her safe, when instead she should have been roasting him for lying to her.

"I wanted to run." She could run. She could do anything she damn well pleased. She didn't need his, or her father's permission, to live her life—and run.

He pursed his lips for a moment. Then dipped his chin. "You were attacked two nights ago. Three of your colleagues were murdered the next day."

"And both men responsible for those acts are dead," she said succinctly. "They are no longer a threat to me. So, I'm going for my run."

She took a step, but he grabbed her arm. "No. Like I told your father, those men were guns-for-hire. Whoever hired them is still out there, and can still pay another hit man to come at you."

"You make them sound like they're some mega-funded criminal gang—"

"You don't know that they're not," he interrupted her. He sucked in a deep breath, then exhaled. "The guy I fought in your hotel room—he was trained. He's not some hood hired off the street to scare you into silence. He was determined to kill you. The guy with the rifle? He was trained, too. Not some guy found on the range and paid to scare. He was highly trained, and ready to kill—and you want to go for a morning jog. Not happening."

He gestured to the street. "I just 'snuck up' on you," he said, moving his fingers in air quotes. "What if I was here to hurt you? Kill you? Kidnap you?" He grasped both of her arms gently, his expression almost pleading. "You're tired. You're wired. I get it. But you can't do this. Not without protection."

She opened her mouth to argue, and he pulled her close. She snapped her mouth shut as he turned them around so that she stood in front of him, her back to his chest. He gently braced his hands on her shoulders.

"Look down the street."

For a moment, she was distracted by his voice, so low, so close to her ear she could feel his breath brush past. His hands were warm on her shoulders, and she could smell him. She blinked, and focused down the street.

"Tell me what you see?"

She frowned. The street was pretty much empty, apart from sporadically parked cars. But nobody was about. Oh, wait, there was a dog. It was taking a dump on Mr. Stewart's front walk.

"I see a dog taking care of business," she muttered.

"See that van? What if someone was inside it?"

She could see his cheek, just out of the corner of her eye, as he bent forward over her shoulder. She followed his line of sight. Oh. That van. She frowned. It had dark windows that she couldn't see into. She swallowed. What if Knox was right? Was someone inside, just waiting to jump out at her as she ran past?

"It's the things we can't see that can be the most dangerous." He raised his arm briefly to point out the figure one block down, and his arm brushed against her sleeve. She bit her lip. The contact was fleeting, warm. She blinked, distracted, then tried to focus on the guy who was turning his phone around, then looking in all directions of the intersection. Was he acting, and waiting for her to come nearer?

"My job is to keep you safe, whether you like it or not."

She trembled. Did Knox's lips just brush against her ear? She could feel the heat of his breath against her ear, her neck, and frankly, it was making her crazy. And a little horny.

She stepped away, frowning. No. He'd lied to her. She folded her arms as she turned to face him. "I know what you're doing, Knox. You're just trying to scare the hell out of me, make me paranoid."

He shook his head. "No, I'm trying to make you aware of the possible dangers," he corrected. "This is what I see, when you come out here alone and unprotected—along with a couple of other dozen potential risks and threats. I'm not messing about."

Well, damn it, he was still making her paranoid. She hugged herself a little tighter. "I will go stir crazy if I just sit at home," she told him. "I need to burn off some of this energy."

He nodded. "I can help with that." He lifted his hand to gesture back down the road toward her home, as though inviting her to precede him. She eyed him suspiciously, and he grinned. "Come on. I promise, you're going to like this."

She gave him a close look as she passed him and started to walk home. He had an idea to burn energy, and she was going to like it. Her heart thudded in her chest. She shouldn't do this. She was angry with him. He'd betrayed her, lied to her.

And yet, going back to her place to 'burn off some energy' with Knox suddenly sounded like something she should at least try …

# Chapter 17

"And block, and block," Knox said as he swung his fist.

Mic obediently raised her arm to block his strike. They were in Mic's tiny backyard, and Knox had to admit, he was impressed with her stamina. For someone who'd gotten very little sleep over three nights, and had experienced everything she had in the last few days, he would have thought she'd spend the day curled up under a blanket, hiding from the world.

But no, not Mic. She wanted to hit something. They'd been at it for nearly an hour, and he wasn't taking it easy on her. She'd stripped out of her lightweight jacket, and her skin gleamed with perspiration, her brow furrowed in concentration as she tried to guess what he was about to do next. She still wore her skintight Lycra leggings, and a top that was part sports bra, part tank top, and all sexy. And distracting.

"You know, this isn't quite what I thought you meant," she said breathlessly as she ducked to avoid the next punch he threw.

His eyebrows rose. "Oh, really? What did you think I meant?" His lips curved in a grin as Mic's cheeks went from workout bloom to radioactive heat.

"Never mind," she muttered.

His grin broadened. He knew exactly what she'd been thinking, and he was thinking the same thing. So damn tempted. All night, on that lounge in the living room, he'd been thinking about her, her luscious body, and about what they'd shared, how good her skin felt against his. Knowing she was just down the hall, warm and curvy in her bed, had meant his night was decidedly uncomfortable. He hadn't gotten much sleep. Now she was standing in front of him, wearing figure-hugging clothes that showed off her athletic physique to perfection. Thank God sweat masked drool.

Knox held up his hands, palms facing her. "Okay, so hit me here," he told her, tapping the center of the palm of his hand. "Remember, fold your fingers—ow."

Damn, that was impressive. "Again." She did it, and he nodded at her in approval. She had a good hit on her. They kept it up for a while, until he could see she was beginning to tire.

"Let's take a break," he suggested.

She shook her head, her dark braid sliding over her shoulder. "No, let's keep going," she panted.

"Mic, you're exhausted."

"Not exhausted enough yet to pass out. Let's keep going."

Knox sighed. She needed sleep. There were dark circles under her eyes, and her complexion was pale, despite her exertions. But he knew what she was doing, had experienced it himself, after Kayleigh's death. He knew how memories could haunt you, how noises could startle, sudden movements and flashes could make you freeze, waiting for the pain to hit, the world to darken. Sometimes it took whatever you could muster, whether it was physical exhaustion, or alcohol, or other illicit substances, to push you into a sweet state of oblivion. He understood.

He straightened. "Okay, let's try some moves."

Her eyebrows rose. "Moves? What kind of moves?"

His lips quirked. "Oh, I've got lots of moves for you, Mic," he teased, and she rolled her eyes, but didn't quite hide the hint of a smile curving her lips.

"Get on with it."

He grinned, then stepped up to her. "Okay, let's pretend I'm attacking you. I'm going to grab you here," he said reaching for her right shoulder with one hand. She immediately grasped his hand with her left as she turned, rolling his wrist over with her movement. He had to step off balance to prevent his wrist from snapping.

"Ow," he said, then grinned when she let go. "You've been holding out on me, sweetness. Where did you learn that?"

She grinned back. "Two older brothers, Landon." She shrugged. "They both wanted me to be able to take care of myself when I was old enough to hit the bars."

He nodded approvingly. "Good job."

She sobered for a moment, and her hand rose to her neck, drawing his gaze to the bruises there. "Can you—can you show me … what I could have done?" she asked in a whisper, and he saw her blink back tears.

Knox nodded. "Of course."

He gestured for her to lie on the postage stamp she'd called 'the lawn' when they got home, then straddled her hips. He kept his weight off her, palms out. "How are you doing?" He didn't want to stress her, or possibly bring back the panic of her attack.

She took a deep breath, then nodded. "I'm good."

"Okay, so it can take about eight to ten seconds to pass out from being choked," Knox told her, and nodded at her shocked expression, "in some cases, maybe six, so you have to act fast."

He grasped her arms. "Tuck your elbows in to your sides, you don't want his knees getting under or over your arms."

Mic brought her elbows in, and looked up at him expectantly.

"In this position, any strike you make towards my head, my face—you won't have the reach. And you could try for my balls, but unless you cripple me with your one shot, I'm going to come back angry," he said, with a mock strike that stopped short of her face. "You understand?"

She nodded. "Yeah. Lights out."

"Okay, so grab my wrist, thumb in," he said, folding her right hand over his left forearm. "Get hold of my tricep here with your left hand," he instructed, and waited until she'd done it. He nodded. "Good. Keep your arms in close, okay? Now, press your left foot down on the ground outside of my foot …" he twisted a little until he could see she'd done it, and smiled down at her in approval. "Great. Now, plant your other foot on the ground between my legs."

He could feel her thigh against his back. "Excellent. Now, if you just lift your hips a little and roll—"

She followed his command, and his bodyweight did the rest, so that he tumbled to the side, and she rolled up over him. She blinked, surprised at the reversal.

"Wow. That was … easy."

He nodded. "It's using your opponent's body mass and momentum against him. Then you strike me, and run," he told her. She did a mock strike, and rose off him, her expression incredulous.

"That's—oh, I need more of this," she told him.

"Well, let's do it a few more times, so that your muscles start memorizing it."

They practiced the move, and each time he did it with her, he noticed she was more confident with her response, her defense. She had good reflexes, with a natural instinct for using momentum to her advantage.

She was beginning to fatigue, though, whether she was prepared to admit it or not. Mic flipped him, then straddled him, panting. Her elbow buckled, hitting him in the shoulder, and she winced.

"Sorry," she gasped, staring down at him. Her skin glistened, and her chest heaved as she struggled to catch her breath.

He smiled up at her. "All good. Ready to call it quits?" He rested his hands on her hips, and the move felt natural, as though her hips were made for his hands.

Her breath hitched, just a little, but he still noticed. And damned if her cheeks didn't get just that little bit rosier. She stared at him for a moment, then nodded. "Okay." Her other elbow buckled, and his hands slid up her sides to catch her as she pitched forward a little, her hands sliding off his shoulders to the ground, so that she almost lay on top of him. He could feel the weight of her body resting atop his, and heat started to coil inside him.

Her eyes met his, full of turmoil as she scanned his face. His fingers spread out, clasping her just above her waist. Her cheeks puffed as she exhaled, and his gaze dropped to her mouth. Her lips were slightly puckered, but relaxed, looking soft and inviting. She leaned forward a little, the movement arching her back just the slightest, and pressing her groin a little more firmly against his.

Knox's body reacted, his cock hardening beneath her.

His hands slid down her body to smooth over her hips and cup her butt. She gasped. Her gaze heated, and she rolled her hips again. He could feel her liquid heat through their thin layers of clothing, and he could feel himself lengthening, seeking her. Desire was flooding him, arousing him, and his hands tightened on her hips. She was so damn beautiful, so effortlessly sensual.

She sighed, repeating that sexy little move that made him want to thrust against her, inside her. He couldn't take it anymore. He'd spent the morning letting her beat him up, in an effort to release their pent-up energy, but instead he found himself wired, coiled for action. He couldn't stand being this close to her and not doing what he craved. He rolled them over, his gaze never leaving hers as he reversed their position. She gave a delighted little gasp, and the gold sparks in her eyes lightened. Her lips curved, parted. He lifted her thigh up against the outer side of his hip, cradling himself closer to her, and lowered his head.

"Hey, anyone home?"

It took a moment for the words to penetrate, to part the carnal haze that had swept through him with annoying awareness.

He lifted his head as Dan walked around the side passage. "Whoa," his colleague said, before clapping his hand over his eyes.

Which would have been almost decent of him, if his fingers weren't parted. "I can't see anything," Dan lied, moving his other arm out in front of him as though blinded.

Mic squeaked, and tried to rise, which just resulted in rubbing herself up against him. Knox growled as he levered himself off her, reluctant and frustrated at the interruption.

"Where is everyone?" Dan asked, fumbling with a potted plant, although how he couldn't see the damn thing, peeking through the gaps of his fingers like that, Knox didn't know. He stretched his hand out to Mic. She grasped it, and he hauled her up.

"Oh, hi," Mic gasped as she straightened. She closed her eyes and covered her face briefly, before lowering her hands, her face scrunching up with embarrassment.

"Dan," Knox greeted his friend. Dan lowered his hand, and made a mock-surprise jolt when he saw them.

"Oh, there you are!" He smiled at them, eyeing them both closely, and Knox didn't miss the tiny frown his friend shot in his direction. "I've come to relieve you." His eyebrows rose as he gestured between Knox and Mic. "Uh, in a matter of speaking, of course." He gestured toward the front of the house. "I didn't think it was an emergency, so didn't use the key."

"Oh, my God." Mic's softly muttered words carried to Knox's ears, and he fought against the smile that tickled his lips. Mic pointed to her back door. "Uh, I'm going to go take a shower." She paused, then grimaced as she eyed the side passage. "Feel free to use that key, next time."

"Sure," Dan said, and gave her a casual wave. Then his friend turned his incredulous gaze back to Knox. "Are you for real? At least take it indoors, dude."

"Your timing sucks," Knox muttered, as he watched Mic's hasty retreat into the house.

"Well, you should have hung a tie over a doorknob, somewhere," Dan said, gesturing down the side passage. "Or something on the side gate—hell, whack it up in neon lights if you have to."

"It's not what you think," he told his friend. Dan gave him a deadpan stare. Knox made a face, then nodded. "Okay, it is, kind of, but it didn't start out that way. I was trying to show her some moves."

Dan's eyebrow rose.

"Self-defense moves," Knox clarified.

"Ah," Dan said, nodding in understanding. "I see. Yeah, that old thrust-and-parry self-defense move can be very effective," he said dryly.

Knox sighed as he climbed the stairs to the back deck. "Seriously. That wasn't … intended."

Dan raised his hands as he followed Knox through into the kitchen. "Hey, you don't have to justify anything to me, I'd be the last person to judge you on something like that, because that would make me … judgy."

"Hypocritical," Knox countered as he walked over to the cupboard, pulled out a glass and filled it with tap water. He still remembered arriving at a stakeout and interrupting Dan with an unnamed woman, with something involving hot wax and a flip flop that he could never unsee. He drank from the glass.

Dan nodded. "That, too." He slid onto one of the stools at the bench. "Smithy got hold of the preliminary autopsy report for that guy Rickerson."

Knox's eyebrows rose, and he looked back down the hall. He could hear the shower running in the bathroom. He tried not to think of what that meant. Mic. Naked. Wet. But if she was in there, then she couldn't be further traumatized by their conversation. He turned back to Dan. "That was quick."

"Well, not quite so much a report as the ME's unedited notes."

Knox hesitated. How did—*nah*. It was best he didn't know how Smithy had managed that. "And?"

"Multiple skull fractures. Looks like he was beaten with a rock."

"Yikes." Sounded gruesome, but he wasn't surprised. The guy had attacked Mic. Karma's a bitch.

"Oh, and we brought Mic's car back," Dan said, fishing her car keys out of his jeans pocket. Knox nodded his thanks. Smithy had brought all of her items back from the resort. It said a lot about Mic's current state of mind that she hadn't even thought of her luggage, or her laptop, phone, keys or the car they'd washed off in the Eagle Express parking lot on Friday night before this whole nightmare unfolded.

"I've parked it in the drive."

The water stopped running, and minutes later Mic walked back into the kitchen, dressed in comfortable, soft-looking sweats that made her look so damn huggable. Knox reached for the glass and refilled it, then passed it to her. "Drink. You need to get hydrated."

She nodded as she took the stool at the end of the bench, and sipped the water. "What's going on?"

Knox leaned back against the fridge. "Dan's just bringing me up to date," he told her.

She finished her drink, and Knox reached for it, refilled it, and handed it back. She took it and looked at Dan expectantly. "So, what's going on?"

"Well, your car's out the front," Dan said, and she set the glass on the table, and cupped her chin with her hand.

"I can't believe I didn't even think of it," she sighed.

Knox gave her a small smile. "You've had other things on your mind."

She nodded, and yawned. He turned to Dan. "Anything else?"

"Your colleague who was shot, she's now stable and moving out of intensive care."

Mic closed her eyes for a moment, her shoulders sagging in relief. "Thank God."

"The deputies want to talk to Sp—Mic," Dan corrected himself, and they darted a glance at Mic. She blinked, her eyes narrowed fleetingly, then she shrugged.

"What about?"

Dan's eyebrows rose. "About what happened. They'll need to go over statements. Once they've had a chance to track where everyone was, and create a timeline, they'll want to check their facts."

She nodded. "Okay." Knox watched her. Her eyes were at half-mast.

"I've told them maybe tomorrow, or the next day," Dan said. "In the meantime, we're sifting through everything we can find to try and track who hired these men."

"Have we been able to identify them yet?" Knox asked.

"No, but they're running prints through military records."

Knox nodded. Both men had training, so military wasn't a bad guess. It was just figuring out which military.

"Smithy's got eyes on bank accounts too, to see if there are any unusual sums being transferred."

"Good."

"The FBI are going to send some guys over, too, seeing as it's a good chance this is connected to their case." Dan looked him up and down. "You're looking tired, old man. You should have time to catch a couple of hours sleep before you're back on tonight."

Knox nodded as he turned to Mic, and he smiled.

Her eyes were closed, and her body was leaning to the side. Ever so slowly, she was sliding off the stool.

He caught her, scooping her up in his arms. Her eyebrows rose, as though she was trying to open her eyes, but gave up, and she settled against him.

"Nice catch," Dave commented as he rose from the stool.

Knox's gaze travelled over her face, so relaxed in slumber. He nodded. "She is."

Dan preceded him down the hall to open Mic's bedroom door, then scooted inside to draw back the coverlet on her bed. Knox carried her through, holding her close as he walked over to the bed. Slowly, gently, he lowered her to the bed, then drew the covers up over her as Dan left the room.

She snuggled into her pillow, turning slightly on the mattress. Knox smiled as she tugged the cover with her. He smoothed it up over her shoulder, then brushed some of her damp hair off her forehead. He crouched down beside the bed to stare at her. She'd been through so much, but she was … amazing. She'd spent the morning learning how to protect herself from an attack. Her strength, her determination, were awe-inspiring. He respected her efforts to make herself safe, regardless of him or Dan, or the others. And she was good. If she kept going, she'd be a formidable badass if someone tried to do her wrong. Right now, though, she deserved her hard-won oblivion.

He leaned forward to press a gentle kiss to her brow. "I won't let anything happen to you, sweetness," he whispered. "Now, sleep hard. Pleasant dreams." He brushed his lips against her skin again, and walked out of her room, closing the door gently behind him.

~*~

Mic rolled over and stretched, then opened her eyes. She gazed out of her bedroom window. *Huh.* She'd forgotten to draw the curtains closed again, and early morning light peeked through. But—she struggled to figure out the time. Had she slept a whole day and night?

She shoved the covers off, then frowned as she sat up. She was in clothes. Her sweats, to be exact. She frowned, glancing about. *What—? How—?* She remembered Dan, talking about deputies … Knox making her drink water … She blinked. Yeah, she was drawing a blank.

But right now, she was busting to use her bathroom, so she climbed out of bed and padded down the hall, yawning and stretching.

The noise of running water didn't quite compute until her hand had twisted the doorknob, and a cloud of steam billowed out from the bathroom.

"Oh, my God, I'm so sorry," she gasped, catching a fleeting glimpse of glorious male nakedness before she forced her feet to move and she turned about, eyes wide. *Oh, wow.*

# Chapter 18

Knox was … stunning. He had a tan line, too.

"It's okay," he said as he turned off the shower tap. She grabbed one of the spare towels from the shelves under the sink and handed it back.

She was such a lousy hostess. She should have made up his bed on the lounge, fetched him a towel, maybe give him some privacy …

"Uh, did you—did you put me to bed?" she queried, and noticed she still hadn't stepped out of the bathroom. Just take one step, that's all. The first one's always the hardest. She could hear his movements behind her in the shower as he toweled himself off. And she still didn't move.

She'd never wanted to be a scrap of toweling so much in her life.

He stepped out of the shower, and his new position brought him into view via the bathroom mirror. *Well, hello there.*

She was seeing his body in the full light of day, and it was magnificent. Sure, she'd seen his torso in the hotel room, and she'd seen more when they'd made love under the stars, but then it had been a little dark.

Now, there was no hiding the fact that Knox Landon was one hell of a gorgeous guy. She swallowed. He must have hurried to dry himself off, because droplets of water still clung to his skin. She could relate to their reluctance to let go of contact with his body.

"Yeah, I hope you don't mind," he said, then ran his hand through his sexily tousled hair. The normally short curls now stood up in tufts and spikes. He met her gaze in the mirror. "You went out like a light, so I carried you."

"You carried me?" she repeated. Damn it, she'd slept through it. She blinked, then shook her head. "I'm sorry, I should leave you to it." She stepped toward the door, but his hand shot past her, closing it in front of her.

She turned. Slowly. His arm was so close. All those muscles, the sinewy cords … she followed the limb along to his chest. That bicep was so damn impressive. His triceps weren't too shabby, either.

Yeah. He was definitely an attractive man.

"I don't mind," he said, shifting a little closer. She stepped back, gaze fixed to his pecs, those nipples, with a little drop of water hanging there that screamed 'lick me'.

"Oh?" she said. Good grief, were they talking? What were they talking about? All she could see was skin, and this tiny white towel that was slung around his hips and tied carelessly in front. Like super-carelessly. She reckoned it wouldn't take much to make that towel drop. Maybe if he'd just take a deep breath in …

Above the line of the fabric was bare skin and a faint line of hair that trailed up in the direction of his navel.

"You can join me in the shower, any time," he offered, his voice husky. His hand slid down to rest on the doorknob, and the move brought their bodies closer.

And yep, that towel slid a little lower. Parted a little, to show her more of that line of hair arrowing down to—

"Any time," he repeated, and twisted the doorknob. "But I'll free it up for you, now."

He opened the door, and his towel started to slide. He caught it, and slung it over his shoulder as he walked down her hallway, whistling.

She gaped after him, stunned, yet still enjoying the view of his pale buttocks as he walked away from her. His broad shoulders, lean hips, and muscly thighs … He looked over his shoulder, and she scrambled to close the door—but not before she saw his wink.

She leaned back against the door. *Holy sex god, Batman.*

A few minutes later, she was having a shower. A very cold shower.

~*~

Mic dressed in a pair of faded jeans and a Seahawks T-shirt that she'd bought in college and that had seemed to shrink after its many washings and didn't quite cover her stomach. She'd worn it intentionally because, although she wasn't about to tell him she was fine with him lying, please shag her, she still wanted him to at least think about it.

She walked down the hall, craning her neck to peer into her living room, which was curiously sex god free. Was that good? She wasn't quite sure how to act around him, not after walking in on him showering. Naked. Wet. Skin all slick. Wow. She fanned herself. She'd been gearing up for an awkward glance, then hurrying along. Now she was overthinking it, which meant it would be truly awkward when she finally saw him. Clothed.

She frowned, turning back to the kitchen. She could hear sizzle. Definitely sizzle—and it wasn't a euphemism. She inhaled. Oh, blessed be those chubby little pigs, she could smell bacon.

She walked into the kitchen then paused. "Wow." It was a word she seemed to use around Knox a lot, but, well, he'd surprised her. He turned briefly to smile from his spot at the stove, then turned to take another longer look, his gaze straying to the raised hem of her shirt. And didn't that sexy glint in his eyes warm her in those unmentionable places …

Her kitchen bench was set with two places for breakfast. Orange juice, little bowls of cut up cantaloupe, co—*oh, sweet Jesus*—coffee, and eggs, hash browns—she wanted to do a jig at that—and Knox was sliding strips of bacon onto the plates before setting the frypan down on the stove.

"What's this?" she asked before she remembered she was going to be tongue-tied and awkward around him.

"Oh, I thought I'd make you my favorite breakfast," he said cheerily as he took the seat next to her. She glanced between him and the feast on the bench, then back at him.

"It's impressive."

"No, my chili con carne is impressive," he corrected her. He pointed at the food with his fork. "I love this stuff, and wanted to share it with you."

She frowned. "Why?" Then she realized how rude that sounded. "Not that I'm complaining," she interjected.

He twisted a little to look at her directly, his elbow resting on the bench—which just happened to make his bicep bulge. She lifted her gaze to his as she reached for her own fork. *Act normal, for Pete's sake.* She felt like she'd stepped into a bachelorette party, and was obsessed with stripping the hot guy.

"I want you to get to know me," he said, his tone serious. She toyed with the fork. "I may have been undercover before, Mic, but where I could, I was completely honest with you."

Her eyes narrowed, and he nodded. "Except when I wasn't—because of the job, and your father's request. So, ask me anything. What do you want to know? I'm an open book."

She cut off a piece of bacon, and chewed on it thoughtfully. "Anything, huh?"

He nodded as he reached for his orange juice. "Yep. Anything."

"Okay," she said slowly as he sipped his juice. She thought about it, about their 'honest' conversations to date, and one factor that had caught her attention, intrigued her. "Who was she? The lady who basically destroyed you before?"

Did that sound jealous? She'd been trying for curious.

Knox coughed into his juice. Mic calmly speared a chunk of cantaloupe and popped it into her mouth—delicious—and eyed him as he wiped his lips.

"What?"

"The other night, you talked about dying, and how you couldn't go through it again. Who was she?"

Knox placed his fork down on the plate, the clink so quiet in the kitchen. She waited, prepared for whatever distraction he could muster to try and avoid the question, like he had the other night.

"Kayleigh Evans," he said quietly.

She reached for her coffee, just to avoid his gaze. "Wife? Girlfriend?" She must have been important, because she could see the hole the woman's death had ripped through Knox.

He shook his head. "No, nothing like that." He dipped his head for a moment, and she wasn't sure if he was fighting tears, collecting his thoughts, or checking if his fly was closed. His expression was neutral and gave nothing away.

"She was an embedded journalist," he told her, his voice low and rough. "Twenty-eight years old. Afghanistan was her first on-the-ground assignment." He rubbed his hand over his mouth for a moment. "I didn't know her very long," he admitted. "She'd only been there three weeks." He swallowed.

It was that moment, that movement in his throat, the tightening of his lips, that glimpse of tightly controlled emotion, that warned her. He wasn't neutral at all, on this topic. She felt like a bitch, making him relive an obviously painful experience as a trust test.

"I'm sorry, Knox," she said, laying her hand over his. "You don't need to tell me—"

"No. I want to be completely honest with you," he rasped. "I don't want to hide anything from you."

He turned his hand over beneath hers and clasped her fingers. "Kayleigh was … ambitious. Fun. Funny," he corrected. "She had a great sense of humor, and she made a lot of us laugh." He sucked in a shaky breath. "Honestly, we got along really well—but not romantically," he said quickly, making a negating gesture with his other hand. "No, she was … she was my friend. Almost like a kid sister."

"She would accompany my unit on some of our missions." He took a moment, sitting silently, breakfast forgotten. "One day we were attacked. Our lead vehicle drove over an IED, and then we took fire when we stopped. She was hit."

Mic took his hand between both of hers, trying to share her strength, her warmth, in response to the pain she heard in his voice. He lifted his gaze to hers, and she saw the ravaged pain in his face, the tortured look the memories left in his eyes. "I lied to her, Mic." He blinked back moisture, and took in a deep breath.

"She was shot. Multiple times. She was bleeding out. I told her she was going to be fine, that we'd go watch a baseball game when we got stateside."

Her heart tore at the pain in his voice, in his face, and she gripped his hands a little tighter, trying to draw in that pain. He raised his gaze to the ceiling. "Oh, boy." He shook his head, the muscles in his jaw flicking as he brought himself under control. "She died in my arms, Mic. Scared, and in pain …" He brought his feet up on the rungs of the stool and leaned forward to clasp her hands. He raised them, and she felt the warm, gentle brush of his lips against her skin. "I've had someone in my care die on me, Mic," he said gruffly. "She was entrusted into our safekeeping. It tore me apart when she died." He took a moment, then, "Shortly after that I commissioned out of the service and started working for SafeKeepers." He lifted his gaze to meet hers, the color of his irises a deep green. "And I swore I wouldn't lose another person entrusted to my care. Whatever it takes. If it means I tell a white lie—or something more serious, I'll do that, Mic, because the alternative, losing you … that's not an option for me."

His eyes narrowed as he looked at her, his gaze skidding over her forehead, her nose, her lips and cheeks before coming back to her eyes. "Do you understand?"

Mic took a deep breath, and blinked at the tears in her own eyes. She nodded. "I think so."

He shook his head. "Then let me make it crystal clear. I'm being completely honest here—I like you. A lot. I hurt you, and I'm sorry. And I will do it again if it means keeping you safe—because your safety is my priority."

Mic sat there silently for a moment. Basically, he was prepared to lie to her again … Could she handle that? She'd promised she'd never stomach another guy's lies. That she'd never trust her heart again if it was going to be ripped apart by deceit. And yes, he viewed those lies as necessary. She, on the receiving end, had a different take. If she'd known the truth, would they still have made love? Would she have trusted him with those stories about her family, her *father*, knowing her father was paying him to be there with her?

She'd like to say hell no, but looking at the man in front of her, his good looks, his own version of a moral compass— honorable, yet prepared to deceive … A man who'd faced great loss and heartache, and who ignored his own personal risk for the good of others …

She was still processing his story. He'd left the marines to make his life all about protecting others. After being in the crosshairs of a killer, she knew she trusted this man with her life. But could she trust him with her heart?

She nodded. "I understand." She did. He was giving her fair warning. It was whether she heeded it, and protected her heart accordingly, that was the question.

He rose from the seat, drawing her up with him. "Good, because I want to get to know you, too." He gave her a heated look that was full of intent, full of awareness, of arousal, and he lowered his lips to hers.

Chapter 19

Knox inhaled her scent. Fresh out of the shower, she smelled like flowers and femininity. Her lips were so soft as he brushed them with his own. Once, twice. She drew in a breath, tilting her head to his, and he accepted her silent invitation, pressing his mouth against hers.

Her lips opened beneath his, and he slid his tongue inside. Her mouth was warm, wet and welcoming. He slid one of his hands into her damp hair, cradling her head at an angle guaranteed to give him deeper penetration. He slid his other arm around her back, his hand beneath the hem of her shirt to stroke against the smooth, soft skin. God, he loved this shirt. He wasn't a Seahawks fan, but he was thinking of converting. He pulled her in tight so that her body was flush against his.

She made this sexy little sound of surprise, and then sighed as her arms slid over his shoulders, her fingers spearing into his hair. His tongue danced with hers, a slick sensation that had him damn near busting out of his pants.

His cock hardened even more as her breasts rose and fell against his chest. He needed to have her. Now. Ever since that night, every waking second he didn't think about making her safer was spent imagining making her scream in pleasure in his arms. His hand trailed around to her front, and he palmed her breast beneath the—*dear God*, lacy bra.

He rolled his hips against hers, felt her tremble, heard her soft mewl. He lifted her so her thighs straddled his hips, and turned to brace her against the wall.

Her head tilted back, and she gasped as he arched against her. "Oh, yes, please," she cried softly. Her fingers clenched in his hair, pulling his head back. "You're so not off the hook," she whispered.

He shook his head. "Didn't think it would be that easy."

"Yeah, you're going to have to keep working at it." She arched a little, her nipples caressing his chest in a way that made him want to strip them both naked. Now.

He nodded. "With pleasure."

She pulled his head back down for a kiss, and it was hot and urgent, and for Pete's sake was that the damn doorbell?

"I'm coming in the door," Dan yelled.

Knox lifted his head and met Mic's wide-eyed gaze.

"I'm closing the door," Dan yelled. "Now I'm walking rea-lly slow-ly down the hall." Knox closed his eyes and rested his forehead against Mic's at the clomp. Clomp. Clomp coming down the hall. "I'm getting distracted at the living room … hey, I love that armchair!"

Knox lowered Mic to her feet, noticed her T-shirt was bunched up over her—well, that was a mighty fine peach-colored lace bra. He pulled the garment down as much as it would go, then lifted her up, turned, and plonked her on the stool.

"I'm going straight past the bedroom and coming toward the kitchen," Dan yelled, then walked through the kitchen doorway. "Why, hello there." He carried a bundle of printed papers that he placed on the bench in front of Mic. "These were in your car."

"Oh, thank you," she said, shaking her head. "I forgot I'd printed these out." She reached for them and started to rise from the bench, but Knox put his hand on her shoulder, stopping her.

He gestured to the plate in front of her. "Eat. You haven't had much since we got back from the resort." She'd eaten like a bird, and yes, an experience like hers could impact on her appetite, but he was going to make sure she got the rest, food and exercise that would help her get through it.

She subsided in her chair. "Thanks."

Dan looked pointedly at the plates. "That smells great," he said.

Knox eyed him and smiled. "It does." He placed a piece of bacon in his mouth and chewed. The guy had interrupted him twice. He did not deserve bacon.

Dan gave him a miffed look and crossed over to the coffee pot. "At least there's coffee."

"Any news?" Mic asked as she took a sip from her own mug.

Dan nodded. "Yeah, the sheriff's still going over the scene, so your interview has been pushed back to tomorrow. As you're on medical leave, it's just you and me today, kiddo."

"I can stay—" Knox offered, and Dan shook his head.

"Walker wants a report from you, so Fitz and Smithy are waiting for you."

Knox's shoulders sagged. Great.

~*~

A strident ringing jerked Mic awake, making her heart pound. No good ever came of a call in the middle of the night. She rolled across the bed and fumbled with the handset.

"Hello?" she answered.

"You think you're safe, don't you?" the caller whispered.

Mic's eyes flew open, and her heart started to thump in her chest. "What?"

She sat up on the bed, and glanced at the clock next to her. Two-thirty-three. She glanced at her windows. It was pitch black outside. She blinked. No, she refused to start imagining the bogey man at her window. Besides, either Dan or Knox were in the house with her. She was safe. When she'd gone to bed at nine Knox still hadn't arrived, but Dan had reassured her he wouldn't leave unless someone came to replace him.

"You're going to pay for what you've done," the voice whispered.

Mic frowned, and irritation, sharp and swift, took over. "What *I've* done? Who is this?" she hissed. After everything that had happened, getting this call was like a match to her dumpster-sized 'so over it' kindling.

"I'm your worst nightmare," the voice whispered.

Mic firmed her lips. *Prick.* "No, you're not." Her worst nightmare had been up in the mountains, watching colleagues getting their brains blown out. "You're nowhere near my worst nightmare, dude." She straightened into a sitting position, feeling all that horror, all that rage, that she had seeing George get killed.

"What you are is a coward," she hissed. "Anonymous calls in the middle of the night, threatening a woman … you're not a nightmare; you're a spineless, gutless snake who likes to hide under rocks."

She looked up as Knox opened her bedroom door, his expression fierce as he switched her light on. A quick sweep of relief, of feeling safe and secure, swept over her at the sight of him, in his gray T-shirt and dark sweatpants. He opened his mouth, but she held up a finger. "Oh, and you're very rude for calling at this time."

She slammed the phone back down on the hook, and then glanced up at Knox.

He gaped at her for a moment, then braced his arm against her door jamb. "Feel better?"

She hesitated, all that anger and hostility still whirling through her veins. "I do, actually." She rose from the bed, then strode over to look out her window. Knox was by her side in an instant, drawing her back from the curtains.

"Easy, sweetness."

"I want him," she said in a low voice, letting that anger creep out. "I want that bastard." Her fists clenched.

"Everything he's done, every life he's destroyed, I want him to pay for it."

Knox covered her fists with hands. "Okay."

She didn't know if she'd finally reached her breaking point, or if learning those defense skills had given her a false and dangerous sense of bravado, or if it was just a simple case of being shot at and witnessing brutal murder that made a phone call in the night seem less than threatening, but she felt like she wanted to rip the head off something.

"I am done being their punching bag," she told him. "I'm done feeling scared, I'm done feeling terrified of what might happen next, what new horror he's got planned—whoever the hell he is."

Knox nodded. "I understand."

"I want to punch him in the face," she confessed. "Really hard. Lots of times."

Knox bit his lip, and nodded.

"Oh, my God, what is happening to me?" she breathed, and he let her hands go when she brought them up to her face. "What am I thinking? This man—hell, I don't even know if that guy on the phone is just another hired hand, or if he's actually involved—I just called him a snake. A *coward*."

Knox nodded. "Yeah, you did. It's normal to get angry over what's happening. It's part of the process."

"What if that makes him angry? What if it makes him angry enough to try and come after me again, or worse, someone else?"

She started to tremble at the thought. Knox cupped her face, drawing her gaze to meet his.

"Hey, you're going to be fine. You're safe," he told her, his voice deep, calm, even. He took a deep breath, his eyes on hers, and she copied him, sucking in air in a slow, inhalation that brought with it a calm rationality. He brought her hands up to his chest, placing them over his heart.

She was surprised by the move and, despite feeling the warmth of his skin beneath the soft T-shirt he wore, and the small measure of comfort she took from the regular beat of his heart, her thoughts still raced around in her head.

"But what if the next time I step out my door, there is someone else lining me up in their gun sights?" she whispered, eyes wide as she looked at him. "Or when I turn up to work, or go shopping?"

Knox grasped her shoulders. "Hey, you're going to be fine." Again, his calm confidence was like a douse of soothing serenity.

"Am I?" she absently bunched the fabric of his shirt with her fists. "How long will this go on? I don't know if I can stand it."

Knox shook his head. "We're going to get these guys, Mic," he reassured her. "Smithy and Fitz are sifting through every connection they can find between Eagle Express and the killers. We're looking into accounts, following the money—and Smithy is one of the best when it comes to finding digital traces of things people don't want found. I'll let him know about this call, and he'll track it from your call log. It's a process, but we *will* find these bastards. We always do."

She took a deep breath in, then nodded. Okay. If he said they were going to get them, they'd get them. The fact wasn't lost on her that she totally believed and trusted him. Even after what he'd done to her.

Which was weird, because if Sebastien dared to cross her path now, she'd like to make a necklace out of his teeth. Knox, though, still made her feel safe. Maybe even cherished. And that was something she just wasn't sure she could address, right now.

"Uh, okay. Thanks," she said. She looked down, surprised to see her hands scrunching up his shirt. It had lifted the fabric a little, exposing the skin of his waist, and his sweatpants sat low on his hips, revealing the crease on either side between torso and hips, the line that kind of arrowed beneath his pants. It took a conscious effort not to bunch the material even further, to gaze at the muscles of his torso. She flattened her hands instead and—yep, there she was, patting his chest.

She swallowed as she forced herself to meet his gaze. "Uh, I'm okay to go back to bed."

Come with me.

His gaze dropped to her lips, and he nodded. "Okay." His eyelids lowered a little, and oh, golly, that must be his bedroom eyes look. Something hot and sensual unfurled deep where her womanly parts recognized manly parts. Did he— was he coming with her to bed? Now she was confused. Had she said that out aloud? Her breasts swelled beneath the storm trooper tank top she wore, and she didn't want to look down, just in case her nipples were doing what she thought they were doing.

His gaze dipped, and halted. Heat swarmed over her cheeks as his eyes darkened. Yep. Her nipples were standing to attention, and he'd noticed. He swallowed.

"You need your sleep," he said, nodding, although she wasn't sure if he was talking to her, or her breasts. His voice was low and raspy. He stepped closer, and his arm slid around her waist.

"Yeah, we both do," she whispered as he lowered his head to hers.

"I'll say goodnight, then."

Chapter 20

Knox kissed her, thoroughly, languidly. He'd been wanting to do it since Dan had so annoyingly interrupted them that morning. No, he'd been wanting to do this since that night in the forest. He was determined to make her forget about the call, about everything that was going on around her, and whatever it was that still bothered her about him, about them.

More than that, though, he wanted to show her just how much she'd come to mean to him. More than Kayleigh, and in a very different way, but also more than any other woman he'd been with. All of that … it felt like it had been practice for him, leading up to this moment, to this woman.

His tongue slid against hers, and he smiled when he felt her shiver in his arms. She tilted her head back, and he followed, licking, biting, tangling. Her hands rose to his shoulders, and twisted the fabric of his shirt in her fists. She dragged at the fabric, and he pulled back long enough for her to drag the garment over his head. He took the opportunity to slide his hands under the hem of her tank top, and smiled when she instinctively arched against him, her breasts swelling against the low neckline of the top.

She braced her hands on his shoulders, and he paused. "This is just attraction, just sex," she told him. "I mean, this is physical. This doesn't mean … more."

He tilted his head to look at her. Behind the desire, the heat of arousal, he could see the hurt, the shadows that went far beyond what he'd done to her, and he ached for her.

He placed one of her hands over his heart. "To me, this means everything. I'm all in."

Her brow furrowed, confusion, arousal, hurt, hope … he could see it all in her golden-brown eyes. He smiled. "I'm in this for the long haul. However long it takes. I'm prepared to wait."

He wanted her—desperately. But he wanted her to want this, want *him*. Free and clear of all the ties of the past, of the painful, regrettable mistakes … He could admit it. He wanted a future with this woman. She meant everything to him, and he would do the work needed in order to deserve her, and her love. But she was wary, and he had to earn her trust. He would, however long it took, because she was worth it. He'd said as much to Walker this afternoon—and a whole lot more—which is why his boss hadn't fired his ass. But he wasn't going to rush her. He was going to let her set the pace.

"I can work with just sex. For now," he told her, drawing her closer.

"Even if it doesn't go beyond that?" She slid her arms up his chest.

"Whatever you want," he told her, lowering his head. He kissed the corner of her mouth.

"What—whatever?" she swallowed, her tone curious, with a tinge of hope, of acceptance. He smiled as he kissed his way to her ear, and bit her earlobe.

"I want you," he whispered. Now. Tomorrow. Forever. "And I'll take whatever you want to give."

"I want you too," she whispered back, then moaned as he bent to kiss her neck, nibbling at the tender cord he found there. He trailed his lips across her collarbone, and found the shoulder strap of her tank top.

"We both have too many clothes on for what I have in mind," he told her, his hands sliding up beneath her top, gliding against the bottom swell of her breasts.

She nodded. "Agreed."

He grasped the hem of her top and she raised her arms, letting him pull the tank off her.

He sighed when he saw her naked torso. "You're so beautiful," he murmured, cupping her breasts, thumbs brushing over her nipples. She traced her hands over his chest, and he felt himself harden when her fingers traced and played with his nipples.

"You're so handsome," she told him. He leaned down, pressing his lips to hers in a hard, carnal kiss. She drove him crazy. So sweet, so smart, yet she made him feel special, strong … worthy.

His hands slid down her body, and pushed her silk boxers down over her hips. Her own hands were busy divesting him of his sweatpants, and they smiled against each other's lips as they stepped out of their clothes. He picked her up—oh, hell, she felt good against him—and turned to the bed. He lowered her onto the mattress, following her down, not wanting to be separated from her body.

Her skin was silken and smooth, her body the perfect combination of muscle and curve. He kissed his way down her body, exploring it thoroughly, loving the sounds she made when he laved her nipples, or bit them gently. He loved the way her body arched when his fingers slid inside her, the way her hands fisted in the sheets. He loved the soft exclamation she made when he kissed her down there, loved how she smelled, how she tasted. He loved the shudders, the gasps, the squeaks, as he brought her to orgasm. And he loved the sensation of her around him, welcoming him as he thrust inside her, wringing another orgasm from her before he found his release. He loved everything about her. He loved her.

~*~

Mic sighed as she circled one of the description lines on the spreadsheet, and sat back. Her muscles twinged, and she bit her lip. She ached. In so many places. Pleasantly. Last night—

well. She'd never had an experience like that. She'd never been so thoroughly—loved. That's what it had felt like. She frowned. But it was supposed to be just sex. She wasn't going to let her heart get entangled with a guy who was so practiced at deceit.

But it's Knox.

He was kind. Gentle—when he wasn't breaking bad men's bones—solicitous. Fantastic between the sheets. And … tempting. So very tempting.

So, what was she truly afraid of? Once this case was over, once she no longer needed a bodyguard, what was going to happen? Knox would get assigned to another 'package'. She circled the description on the report again, this time a little harder, leaving a darker, heavier imprint.

He'd leave her. Sure, he'd said he was in it for the long haul, but didn't that mean until his next assignment? Until he had to leave? She still remembered the shock, that searing pain when she'd accidentally picked up Sebastien's phone instead of her own, and seen the string of texts on the screen from his female business partner—who turned out to be more than just a business partner. The way they'd talked about Mic, and her family … the things he'd promised to do to his lover, once he could get away from playing attentive beau to Mic.

She remembered the lies he'd told her. He loved her. He wanted forever with her. All those compliments she'd thought were sincere. The things he'd done to her and—she squeezed her eyes in mortification—the things she'd done to him, believing they were a couple, planning a future.

The utter sense of betrayal, of hurt … it was something that wasn't so easy to forget, and she was more than wary of repeating the same mistake. But now that she knew Knox was hired by her father, did that make a difference? Apparently not, because she'd still slept with him. Well, spent the night with him. There wasn't much sleeping involved.

But what she'd experienced with Knox made whatever she'd had with Sebastien fade to a dull, indistinct gray blur.

She stared down at the report. Ugh, all this second guessing was giving her a headache. She slid her pencil into the hair at the base of her ponytail.

She looked up when Dan entered the room, a coffee mug in one hand, and his cell phone in the other. He placed the mug down in front of her.

"Thanks."

"We've just heard from your boss. They've got a detective coming in to talk this evening, after the final dispatch—whatever that means."

Mic nodded. "Once all the afternoon pickups have been sorted, packed and sent." She wracked her brain. She was losing track of the days, and couldn't wait to get back into her normal routine. Gym. Work. Microwavable meals. Repeat. "It's Wednesday, right?"

Dan nodded as he sat in her armchair. "Yep."

"Our road freight departs at seven-thirty, sharp, and the last flights need to be lodged out at the airport by eight. I can understand coming in after that—with everything the staff have been through, anything that doesn't directly involve or impact them should be behind closed doors. Let them get on with living normal by doing normal things." No sense in everyone living the hidey-hole life she currently found herself in.

"We'll take you in after that, then."

Her brain locked onto that little detail. "You'll take me in?"

Dan shrugged. "Either me or Knox."

Her cheeks heated. She wasn't sure what to say to Knox now, or how to act. He'd clearly indicated he wanted more between them, but she still had that instinctive reflex to draw back, to avoid hurt.

"Maybe … you?" she suggested.

Dan tilted his head to the side as he looked at her. "Technically, that's Knox's shift."

"Oh." She frowned.

He crossed his ankle over his opposite knee, settling himself into the chair. "I couldn't help noticing you guys were really quiet this morning when I arrived."

"Oh?" Her frown deepened as she turned her attention back to the papers on the coffee table. She'd found it hard to talk to Knox, when she wasn't telling him how gorgeous he was, or how good he felt—that, she was fine with. It was the other stuff, the 'them' stuff, that felt like talking around a glob of peanut butter.

"Yeah."

"I didn't notice," she lied, and shrugged.

Dan pointed a finger at her. "You'd be lousy at playing poker, you know?"

Her cheeks bloomed with heat. "Maybe I'm just focused on work," she told him, gesturing to the papers. "I'm going through these reports. I know the FBI is still working on the case, but I wanted to make sure we weren't missing anything."

Dan rose. "You found something?" He came over and sat next to her on the sofa. She pointed to some of the entries she'd circled.

"We ship out heaps of stuff," she told him. "You name it, we've moved it. Clothes, food, furniture, horse semen—"

"Seriously?" Dan's eyebrows rose.

She nodded. "Seriously. But I've noticed we are shipping a lot of soda."

"Soda."

"Soda." She flipped through the pages and pointed to the entries. "Three companies have started to seriously up their orders to the Asia-Pacific region in the last two months."

Dan leaned forward to scan the entries. "Cola?"

"Yep."

"What are you saying?"

She shrugged. "Nothing, yet. I'm ... spitballing. It's just a curious trend I've noticed."

Dan looked at her dubiously. "This is what you do with your spare time? Look for quirks in shipping?"

She met his gaze. "I don't want the company I work for to be a front for any kind of trafficking," she told him. "I'm being cautious." And that was nothing to feel embarrassed about. Even if it did make her sound like a conscientious dork.

He pointed to the papers. "And you found this in printouts. No searches, no databases or algorithms …"

"The very definition of smuggling is to convey goods surreptitiously," she told him. "These people do everything they can to not trip alerts or gain attention."

"But cola caught your attention?"

She frowned. "Lots of things catch my attention." She hadn't intended for the words to come out so brusquely. She was crabby, and she'd been pretty much monosyllabic with him for most of the day as she grappled with her thoughts. She sighed.

"Sorry, I think I've been cooped up too long, I'm forgetting my manners."

Dan waved a hand. "Oh, don't apologize. We tend to ignore that stuff." He took one of the papers. "Mind if I get Smithy to look into this?"

"Please."

She reached for her mug and settled back on the sofa, her gaze on the living room windows. The curtains were drawn. She sighed. Okay, so she'd been home for three days. She was beginning to get cabin fever. Dan or Knox brought in groceries, and apart from that failed attempt to go for a jog, or when she and Knox had sparred in the backyard, she hadn't actually stepped outside.

But she would be going out, tonight.

Her stomach muscles tightened. She was eager to get out, but still anxious. Stepping outside into the world sounded beautiful. Terrifying. Exciting. Chilling. The prospect filled her with anticipation, and with dread.

She just wanted her normal life back. One that didn't involve threatening phone calls and bullets. One that didn't involve Knox?

She frowned. She wasn't ready to risk her heart, but was she ready for him to disappear completely from her life? She didn't want to think about the empty void that would leave. She firmed her lips. Which was why it could only ever be physical between them, and nothing more. Once this was over, he would leave, and she didn't want to go through those same emotions she'd felt at the hospital, or after Sebastien. Sure, leaving isn't the same as lying, but lying—well, it always kind of resulted in leaving, didn't it?

She rubbed her forehead. Oi, it hurt to think today.

~*~

Knox nodded at Dan when he arrived. Dan looked down the hall, then sidled up to him. "Hey, this is completely none of my business—" he started in a whisper.

"Which is never a good way to start a conversation," Knox said dryly.

"Sparrow's been a little off today," Dan told him in a low voice, glancing about to make sure Sparrow wasn't around.

Knox frowned, and immediately started to walk down the hall. He'd stopped thinking of Mic as Sparrow ages ago. "Is she okay? Is she sick?" Was Mic struggling with the memories of what happened on the weekend? His worry for her rose. Dan grabbed him, forestalling him.

"No, nothing like that. I think—I think she just needs some time."

Knox hesitated. "Time?"

Dan made a shushing gesture with his hand. "Yeah. Or space."

"Space?"

"Look, she's a little cranky. I don't know what's going on between you," Dan said, and held up a hand, "and unless it's

X-rated, I really don't want to know, you can keep all that complicated relationshippy stuff to yourself. Or Fitz. Yeah, tell Fitz, he likes to overthink things, dwell on stuff."

Knox sighed. "She's … cranky."

"Yeah. Look, she's been cooped up in this place, and she's been good about it, no complaints, but I think she's feeling a little …"

Knox raised his eyebrows as he met Dan's gaze, waiting for him to finish his sentence. Dan grimaced, then shrugged. "I have no idea what she's feeling—I don't do that thinky-feely stuff with chicks. But she wanted to know if I could take her in tonight instead of you."

Realization had Knox tilting his head back. "Ah." She was doing it again. Every time they got a little bit closer, she tried to put some distance between them. Which meant he'd gotten closer to her last night. *Good.*

And now she was trying to do her version of the duck and run. *Not so good.*

"It's classic Mic." He didn't know how to overcome that, though, and it was driving him crazy. It felt like two steps forward, one step back. He knew she needed to set her own time frame on this but, well, he was damned confused.

Dan blinked. "I have no idea what that means."

"We got closer, and now she's trying to back off."

"Oh, so it is X-rated." Dan nodded, then frowned. "You know," he said, wagging a finger, "this seems to be a common occurrence. You have sex with the woman, and she shuts you down. Maybe you do need some tips …?"

Knox shot him an exasperated glare, then realized he was talking with *Dan.* He hesitated. "Actually, that might not be a bad idea," he said, stroking his chin.

Dan made a face. "Ew. I was joking. I really don't want to advise you on your sex life."

Knox waved a hand. "No, no, that's not what I meant. You run," he said to Dan, as pieces started to come together in his mind. "You. Run. Why do you run from women?" Dan had sex, and then he'd leave. He was notorious for it. Mic and he had sex, and she couldn't physically leave, but she tried to, emotionally.

Dan cocked an eyebrow. "I don't run from women. I run toward them. I like to chase, if you will."

"But then afterwards, you run."

Dan put both hands on his hips. "I don't run," he argued in a whisper, looking down the hall briefly. "I might depart hastily, but usually there is a time constraint involved."

Knox nodded. "Yeah. Before they wake up."

Dan shook his head. "I'm not there for touchy feely— well, we do touchy-feely things, but I'm not there for the thinky-feely stuff afterwards. I'll be in a different city, maybe even a different country at the drop of a hat … I can't commit to anything more, and I make sure they know that."

"But, if they know that, why do you run?"

Dan folded his arms, frowning. "I don't like being your sex therapist."

Knox held up his hands. He thought he might be getting somewhere. There were certain things Dan did that Mic did, but on a different, more subdued level. "Let's pretend you're a woman—"

"Geez," Dan said, shaking his head.

"And I've slept with you—"

Dan made a gagging sound in his throat.

"And it was good—I mean, *really* good," Knox said. "Why do you want to back off?"

Dan looked at him as if he'd grown three heads. "Seriously?"

"Yes. I'm stumped. Okay, maybe there was some lying involved earlier on …" Knox admitted.

"Oh, this is painful." Dan turned away, dragging his hands over his face.

"But it's really good between us," Knox said, and Dan turned back to him.

"But you *lied*," he pointed out.

"But I think, deep down, you understand why I lied."

"You hurt me?" Dan suggested.

"Yeah, but—sometimes it seems like you're forgiving me … and then we kiss—or more—and you back off again."

Dan sighed, and looked up and down the hall before meeting his gaze. "Because I'm scared?"

"Of what?"

"Of what you might mean to me?" Dan said, waving his arms out aimlessly. "Of being hurt again, of repeating the same mistakes, of never finding that one person who understands you, and is there for you …"

Knox nodded and rolled his hands. "This is good, keep it coming."

"Or maybe, just maybe, you know deep down you're so damaged that you're only good for a roll in the hay, and run before they can see what you're really like on the inside?" For a moment, Dan looked surprised, then borderline horrified.

Knox eyed his friend, then frowned. "I don't think that's it," he said, shaking his head. No, Mic was pretty fantastic, and she had this self-awareness, this insight into what she deserved and what she wasn't going to accept. "I think you were on to something before, though." He turned and looked down the hall. "I'm going to think on it."

Dan sagged against the wall, looking slightly drained. "You do that."

"Good talk."

"I hate you."

"I'll take Mic to the depot," Knox said over his shoulder.

"I'll go find a bottle of scotch to crawl into. Oh, and Knox?"

Knox turned. "Yeah?"

"We are never doing this again," Dan said, making a slashing gesture with his hand.

"But you're so good at it."

"You suck."

Knox chuckled softly as he walked down the hall, but sobered when he reached Mic's bedroom door. Mic was afraid of something, but what exactly? Of being lied to? Of being left? How did he convince her he'd never hurt her, not again? Should he push, or should he let her retreat?

He knocked on the door.

Chapter 21

Mic stared out of the passenger window as Knox pulled into a space in the near-empty parking lot. She noticed the light at the back of the lot had been replaced. Finally. There were a few more cars in the lot—night staff, Doug's car, and one that looked like it probably belonged to a detective who didn't get much in his pay packet, going by the state of the depressed-looking silver sedan.

Knox killed the engine, then sat for a moment, silent. She chewed the inside of her cheek. He'd been very nice, very respectful. When he'd walked into her room earlier that evening to greet her, he'd been completely professional, polite. His easy-going, relaxed manner had dispelled most of her awkwardness, her tightness. She'd had a chance to relax …

Her brow dipped. But he hadn't once mentioned what had happened last night. No reference, no smoldering looks, no half-lidded bedroom eyes, no kisses, no casual but intimate touches …

As if he hadn't made love to her through the night and into the morning.

Was it a case of now he'd had a taste, he was no longer interested in the rest of the cake? God, was that her mother's voice she could hear in her head, echoes of the pre-prom Mom-and-Daughter Chat About Boys?

She didn't think so. She glanced at him for a moment, before looking away. Knox didn't strike her as that kind of guy. Hadn't he said he was in it for the long haul? However long it took? She didn't mind admitting, she was confused.

Knox rested a wrist on the steering wheel, and turned his head to look at her. "Do you mind if I ask you a question? You don't have to answer it," he told her quickly, "I'm just … curious."

Her eyebrows rose. "Uh, sure. Fine. Go ahead."

"Who was he?"

Mic stilled. Blinked. "What?"

"Who was he? The guy who lied to you? The guy who hurt you?" His voice was low and husky.

Mic turned to look out of the windscreen at the parking lot garden. *Huh. Didn't expect that one.* But if he could share his story about his friend, Kayleigh, with her, with all the pain and heartfelt agony that had entailed, she could probably share this embarrassing, humiliating memory from her past.

She sat still for a moment, then clasped her hands in her lap. "I thought he was the man I was going to marry," she said quietly.

The muscles in Knox's jaw flexed. "What did he do?"

She glanced down at her hands. "We met at a charity fundraiser for one of the organizations Dad's company supports. He literally bumped into me. He spilled champagne on my dress. He apologized. We laughed. We got talking, and he asked me out on a date."

Knox sat quietly, staring out the windscreen, but he was still, so incredibly still. Listening.

"We dated a lot," she said, then laughed, although there was nothing really funny about it. "He'd planned this special dinner for us, one night." She shook her head, still amazed at how gullible she'd been. "I found out, and thought he was going to propose. Until I found his phone."

Knox winced.

She waved her hand. "We had the same model phone, even the same case—like, how amazing is that? How in sync were we?" She rolled her eyes. "I realized I'd taken his by mistake, but I really had to make a call … so I unlocked it."

Knox frowned, and turned to look at her. "How? Those encryptions are nearly impossible to break."

She sucked in a breath. "Well, he was often on it when we were together," she held up a hand, "I know, I know, red flag when the guy spends most of his time with you on the phone to another woman, but I honestly thought they were just business partners. I'd seen him key in his code a hundred times, so it was easy getting in." She leaned back in the seat and rested her elbow on the interior passenger window frame. She fiddled with the pencil she still had speared into the base of her ponytail.

"They'd been messaging each other—not just about business. About me, how soon they could present their application proposal to my father for investor buy-in, how they were going to make bajillions once Dad saw their idea, if he could just muster up the gumption to close the deal with me … and he could always get half in our divorce to make it worthwhile."

Knox swore, and leaned forward to rest his forehead against the wheel. "Oh, God, Mic, I'm so sorry."

She lowered her hand and shrugged. "It is what it is."

Knox shook his head. "No. That should never happen. I'm so sorry." He squeezed his eyes shut. "Damn. I get it. I get now why what I did hurt you so much." He swung his head around to meet her gaze, remorse and regret so evident in the harsh lines of his face. "I'm so sorry."

"But that won't stop you from lying if you think that's what is necessary," she said in a whisper, and felt tears well in her eyes.

"No," he whispered hoarsely. "I—I can't do that. Not now." He leaned forward and grasped her hand. "I will always, *always*, be honest with you, sweetness. No matter what."

She stared at him for a moment, stunned by his ferocity, his intensity, his pain on her behalf … like how she'd felt for him when he'd told her about Kayleigh.

Something tiny unlocked inside, a release, a lessening. Something that she felt, but couldn't quite name. It felt … weird. Like when she'd finally had the plaster cut off her arm at twelve, and she'd felt a little floaty without the weight of it. Like … she was in an area that didn't quite have an anchor to it, and she could drift in a direction she wasn't sure she was ready for.

"I, uh, should go inside," she said distractedly. He blinked, then looked behind them, toward the gloomy building.

"Okay," he said, nodding, and reached for his seatbelt. She stopped him. She needed to think, needed—oh, heck, needed to get some distance, just so she could make sense of all this mush in her head.

"No, don't worry, I can handle this."

He gave her a look that could only be defined as patient exasperation. "I'm your bodyguard."

"Knox, I'll be in there," she said, gesturing to the building. "It's work. It's fine. There are cops in there. Well, deputies. I'll be fine."

He shook his head, but she leaned forward. "Please. I just—I want to do this on my own. I need some space." She didn't want to have to sit through an interview with law enforcement with him there, knowing she'd just shared her most mortifying experience to date. It so eclipsed that time when Timmy Bradshaw walked in on her in the bathroom at Cindy Myers' fourteenth birthday party. It was uncomfortable, a little embarrassing, and she hated reliving it. She needed … distance. Space and time to think.

He slid his seatbelt off. "I'll walk you to the door," he told her. She nodded. Fine.

They climbed out of the car—once Knox gave her the all-clear sign, and walked in silence around to the main front door. She paused at the front, gazing up at the structure. So much had happened since the last time she was here. Something was different, and it took a moment to realize the difference was with her. She felt she'd changed so much, had experienced a lifetime since she was last here …

Knox stopped at the door and frowned down at her.

"In the spirit of being completely honest with you, I'm going to tell you I don't like this," he said.

His borderline sulky expression brought an unexpected smile to her face. "Thank you for the concession," she said, and swiped her access card through the security pad on the doorframe. "I'll be fine. It's the cops."

The main lights of reception were on, giving it a bright, cheery look despite the darkness outside. She could clearly see Doug inside, waiting for her, and the CEO gave them a wave, although his gaze was curious as he took in Knox's presence. Oh, right, he didn't know the man was her undercover bodyguard. No wonder he was looking just a little perplexed. Knox nodded a brief greeting in return.

"Where are the cops?" he called out.

Doug gestured with his thumb over his shoulder.

"See, nothing to worry about. I'll be fine."

Knox's lips tightened in exasperation, but he gave her a begrudging nod.

There was a click, and Knox opened the door for her, stepping aside to let her enter. "Call me if you need anything," he told her gruffly, and she nodded as she walked past him. He'd set up her phone with all of the team's numbers on direct dial.

"I will."

She stepped into the quiet reception, and looked over her shoulder, waiting as the door slowly swung closed. She swiped her card through the second access door. Reception had a two-door entry setup, and once the night bell was switched on, the security measure kicked in where the first door had to close completely before the second door would open.

She stepped inside, and slid her light jacket off her shoulders. It felt weird, walking into work wearing jeans and a T-shirt. She rarely did casual attire in the office. Doug stepped forward, a warm smile of welcome on his face.

"Michaela, it's so good to see you—how are you?"

"I'm good," she told him, and looked briefly at the man who was now striding back to the car in the parking lot. It was true, she realized. She was … good. She felt good. Strong. Confident.

She turned to her boss. "How's the head?" She indicated the green and yellow bruises on his face.

He gave a dismissive wave as he turned toward the door that led to the back-office areas. "Bah. Fractured cheekbone, slightest of concussions, bruising—nothing that won't heal."

"I'm glad," she told him truthfully as she walked through the customer service call center area, toward the stairs that led to the other offices upstairs.

"Uh, did I miss something? What is Jones doing here?"

Oh, yeah. She'd fired Knox at the hospital, but hadn't gotten around to doing anything from an administrative perspective. She didn't really want to go through the whole 'my dad hired a bodyguard' story with her boss. She shook her head. "No. It's a long story." She looked around. At this time of night, they had one customer service representative to take the calls, one operations hand to sort any leftover freight and prepare ad-hoc shipments for the morning, and an IT administrator to ensure all the systems kept functioning, but she couldn't see anyone around at the moment. "Who's on tonight?"

Doug turned, his expression surprised. "Oh, I think it's Jenny Gilmore," he said, and scanned the long call center room. "She must be on a toilet break." Mic nodded. Her nightshift operations hand, Graham West, would be out in the warehouse, going over volumes and documentation for the morning flights, and Johnathan Leung, their night IT administrator, was probably curled up under his desk, taking a cat nap before checking the server room.

She followed Doug up the stairs and along the hall to the small boardroom. "How is Camilla doing?"

Doug nodded as he opened the door and gestured for her to enter first. "She's doing well. She'll be leaving the hospital in about a week."

"And Luis?" She would be the first to admit she was a little ambivalent when it came to her air operations supervisor, but ultimately believed he was a good guy in a bad situation. Having a few days distance from the attacks, she honestly didn't believe he could be a part of this. But she knew the man was under investigation by the FBI, based on Knox's report.

"He's back, but restricted hours. Everyone on that orienteering activity is either on medical leave or reduced hours."

She nodded. "Good. I can come back tomorrow, if you like?"

Doug smiled, and shook his head. "No, not yet. I think you're going to have to get clearance before coming back in."

She frowned. "How so?"

Doug grasped her hands, and she was a little surprised at the gesture. "Michaela, you've gone through so much. Not only did you witness a colleague's murder, you suffered an attack the night before. I want to make sure you get all the support you need to get through this."

She smiled, touched by his consideration. "Thanks, Doug. I appreciate that. I'd like to come back though, I'm going stir crazy at home."

He chuckled, and patted her hand. "Don't worry. That feeling won't last long."

Mic turned and looked about the boardroom. "Where is the detective?" She thought Doug had said the men were inside.

Doug fished a cell phone out of his pocket. "I'll call him and tell him you're here."

"Him? Not them?"

Doug shook his head as he held the phone to his ear. "They're short-handed," he whispered, then turned his attention to the call.

~*~

Knox reclined the driver's seat, just a little, and gazed out the windscreen. He sighed, his cheeks puffing. God, he got it. He finally understood. He shook his head. He'd like to track down the bastard who'd hurt Mic and pound him into the dirt.

Hell, no wonder she'd flipped when she'd found out about him. She'd already had someone get close to her under false pretenses, spend time with her because of her father. Sure, he could convince himself his lies were for completely protective purposes, but it was a means to an end for his job, just as it had been for this SOB. His clenched fist pounded the steering wheel rim. Damn it. His lies, his justifications—he'd hurt her. His gut churned. He felt like a schmuck. He got it. SOB had lied to her, and had gotten close to her, because he'd wanted to get in her father's good graces. Hell, he'd even been prepared to marry her. Knox was so damn relieved that Mic had discovered the man's duplicity before that had happened.

But he, Knox—was he any better? He'd lied to her, pretended to be someone he wasn't, because her father had hired him to. And he'd kissed her. Knox shifted in his seat. He'd made love to her. Damn, after what had happened to her, no wonder she'd recoiled from him. An overwhelming need to protect her, to shield her from further harm or hurt flooded him.

He couldn't stand waiting for her in the car. He wanted to go to her, apologize again, hold her, soothe her, tell her—

what? Tell her that he finally got it, he finally understood her need for honesty, for sincerity? Would she believe him, after his little forays into mistruths? His hand rested on the door handle. He wanted to be there with her, shield her, and be totally honest with her--but what was he going to be honest about?

Would he, could he, tell her how much he thought about her, that she was the first thing to enter his mind upon waking, and the last thing he thought about before he drifted off to sleep? That he felt better, calmer, when he knew she was safe? That when she was upset, he wanted to do anything to get rid of her pain, and bring back her smile? That he wanted to do that every day for the rest of his life?

Hell. He was turning into a Hallmark card. He hated sitting in this damn car, waiting for her. But she'd told him she needed her space.

Damn it. He didn't want any space between them. No more distance.

But it wasn't about what he wanted. He sighed. Patience. He needed patience. Ugh. Patience sucked. He needed a distraction.

Knox reclined the driver's seat, just a little, and dialed Smithy as he slid the Bluetooth speaker and mic in his right ear.

"Hey." Smithy was always so communicative. Not.

"Hey, Smithy. Any updates?"

"Yeah, apparently you're not too flash in the sack," Smithy stated, and Knox rubbed his forehead.

"Don't listen to everything Dan tells you," he replied.

"He's not actually saying much, after he dropped that gem. He's just sitting on the lounge, staring at the wall. What did you do to him?" Smithy asked, a little awed.

Knox frowned. "Nothing. He helped me work through some stuff, that's all."

"Dan did?"

"Yeah."

"Our Dan?"

"Yes."

Smithy started to chuckle in a whisper over the phone. "Wish I'd been a fly on the wall for that."

Knox thought about his conversation with Dan, then grimaced. "No, you don't. Anyway, back to the case," he said purposefully. "I've just dropped Mic off with her boss. She's giving a statement tonight to one of the detectives from San Bernardino."

"Oh, really?"

Knox heard Smithy tap on the keyboard. "I thought they were still going over the physical evidence. The coroner has only just released the interim autopsy report on the victims."

"Well, one's taking statements here. Dan mentioned you got a glimpse of the report …"

"Yeah. Two victims received fatal bullet wounds, ballistics still to be completed, and one victim with multiple skull fractures from a blunt object."

Knox eyed the dark parking lot. "You know, when I first heard it, it never occurred to me to question it."

"What do you mean?"

"Well, I saw the shooter. He was armed. Rifle, knife— God only knows what else."

"Yeah …?"

"So, if you had such effective weapons that would take out a target quickly with minimal effort, why beat the guy over and over again with a rock?"

Smithy was silent for a moment. "Good question."

Knox shrugged. "I don't know, but it's been bothering me. How did you go with the phone?"

"Believe it or not, the guy's passcode was boob."

"What?"

"Four-letter word encoded by the number pad. Two-six-six-two."

Knox gaped. "What?"

"It's a fun game I play sometimes, type out names or phrases as passcodes. This guy's was boob. I didn't have any other info—name, birthday, etc. So, I tried words."

"You tried boob?"

"I'm a boob man."

Knox shook his head in amazement. "That's got to be a fluke."

"Tell me about it. Who knew there was another boob man out there?"

"Tell me what was on the phone."

"Well, there are lots of coordinates, lots of code talking that Fitz is slowly deciphering—you know, the usual, where and when to meet, etc."

"With who?"

"Well, there's only a few contacts in the phone, and none of them have names, which I think is rather inconvenient."

"Yes, it is."

"But we're tracking what we can. None of the numbers are registered, they're all attached to prepaid SIM cards, so that's slow going, but we're also doing geotraces now to see if we can—whoa."

Knox could hear a faint pinging sound through the phone. "Whoa, what?"

"One of the contact numbers is currently in use."

"Great, are you tracing it?"

"Yes."

Knox leaned forward. "And?"

"Keep talking, keep talking ..." Smithy muttered. Then he swore.

"What?"

"It's coming from your area."

Knox peered out into the parking lot, scanning the area from side to side. "What do you mean, my area?" Traces took a little time to narrow down. Depending on how long the call lasted, they might only get a suburb.

"Okay, got it. It's coming from a site on the corner of Billings and Haversham."

Knox flung open his door and started running toward the building. "Quick, send backup," he rasped. "That's the Eagle Express building—and Mic's inside."

Chapter 22

Mic looked up when a knock sounded at the door, and Doug rose from his seat. She glanced casually out the window to look down on the warehouse floor. She craned her neck. The warehouse was dark, which was weird. Usually minimal lighting was kept on overnight, purely from a safety perspective for the shift hand, but now only a light over the inter-office door was on, and moonlight streamed through the light strips in the roof. She glanced at her watch. Nearly nine o'clock. She hadn't seen Graham yet, which was unusual. She could see a half-packed AKE freight container sitting in the gloom on the conveyor belt. Where was her staff?

"Michaela, this is Detective Smithers," Doug said, and she turned. The detective walked towards her, a polite smile on his face. His hair curled over his collar, and his tie was slightly askew. His shirt was creased beneath the jacket. *Must be having a long day.*

"Michaela, pleased to meet you," he said, holding his hand out to her.

She shook it, surprised when he didn't immediately let go. He looked at Doug over his shoulder.

"The others?"

"All out," Doug said.

Mic tried to withdraw her hand, and the detective's grip tightened. He turned his attention back to her, and his smile grew.

Mic paused. He looked … creepy. Scruffy. Cold. Not shivery cold, but lack of personal warmth and empathy cold.

"This won't take long, Michaela."

She frowned. He was being very familiar. The other officers she'd dealt with had been politely formal, calling her Miss Robson. She again tried to withdraw her hand, but now his grip tightened painfully.

She gasped, then froze as he reached for something in his belt and withdrew a gun.

Mic felt the blood drain from her face. Her panicked gaze flicked to Doug, who shrugged, then smiled.

"Sorry, Michaela, but you really were too nosy for your own good."

~*~

Knox raced up to the front reception door, then swore as he rattled it in its frame. He no longer had a swipe card. Mic had made him return it to her as they'd left the hospital. He lifted his phone back to his ear. "Smithy, find me a way in," he said, backing up and pulling his gun out of his belt holster.

"On it," Smithy responded, and Knox could hear the furious tapping of keys.

The building was on an intersection, and the complete ground floor had toughened laminated glass on its floor-to-ceiling windows. He and Amber Simpson had done a threat assessment on the building when they'd first taken on the case, and he wasn't going to shoot his way through that glass any time soon.

He ran back down the path toward the parking lot, and raced around the side of the building. The large roller doors were closed. His heart pounded in his chest. Mic was inside, and someone who'd been in contact with the shooter from the resort was in there with her. Damn it.

"Okay, everything is locked down, and I can't release the doors remotely," Smithy said. "I'm studying the schematics, though, and I can hack into their ventilation system. Go to the west side of the building."

Knox kept his pace up as he ran around the building, eyeing the high-set windows as he went. Interspersed between the windows were slats of metal. "I don't see it."

"Eagle Express handles dangerous goods, and their building has installed a state-of-the-art ventilation system. If I can make it think there is a fire in the warehouse …" Smithy trailed off, and Knox watched as the large steel slats grated open like vertical blinds. "They should open to release fumes and re-oxygenate the store."

Knox stared at the slats. There was enough space for a man to squeeze through. And there was a very convenient drainpipe nearby that he could climb up. "You're a freak of nature, Smithy."

"No, I'm awesome," his colleague corrected. "Dan and Fitz are on their way, and I've alerted local police, as well as highway patrol."

"Thanks," whispered Knox as he shoved his weapon back into his holster, grasped the drainpipe, braced his feet against the wall, and started to climb. He was panting softly by the time he reached the level of the slats. He stretched one leg over, his foot catching the base of the frame, and then carefully shifted his weight across. He grabbed the open slat, and pulled himself over, then balanced on the sill to look inside the warehouse. He frowned. It was really dark inside.

He knew there was supposed to be emergency lighting on, especially in the main traffic zones of the warehouse, but even that had been switched off. He slid inside the warehouse. The conveyor belt used for sorting freight ran around this side of the building, and he could jump across to one of its uprights. He did so, grasping the metal pole and then sliding down into the darkness. Where the hell was Mic?

~*~

Mic's gaze was fixed on the barrel of the gun, her body going cold as though her blood had drained to her feet. "Noooo," she gasped. Everything slowed down as horror surged through her, filling all the spaces within her until there was just dread, and that gun barrel. It was like a movie screen displaying a film in her mind of all the things she had to regret, to grieve.

No, she wasn't ready to die. She wasn't ready to not be present. She still needed to show her father she could make it on her own. She needed to ask her mom for the pumpkin pie recipe she used at Thanksgiving. She needed to beat her brothers just once at poker. She needed to tell Knox she loved him, and that she understood why he'd lied to her, and she understood the kind of job he did, and yes, she forgave him— *of course* she forgave him. He'd saved her life. She may not have him for long, but she wanted to grab hold of whatever time she did have with him with both hands and enjoy it. Experience it. No regrets.

And yet, that's what filled her, looking at the gun pointed at her. All those things unsaid, undone, unrealized.

She didn't want to die. Her eyes filled with tears as her gaze left the barrel and rose to meet the cold eyes of the man holding the gun. "No," she said.

"Sorry," he told her, and she didn't for one moment believe he was being sincere. He flicked the safety catch on his gun.

It was that sound, that click, that spurred her, like a match to a puddle of gasoline. She pulled the pencil from her hair and jammed it into the man's shoulder.

His eyes widened in shock, in pain, and he dropped the gun, bellowing as he let go of her to clutch at the pencil protruding from his joint.

"Argh, you bitch," he snarled, his arm hanging limp at his side.

"What the—" Doug exclaimed.

Mic shoved at the man in front of her, and he tumbled backward, upending a chair at the table as he went. Mic spun to the window and slid it open, then climbed into the dark void of the warehouse.

"Michaela!"

She ignored Doug's yell as she dropped down onto the stack of pallets that were placed under the window. *Oh, God.* She flung her arms out for balance as the pile of pallets moved with her weight. She had visions of the stack tumbling to the ground, taking her with it. Her pulse thudded in her ears.

The fixed pallet racking was to her right, and she leaped, wincing as she caught one of the shelves with her arm. Her body slammed against the frame, and she scrabbled with her legs to find purchase as her fingers slid over the smooth, powder-coated steel. She managed to jam her foot in between the rack and a shrink-wrapped pallet of photocopying paper.

"Give me the gun," she heard Doug scream, followed by scuffling in the office. She crab-walked along the shelving, heart thudding. Hands on the rack above, feet on the rack below, she sidestepped along. *Don't look down. Don't look down.* She glanced over her shoulder. *Oh, crap.* She was three levels above the ground. She bumped into another upright, and had to hug it as she navigated around it. She kept looking back toward the window, and froze when she saw Doug's head lean out.

"Michaela!" her boss gazed out over the warehouse floor. She squeezed herself in between two storage locations, using the pallets as cover between her and the boardroom window. She peeked around the rear corner of a stack of boxes. She was in gloomy darkness, whereas the men were clearly visible with the lights of the room behind them.

"Can you see her?" the other man called out. He joined Doug at the window.

"No, but she can't be far. I've locked all the doors, and I deactivated her card when I stepped out to call you."

Mic mouthed a swear word when she heard that. She squeezed her eyes shut. Damn. She'd left her bag in the room. With her phone. She couldn't call Knox—unless she managed to climb down to the warehouse floor and use one of those phones.

"Get out there," Doug growled, gesturing to the warehouse.

The phony detective looked down, then shook his head. "I'm not climbing out there. Those pallets don't look secure."

"I said, get out there. I want to find her," Doug insisted.

"The bitch screwed up my arm," the phony detective snarled. "I can't move my hand."

Mic's eyebrows rose. She must have somehow hit a nerve. Literally.

"Damn it." Doug slammed his fists on the window frame. "Let's go downstairs, then."

They withdrew from the window. Mic squeezed through the gap to the front of the shelving, and sidestepped back toward the upright. Biting her lip, trembling with fear, she wrapped her arms and legs around the post and did a stop-start slide down the pole. As soon as she'd start to move, she'd clench her muscles to prevent falling, then would have to relax, slide, then clench again.

She could feel her hands getting slippery with sweat. She got down one level, then realized the forklift was parked in the next bay. She sidestepped along the shelf, trying to shore up her trembling arms and legs with strength until she reached the tines of the fork, then clambered over and down that. She dropped to the ground, and paused, swallowing.

She never wanted to monkey-climb a three-story pallet rack ever again.

She gazed around the warehouse. Graham obviously wasn't on tonight. Freight had been left around, and while it provided plenty of cover in the warehouse, it was also a dangerous trip hazard.

She sidled along the forklift, then peered out beyond the rear gas cylinders. Her eyes widened. Oh, hell. She didn't want to be anywhere near a gas cylinder if bullets were flying around. She bent low and scuttled toward a stack of boxes, then crouched behind them.

The door leading from the office area opened, and she caught a brief glimpse of two dark figures emerging from the lit hallway into the gloom of the warehouse. She swallowed. Oh, God, this was not good. She covered her mouth. She wanted to cry. She wanted to scream, but that would just alert them to her whereabouts—and Knox wouldn't hear, parked all the way out in the parking lot.

Phone. She had to find a phone. The exports office was too obvious, a point made clear as she saw one of the dark figures jog in that direction. There was a phone near the hallway exit, and one more down near the roller doors. The one near the hallway was too close to where she'd seen the other figure. She bent low, and slid her shoes off. She had a moment of surprise at herself—no bare feet permitted in the warehouse—but they also squeaked a little on the painted surface. She placed them neatly against the side of the box— she didn't want to trip—then ran toward another crate.

"Michaela," Doug called out conversationally.

Ugh, that didn't sound creepy at all.

"You can't go anywhere, love."

She ducked behind the crate, then eyed the distance between her and the pallet racking. There were some shrink-wrapped pallets that were lined up in a cross-grid pattern, ready for easy loading the next morning. She ran toward the closest one.

"Come on, stop making it hard on yourself," Doug yelled.

Oh, she planned on making it very hard. For him. She glanced back into the dark gloom of the warehouse. Where were they? God, it was so damn dark in here. She walked back a little. She eyed the pallets behind her, and scooted off toward another one.

A hand clapped over her mouth, jerking her to an abrupt stop, and she was swept up off her feet, and brought flush against a hard body.

Chapter 23

"Shhh." Knox breathed the words against Mic's ear. He was relieved when she instantly relaxed against him. She trusted him. Good. He lowered her to the floor, then pulled her against him. He walked backward, scanning the warehouse as he did so. There. A darker shadow moved near the exports office, hiding against the wall behind the sorting desk.

Were there more? And had he heard right? Was that *Doug*?

The shadow detached itself from the wall, and started to creep forward in their direction, pausing every now and then to listen.

There was a click, and music blared from the speakers, a heavy rock tune with a thumping base. Damn it. They were masking themselves.

Knox pulled out his weapon. "How many?" he whispered against Mic's ear. She held up two fingers, pale and trembling in the gloom. He nodded against her cheek so that she knew he'd seen her gesture and understood. He turned her around to face him.

"Do you know where the other one is?"

She shook her head. He looked about. The fire exit door was a good thirty feet away from them. It was probably the one exit they could escape through.

And he was pretty sure the other guys knew that.

He looked back at her, and he could see the worry in her face. He was tempted to tell her everything was going to be all right, but her story in the car haunted him. He'd promised he'd never lie to her. And the truth was they were in real danger.

"We need to get to that door," he said, gesturing toward the fire exit.

She nodded.

"But they'll be expecting that."

Her eyes widened, and she shook her head rapidly.

He held up a hand. "To be honest, we have backup coming, so we can either head for the door, or sit tight and wait, but both options have their risks."

A noise, a soft scrape, from a few feet down, had her pointing furiously at the door. He nodded. "Okay, fire exit it is."

He grabbed her hand and turned, hooking it into the back of his belt. "When I move, you move. When I stop, you stop."

"Okay," she whispered back to him.

Clasping his weapon, he peered around the pallet. There were shadows on shadows, damn it. He scooted around pallets, paused, ducked, scuttled behind boxes, stopped … each time, Mic was at his back, mimicking his every move in perfect synchronicity. The blaring rock music was effective in masking footsteps—and mildly annoying.

They were about twelve feet away from the door, when he ran over to an empty freight container and used it as cover. She kept up with him.

He pointed to the door, and she nodded. They were going to make a break for it. He held his gun up, peering down the sights as he checked to see if the coast was clear. He took one step, and felt the heavy weight of a body topple onto him from above.

His gun clattered to the ground, and he wheezed when a fist hit his back, somewhere in the vicinity of his left kidneys. Strong legs wrapped around his waist, calves braced against his thighs and preventing him from rolling forward. An arm was around his neck, pressure against his larynx increasing in an effort to choke him. He could see Mic run toward him, calling his name, but it was the figure that ran at her from behind that caught his attention. Doug Danvers dove at her, tackling her to the ground.

Knox pulled at the hand that only lightly pushed against the top of his head, and yanked it forward and under his head, putting pressure on it to twist so his attacker had to follow the drag, else have his wrist snapped. Knox turned to face the man and punched him twice in the face.

A shot rang out, and Knox whipped around. Doug held Knox's gun above his head, but lowered it when he realized he had Knox's attention.

"Get off him."

Knox looked past him to Mic, who was sitting on the concrete floor, holding her cheek. His eyes narrowed as he met Doug's implacable face, and he put his hands out as he rose to his knees, and then his feet. His attacker lurched to his feet, swearing as he pressed his hand against his bleeding nose. Knox noticed his other arm, and realized why it had been so easy to break the choke hold. His arm was limp, and he could see a bloodstain on the shoulder.

"You really are inept, aren't you?" Doug muttered at the man. The man didn't reply, but sent the CEO a filthy glare.

Doug waved the gun, gesturing for Knox to join Mic, which he did, helping her to her feet.

"Doug, what are you doing?" she cried softly, cupping her cheek.

"I'm protecting my investment," the CEO said. "You've made life quite difficult for me."

Knox shifted in front of her as she shook her head. "I can't believe you're involved in this."

Doug barked with laughter. "Honey, I run the show."

Mic tried to move Knox out of the way, but he refused to budge. He was mentally counting down the seconds, trying to gauge how long it would take Dan and Fitz and the locals to arrive.

"How could you do this?" she cried.

Doug made a scoffing noise. "Quite easily, Michaela. Money does interesting things to a man's conscience."

Knox kept his eyes on the man with the gun. The other guy, the one nursing a bloody nose and a useless arm, wouldn't take too much effort to neutralize. Danvers, on the other hand, had a weapon Knox knew was loaded. Keep him talking, and maybe prevent him from shooting. *Watch the gun.*

"He needs you dead so the men awaiting trial don't rat him out. Right?" Knox said.

Doug tapped his nose. "Very good. If there is hope that they won't be found guilty, then they won't give their own testimony. That means I need to get rid of the key witness."

"But there's other evidence," Mic protested. "I'm not the deciding factor, here."

Doug smiled. "Evidence has a habit of getting lost, or destroyed," he told her. "Get rid of a witness, even better."

"What about George? And Wayne?" she cried. "They weren't testifying."

"No, but they were getting nervous, and I couldn't trust them not to squeal."

"Oh, my God, Doug. You killed two people!"

Doug held up a finger. "Actually, no, that man who was shot at the scene did that."

"But what about Camilla? Are you trying to tell me she was involved in this? And Luis? Your man tried to kill them, too."

Knox shifted a little, trying to angle himself a little closer to the CEO. He glanced between Mic and her boss, to try and hide the movement.

Doug winced apologetically. "Yes, well, that was a miscommunication. I told my man to shoot everyone connected to the operation, and he heard 'shoot everyone'." He eyed his accomplice. "Good help can be so hard to find, these days. You know how it is."

"He killed Rickerson," Knox told Mic, and she looked at him in horror.

"What?" she gasped.

Doug's eyes narrowed. "Very good, Jones—or whatever the hell your name is. How did you figure that out?"

Knox glanced back at Mic. "Rickerson had a number of skull fractures. He was beaten to death by a rock. The man I tackled drew a knife on me, so why wouldn't he use that on Rickerson? Or his revolver, or his rifle? So, I figured there were two killers out on that mountain. Then Doug got his man to hit him in the face with the butt of the rifle, right?" He glanced over at Danvers.

Doug nodded. "Had to make it look realistic."

"Oh, my God. But why kill Andy at all?"

"Oh, he took exception to my decision to clean house," Doug stated. He shrugged. "I had to get rid of him, too, especially after he threatened to go to the Feds and confess everything." He brightened as he looked at Mic. "And you're my last thread. Get rid of you, the case falls apart, everything goes back to normal."

"You're good," Knox commented, nodding. He glanced at Mic. "He's good. He's thought of pretty much everything."

She stared at him in consternation. "Don't say that."

"No," Knox said, raising a casual hand in the man's direction. "We're screwed. He's got the gun, he's got the …" he eyed the injured man, "whatever you are. He's cleaning up. We're pretty much done for."

"Knox," Mic said in panicked disbelief as her gaze flicked between him and her boss.

"I told you, I will always be completely honest with you," he said, turning to grasp her hands.

She frowned at him. "I think I'd prefer less honesty," she told him bluntly

"I can't. He's going to shoot us," Knox said, tilting his head in Danvers' direction, "and I don't want to die before I get a chance to tell you how I feel."

She gaped at him, then shook her head. "So not the time, Knox."

"This is really quite touching," Doug interrupted, stepping closer, frowning, "but I don't have the time, nor the stomach for it."

"Please, before we die—"

"Oh, my God, Knox," she said, paling, her eyes welling up with tears.

"Hurry up," Doug muttered, looking bored as he glanced over at his injured hit man. "Can you believe this?"

"I wanted to tell you …" Knox started, his hands sliding up to cup her arms, and his thigh muscles tensed, "*duck*."

He shoved her down and raised his leg to kick the gun out of Danvers' hand. The CEO bellowed in rage, and the other man made a dive for the weapon that slid along the concrete floor.

Knox bolted after him, lunging at the man as his arm stretched out for the weapon.

~*~

Mic screamed as the phony detective did his best to fight off Knox. She started to run toward him, but something crashed into her from behind, and she tumbled to the ground. She twisted around, but Doug was faster and stronger, straddling her hips.

"I'm going to end you," he rasped, his hands circling her throat. Mic's eyes widened, as memories, sensations, bombarded her, like a flick book of cartoon images. Her attack in the hotel room, the fear, the cloying darkness, and Knox, talking to her calmly.

Doug squeezed, levering himself up so he could bring his weight down on his hands around her throat. Red, flashes of red, noise screeching in her ears. She could hear her name being called, as though from down a long tunnel.

Knox.

She tucked her elbows in tight to her body, grasped one of Doug's wrists with one hand and dug her nails into the soft underside of his tricep. His eyes widened, his teeth bared. She bent her legs and planted her feet, and then lifted her hips and rolled.

Doug toppled to the side. Mic rose above him, hot rage filling her. This man—this man had wreaked a path of destruction through the lives of so many people. She shoved his wrists to the side as she followed through with fierce punches to his surprised face.

"This is for Wayne," she said, her fist connecting with the bruises on his face. "And George, and Andy," she yelled, punctuating each name with a jab to that smug, evil man. "And for Camilla, and Luis, and Kelly, and Aidan—"

Strong arms wrapped around her waist and pulled her off him. She kicked and yelled, trying to get to the dazed and bloodied man on the floor. "It's over, Mic," Knox whispered, and Doug's eyes closed.

"You bastard," she screamed at Doug, still trying to reach him, to cause him as much pain and anguish as he'd caused her, and her co-workers.

"Hey, hey, it's okay," Knox said as he carried her away from the man as police officers swooped in, holding her boss's arms down—not that he was giving any indication of resisting arrest. She got a brief look at the other man—unconscious on the floor, his arm at an unnatural angle.

Knox pulled her behind a pallet of goods, murmuring soothing words as he blocked her sight of the injured man. He set her down and clasped her face between his hands, his gaze scanning her face.

"It's over," he said quietly. His words pierced the angry haze, and she blinked, looking up at him.

"Really?" she panted, tears filling her eyes.

"Really," he reassured her.

"Knox," she sobbed, and he enveloped her in his arms. She rested her head against his chest, his heart thudding strongly in her ear as she cried with relief.

It was over.

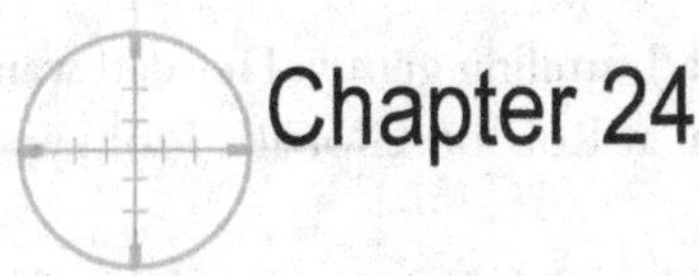

Chapter 24

Mic leaned back in her chair and slid a pencil through the base of her ponytail. "That's it, then."

Gerard Robson nodded, and shut down his tablet. "Yes, that's it."

He father leaned back in the chair and glanced across the boardroom table at her. "You're amazing, you know that?"

She nodded. "Yeah, I do. But it's good that you know that, too," she said, and smiled. Her father shook his head, grinning. "But thank you, for helping me with this."

"No, thank you. You've reminded me that good managers really do go the extra mile for their employees."

She closed the folder on the table and added it to the pile. In the month since Doug's attack, Eagle Express had been dissolved as a company. The three men who were originally arrested were singing like canaries, as Dan put it. The Feds and local law enforcement had taken the place apart, seized records. Doug wasn't about to see the light of day anytime soon.

And she and her father had sat down and used all their available contacts to find jobs for the remaining Eagle Express staff. Mic had insisted—there were people at the company who'd worked damned hard, and had had nothing to do with the drug trafficking. They didn't deserve to lose their livelihoods. She glanced around the room. So much had happened in here. A slight smile curved her lips when she remembered that day, eons ago, when the FBI had set up their sting operation. She eyed the window, and shook her head. She never wanted to leave a boardroom like that, ever again.

"Are you sure you won't reconsider?" her father asked softly.

She shook her head, smiling gently. Her dad wanted her to come work for him, at Robson Global. "I told you, I have another job offer."

Jesse Walker, CEO of SafeKeepers Inc, had offered her a job as the director of logistics at the company. Apparently, he'd been impressed with the reports he'd received from his bodyguards. "It's a good job, Dad, doing good work." It wouldn't get boring.

And she might see Knox.

Her father sighed, and dipped his head. "I don't suppose your decision has anything to do with a particular six-foot-four bodyguard, does it?"

She looked away. "Maybe," she admitted, then shook her head, "but the main reason is the job itself, and the type of work they do." She frowned. "Why, you don't think I'm up to it?"

Gerard winced. "I guess I deserve that." He rubbed his chin. "You know, I didn't choose my words well," he admitted. "I'd heard stories about Danvers, about some shady stuff going on here … but I'd heard those stories for years, and nothing actually came of them. I didn't think this was the right place for you, but only from a position that they weren't good enough for *you*."

"Oh," she said softly, and rose from her seat to walk around and give her father a hug. "Thank you for that, Dad. That means a lot."

He clasped her close for a moment, then cleared his throat as he stepped back. "I have to get going. Your mother is waiting for me." He winced. "She's still not happy with me."

"I'm sure you'll make it up to her."

He nodded, and gathered his coat and tablet, and left the boardroom. Mic followed, then looked up in surprise when she saw the tall, broad-shouldered figure waiting for her in the hall.

Her breath caught. He looked so good. He wore a green T-shirt under his black jacket, and it brought out the color of his eyes. His long legs were encased in black jeans. He looked dangerous and sexy and strong and so damn gorgeous.

"Hi, Knox," she breathed.

His lips quirked in that sexy smile of his. "Hi, Mic."

She looked up and down the hall. "What—what are you doing here?" She hadn't seen him much over the last two weeks, and when she had, he'd always been in the company of his colleagues. She hadn't had the opportunity to talk privately with him since the case was officially brought against Doug and everyone was arrested. Basically, when her need for a bodyguard was over. He'd gaze at her with such heat, such ... intensity, but then would step back, the consummate professional.

She blinked. That's okay. She knew that was coming. She'd expected it, hadn't she? But, now? She didn't understand what his presence meant.

"I thought I'd escort you home on your last day at Eagle Express," he told her, gesturing for her to precede him down the hall toward the stairs that led down into the warehouse.

"I think I can find my own way home," she laughed, conscious of his large body so close behind hers. "Unless this is a value-added service from SafeKeepers?"

He jogged down past her and turned to face her. She halted so that she didn't run into him, and her eyes widened at his move.

His eyes were on a level with hers, and she could clearly see the seriousness of his green gaze. "This has nothing to do with SafeKeepers," he told her quietly. "This is all me."

"Oh."

His gaze skimmed over her face, pausing on her lips. Warmth stole into her cheeks, and her heart picked up a little in pace.

"You look good, sweetness."

Now her cheeks were more than warm, and so was the rest of her body. "Uh, thank you," she murmured, eyeing him up and down. "You look pretty good, yourself."

He lowered his head toward hers.

Her breath caught, and her gaze dropped to his lips. So close. She even rose a little on her tippy toes.

He straightened, and his sigh gusted across her lips. "I want to take you home."

She nodded. "Okay."

After facing a gun, and nearly being killed several times, Mic was determined to make the most of her chances, however and wherever they arose. If this is what it could be like, seeing Knox occasionally, especially through work, then she would take that. No regrets.

He slid his hand into hers, and a thrill went through her at the warm, solid contact. "Come on," he said, and walked down the rest of the stairs with her.

He opened the door to the warehouse, and pushed her gently through. She tore her eyes away from him so that she could see where she put her feet, and halted, eyes wide.

Two lines of now-former Eagle Express staff had formed between the door and the exit. Luis was closest, and he started to clap.

Others turned at the noise, and then joined in. Mic looked up at Knox. "What's going on?" she asked breathlessly, turning back to the cordon of employees. Kelly was about half-way down on the left, and Aidan stood next to her, clapping furiously.

"I think they're saying thank you. Or sorry. Or both," Knox suggested.

Mic took a step forward, and Luis approached her. He was shaking his head, and oh, gosh, were those tears? She gaped as Luis stepped close.

"I'm so sorry," he told her, although she could barely hear him above the applause. She smiled, and shook her head.

"It's okay," she said. "I understand."

Luis shook his head, his lips tight, and he sucked in a breath. "No. I was a dick. We all were. We didn't know—"

She patted him on the arm. "None of us did. We believed in the wrong people, that's all."

He closed his eyes briefly, and sucked in another breath, before again meeting her gaze. "Thank you. From all of us. We all got the job offers."

She grinned. "Well, don't thank me yet," she told him. "You're going to be working with my brother."

He laughed, then stepped back to allow her through, clasping his hands to his chest in a sincere gesture of gratitude.

Mic walked through to the roller door, stunned at the response of the employees. Knox stepped around her to open the passenger door of his car, and she climbed in, waving to the faces that she'd thought hated her. Knox walked around to the driver's side and climbed in.

"I think I'm having a Sally Field moment," she murmured, smiling at the group of people who trailed out of the warehouse as Knox drove out of the lot. "They like me. Right now, they like me."

Knox chuckled as he steered the car in the direction of her home. "What's not to like?"

She averted her gaze. She could read so much into that, but shouldn't. Since that night in the warehouse, he'd been the perfect gentleman, and completely professional. *Ugh.* She didn't like that word, not when it came to Knox.

She wanted him to get personal. To get all up into her face, into her business, into her life.

But he'd maintained a frustrating distance, so now she wondered if what they'd had was just a dreamy, foggy memory, influenced by proximity only. Cooler heads, et cetera.

"How are you?" she asked quietly.

"I'm good," he told her. "Work is keeping me busy …"

"Oh?" she tried to sound casual. They were going to be colleagues, after all.

She stilled. *Colleagues.* Of course.

He'd told her, when he'd dropped her home after the hospital, that he never mixed work with pleasure. That he'd never once broken that rule—until her. Even though Kayleigh's death had rocked him, he hadn't been romantically involved with the woman.

Good grief. She'd sabotaged any chance with the man the minute she'd signed that employment contract with SafeKeepers Inc.

"I've got a new assignment, but it's only temporary—and local," he added, then shrugged. "But you'll learn more about it when you start at the company."

She nodded. "Okay."

He pulled up in front of her house, and got out of the car. She opened her door and got out before he reached her. He held his palm out, and automatically she handed him her keys, then blinked as he strode up the path. Old habits, she guessed, as she followed him.

He unlocked her door and opened it, then turned to face her, dropping the keys back into her palm.

"I, uh, guess I'll see you when I start work," she said, curling her fingers over the keys.

"Yeah, you will," he said, nodding. He eyed her intently. "You could see me before then, if you like." His suggestion was uttered in a tone that was low and silky smooth, and caused all sorts of reactions, from the thumpity-thump of her heart, to her breath stuttering a little, to her breasts growing heavy and full in her bra.

She stared at him for a moment, and her stomach clenched. "What—what are you saying?" she asked. She shifted on her feet as she glanced down her front hall, then back at him. She was fully prepared to take what she could get, but she wanted to set herself some realistic expectations. She didn't want to eat her heart out for something that would never eventuate, but if all he could offer was 'right now'— then she could accept that. She just needed to know. "I want to make sure I'm not getting the wrong idea," she told him.

~*~

Knox braced his hand on the door jamb and leaned closer. He inhaled, closing his eyes for the briefest of moments. She smelled fantastic. Delicious. Floral, feminine, with a hint of fruit. He'd missed her so much, but he'd been determined to give her the time and space she'd told him she needed. After what had happened, it was easy to mistake relief and gratitude for something more … He wanted to give her the opportunity to sort all of that out.

And he'd hated every second of it. But this was about her needs, not his, and it was something he'd had to do.

He'd also told Jesse that he totally planned to have a very personal relationship with the new logistics director, if she'd have him, and if his boss wanted to fire him for that, then do it. Jesse had merely shrugged, and told him that the woman had punched the living daylights out of a kingpin drug trafficker, so if he was brave enough to take her on, good luck to him. Knox just needed to find out if she felt as crazy about him as he did about her.

"I'm saying," he said slowly, as his finger toyed with the collar of her shirt, "that I want to see more of you." She was wearing a soft pink business shirt tucked into a pencil skirt. He looked down. This could be the first time he'd seen her in a skirt—and heels! She looked good. Damn good. Her legs were slender and toned. But then, she looked good in anything.

Or nothing.

"Like … naked? Or more often?" She said, and he blinked. She looked … confused. Was she not expecting him to want to be with her? Or for him to return? Was he really the only one feeling all these—what did Dan call it? The thinky-feely stuff?

Something deep inside him clenched. What if he'd gotten it all completely wrong with Mic?

"Like naked, *and* more often," he said, then swallowed. "I want to be with you."

"Do you mean … tonight? Until you need to go on your next assignment, wherever and for however long it might be?" She glanced out down the street, as though making sure the neighbors couldn't hear their conversation. But she hadn't invited him in—did that mean she didn't want to invite him in?

"Uh …"

"Are you asking for more sex?" she asked, then touched his chest, and oh, that felt good, just having that minimal contact with her. "Because if that's all you want, I'm okay with that," she said earnestly. "I mean, you know, just sex." She scratched her temple. "I just need to know what's on the table."

All this talk of sex, and now sex was on the table. Knox swallowed.

"I want sex on the table."

Mic's eyebrows rose, and her mouth parted a little. "Oh."

He frowned. She sounded disappointed, and looked a little despondent. "Or wherever you'd prefer …" he said hastily.

"Just sex, then. Okay."

"No!" What? How the hell could he keep screwing up the most important conversations with this woman? It was like he'd taken a leaf out of Fitz's book, and refused to use his words properly.

"You don't want sex, then?" Mic looked confused, and Knox could relate. He took a deep breath, then straightened.

Screw it. He was putting everything on the table. Right next to the sex.

"I want you," he told her, looking at her squarely, and fighting the urge to hurl. He'd never felt so damn nervous, not even in his first skirmish outside Kandahar. "I want to be with you, all the time, and it's going to tear me up to step away for an assignment, but then I want to come back. To you. Always. Only you."

He cupped her cheek, and she tilted her head, leaning into his touch. "I'm all in, sweetness." He tilted his head until his forehead rested against hers. "I'm asking you, what do you want? Whatever you need … I'll do it. If you want me to keep staying away—"

She reared her head back, frowning at him. "I never wanted you to stay away," she told him.

"I thought I'd give you time. And space." Time. Space. He hated those words, for the control they wielded over him. "I don't want to rush you, I don't want to pressure you. I know you have good reason not to trust me—"

Her lips cut off his words, and he closed his eyes as he pulled her in close, responding immediately to her kiss. She drew back, her eyes shining as she looked up at him.

"I do trust you, Knox," she whispered. "You saved my life—"

"I don't want you to feel like you have to be with me because of that," he said hoarsely, his hands resting on the indent of her waist.

"Oh, I don't want to be with you out of a sense of obligation," she told him as her hands slid around his neck. He instinctively brought her in close, sighing as her body pressed against his, chest to chest. "I want to be with you because you're amazing. You're loyal, you have a sense of honor that won't quit, and you're great in bed. You're my unicorn."

He chuckled against her lips. "Really?" That was … interesting. She nodded.

He took her lips in a deep kiss, rubbing his tongue against hers, over and over, until he had to stop or give the neighbors a show. He drew his head back. "I love you, Michaela Robson," he whispered. "I love the way you think, the way you put others' needs before your own, that you'll give people the benefit of the doubt, that you're so damn fair, even when it would be easier to hate people, and how strong you are."

She eyed the hallway, then the street. "Shall we continue this conversation inside?"

"I thought you'd never ask." He tightened his arms around her and lifted her up, walking into the house with her. He kicked the door shut behind them, and started kissing her all over again.

"God, I love you, sweetness."

"I love you, too," she said breathlessly, and he pressed her against the wall, holding her up with his hips and arms. God, she felt fantastic.

His heart felt damn near to exploding in his chest as he kissed her again. He couldn't get enough of her, would never get enough of her. He finally understood what his mother had had with his father, and felt, deep down, he'd found that with Mic. There was no other woman after Mic.

She pulled back a little, then smiled up at him, and there was something so cheeky, so wickedly mischievous in her eyes, that he was hooked. Always and forever.

"Do you think you could show me some more of your moves?"

Desire shot through him, straight to his groin, and he grinned. "Oh, I've definitely got some moves for you."

He scooped her up in his arms and strode down the hall, capturing her lips in a sensual kiss. Her shoes fell off somewhere—he didn't care. He shouldered his way past her bedroom door, and dropped her on the bed.

She laughed as she bounced on the mattress, leaning back on her elbows, but he noticed she stopped laughing when he shucked off his jacket and drew his shirt up over his head and flung it … somewhere. He toed off his shoes, his body throbbing for her. He crawled on to the bed, his gaze going up her sexy legs, over the curve of her hips that gave him so much pleasure, to her cotton-covered breasts and further. He let her see his desire, his arousal, his need for her.

She caught her bottom lip between her teeth as he crawled up her body, and that look of wonder, of delight, of love, in her eyes, filled him with a sense of hope, of happiness he'd never thought he'd experience.

"Oh, Knox," she breathed as he started to unbutton her shirt.

"Oh, Mic," he said right back, and rose up to take her lips in a kiss he poured his soul into. He slid his hand up beneath her skirt, lifting the garment as he caressed her silken skin, until he found her tight, wet epicenter.

"Oh, Knox," she gasped in ecstasy, her head thrown back, as he showed her he did, indeed, have some moves for her.

The End

Dear Reader,

I hope you enjoyed reading *Easy Target* as much as
I enjoyed writing it! While I have you, would you mind if
I asked you a favor? Honest reviews on Amazon and
Goodreads are very important. They help other readers who
haven't tried my writing to decide whether or not it might be
for them. Reviews also help readers discover my books in
searches, and I can always do with more! If you have a spare
moment, I'd be ever so grateful if you could leave a few
words. Reviews can be as short as you like, and I can assure
you I need every one!

If you've already left a review, thank you soooo much for
your time! This means the world to me, and I don't take your
support for granted.

Happy reading, and stay awesome!

Shannon

Want to know when Shannon's next book comes out?

Sign up for her newsletter to receive all the updates and exclusives at
her website: www.shannoncurtis.com, or directly here:
http://eepurl.com/eaYa9 and receive a free read!

Other ways to contact Shannon:

contactme@shannoncurtis.com
www.shannoncurtis.com
http://twitter.com/2BShannonCurtis
http://www.instagram.com/shannoncurtiswrites/
http://www.facebook.com/Shannon.Curtis.Writers.Ink/

Keep reading for an excerpt from

Available March 2021

Chapter 1

He ran across the rooftop, his thigh muscles bunching as he leapt. He sailed through the air for a moment, lifting his feet to avoid the sheet flashing, and then landing in a roll to absorb the shock as he hit the neighboring roof. He rose with the momentum to take off running again. He paused briefly to open the maintenance door that led to the fire stairs, then jogged down the seven flights until he reached the eighteenth floor. He opened the stairwell door and removed his sunglasses and cap as he stepped into the hall. He lowered the hood of his jacket, and pulled down his scarf as the heat inside the building enveloped him. The elevator dinged as he approached, and he slowed as two men stepped out. They both saw him, and one of them rolled his eyes.

"You know, you could always try the front door like a normal person," Dan Demetre commented. He pulled his knitted cap off his head, and ruffled his dark hair.

Smithy Johnson grinned at his colleague. "Where's the fun in that?" He pulled his leather gloves off. It was cold outside, threatening snow, but inside this commercial building in downtown Seattle it felt like a sauna.

"One of these days, you're going to fall and break your neck," Angus Fitzgerald said as he keyed a code into the access panel next to the glazed glass doors with SafeKeepers Inc emblazoned in red across the middle. Fitz didn't seem to feel the cold. No scarf, no cap—the only concession he made to the weather was gloves, and in their line of work, that was more practical than a fashion accessory. The access panel flashed a green light, and Dan pushed it open.

"Ah, but you'll be there to catch me, won't you, Fitz." Smithy patted the man on his back and followed him into the office. Fitz grunted, but refrained from comment.

Smithy smiled as he walked through toward the office kitchen. Amber, the SafeKeepers intelligence officer, and Clem, their CEO's executive assistant, paused in their conversation as he entered the room.

His eyebrows rose. "Am I interrupting?"

Clem shook her head, but Amber nodded. "Yep, I'm getting the lowdown on Knox and Mic's wedding."

Smithy's eyebrows rose even further. "Really?" He poured himself a cup of coffee and leaned his hip against the counter. "Do go on."

Knox Landon had met his fiancée, Michaela Robson, on a case, and while things hadn't started smoothly for the pair, they were now planning their nuptials. Their closeness was beyond sickening, as far as Smithy was concerned.

"Mic's father wants a big, flashy affair, and Mic and Knox … don't," Clem informed him.

Amber leaned forward, her expression conspiratorial. "Mic's father has also invited nearly eighty more guests— business associates, et cetera, and Knox isn't impressed—"

"Neither is Mic—" Clem interrupted.

"So, they're both talking about putting the wedding on hold," Amber finished.

"It's a pretty easy fix, though, isn't it?" Smithy queried.

Both women frowned, and glanced at each other before they met his gaze. "How do you figure?" Amber asked. Clem tilted her head, waiting for his response.

Smithy shrugged. He thought it was fairly obvious. "Elope."

Clem's jaw dropped. Amber's eyes widened, and she shook her head. "No," the women chorused.

"Why not?"

Clem's mouth opened a couple of times, as though each response she thought of wasn't suitable.

Amber cleared her throat. "Uh, because it's important to have family at these sorts of events," she told him gently.

Smithy grimaced. "Well, there's your first mistake. Family is way overrated."

"If you folks have had enough gossiping, would you care to join our meeting?" Jesse Walker, CEO of SafeKeepers, asked pointedly from the doorway. Smithy smiled and lifted his mug in a salute to his boss as he left the room and walked down the hall to the boardroom. Perfect timing. He didn't want to get into any debates about how important family was—or wasn't.

Jesse followed him into the boardroom, where Dan, Fitz, Knox and Mic were already seated. Jesse took his seat at the head of the table, and Smithy took his down the other end, as Amber and Clem joined them. He smiled when he saw the plate of breakfast muffins on the long table. Clem always had food on offer at these meetings, bless her. He reached for one—oh, sweet Jesus, it looked like it might even have bacon in it.

Jesse opened up his tablet. "Right, we've got a couple of things on the go. Fitz, do you want to update us about the Acevedo case?"

"We believe he's now in Toronto, thanks to Smithy tracking his new cell phone. He used coach services to go up the coast to Vancouver, and then trained it across to Toronto." Fitz waved in Smithy's direction. "We've been tracking him since he called his girlfriend. He used a fake ID to get across the border. I'll fly up this afternoon and monitor, but I'll look to bring him back tomorrow—the day after at the latest."

Mic raised her hand. "How are you going to get him back across the border? I can imagine the red tape involved in getting a fugitive under a fake ID brought back stateside."

"We'll use the same ID he used going up. He's not wanted in Canada for anything—unless we include the counterfeit passport. We'll get him out, then deliver him to the Marshall's field office in Chicago."

"But what makes you think Acevedo will come willingly with you, and cross the border? It would be in his best interest to alert Canadian officials and hold up his transport, maybe give him another chance to escape." Mic was already making notes in her folder. As their logistics manager, the woman could probably see a myriad of consequences, and was planning counteractions.

Smithy's eyes narrowed. Fitz's lips twitched—that was about as close to smiling as Fitz got.

"I can be very convincing," Fitz assured her.

"What do you need?" she asked him.

"A van. I'll take care of the rest."

She hesitated, then nodded, and made some notes. "I'll have one ready for when you arrive."

"Okay, then," Jesse said, scrolling down his notes on his tablet. "Knox, you can provide backup—I'll let you and Fitz figure out the details, and Mic can provide support."

Clem made some notes in one of the pretty notebooks she always seemed to carry around, despite having a perfectly good laptop on the table in front of her. Jesse looked over at Amber. "Looks like we may have a case in New York. Watkins wants to make another delivery, but to a new client. I'll want you to go and scout the location, learn whatever you can."

Amber nodded. As their intelligence officer, she surveyed locations, routes and people before they committed further resources.

"Right, that leaves us with Optimax, here in Seattle." Jesse arched an eyebrow in Smithy's direction. "What have you got?"

Clem handed Smithy her laptop, and he nodded his thanks as he quickly pulled up the access to the larger screens on the wall.

"Our client believes a competitor is working on stealing the formula for their latest weight-loss product, but I'm not so sure. Obviously the client isn't about to give us access to their IP data, so it's hard to see who, exactly, has accessed what, but I've been hitting the forums, and I've found one guy who wants to get the information out, but he's not selling it …"

Dan frowned. "He's giving it away? What is he, some sort of disgruntled ex-employee?"

Smithy shook his head as he pulled up an image. The client wouldn't willingly let them access data, but that had never stopped Smithy. He'd managed to trace this guy back from a forum, and hacked his email. "This is Andrew Fisher. The current clinical operations manager."

He looked up at the screen. If there was ever the quintessential nerd, this guy was it. He was even wearing a cardigan, for crying out loud. The man was aged somewhere in his fifties, and had a receding hairline, thick glasses, and a pudgy physique. Smithy eyed the image. The man didn't appear to be availing himself of the new weight-loss formula he was wanting to release beyond the firewall of the nutraceuticals company.

"He's still working there, and seems to have been a loyal employee since he started twenty years ago." He looked up at Jesse. "I've set up a meet with him. One of us can go and retrieve the data, and we can have him arrested for selling trade secrets."

"Won't he just send it to us—or anyone else, for that matter?"

Smithy shook his head. "This company takes its IT security very seriously. He can't figure out how to send the data electronically without triggering alarms and a trail that leads back to him, so he's taking a physical copy of the data and handing it over."

Jesse nodded. "Okay, if you run point on that one—we're going to need someone to verify the contents of the data, and make sure he's giving away what our client thinks he's giving away. Dan, you can run backup."

Dan nodded. He glanced down the table at Smithy. "When was the meet set up for?"

"Tonight. I'll go into his office—"

"His office? If the guy doesn't want to get caught, why the hell is he setting the meeting up on his home turf, where we can identify him?" Dan queried, frowning.

Smithy shrugged. "I'm not sure, either, but this particular product has already made the company several million dollars in sales—they don't want any chance of it leaving their premises, so we're doing the sting on-site."

"Have we notified the client?" Jesse asked.

Smithy nodded. "They know we've established contact, and will be organizing a meet and exchange, but I haven't given them the details. We wanted to minimize the number of people who knew about this, just in case someone who actually knows this guy wanted to give him a heads up."

Mic leaned forward to look down the table. "Do you need anything?"

Smithy grinned. "Nah, I'm good." He didn't need much, and whatever he did, he could source himself. Besides, the things he used, he didn't think Mic could get hold of—not legally, anyway.

"Do you foresee any issues?" Jesse queried.

Smithy shook his head and pointed to the screen. "Look at him. At worst, we're looking at paper cuts. Or maybe he doesn't actually have what he says he has." Smithy shrugged. "Dan and I will be fine."

"Okay, then," Jesse said, closing the flap across his device. "I think we're done. Good luck, everyone."

Dan remained seated, and raised his eyebrows. "So, you're going in, huh? This place takes its security seriously. It's not like you can walk through the front door—and this guy is expecting a little cloak-and-dagger."

Smithy smiled as he rose from his seat. "No place is impregnable, Dan. Where there's a will, there's a way." He winked.

Dan's eyes narrowed as Smithy donned his knitted cap. "You're a little scary, you know that, right?"

"Come on, let's get our kit together and go."

"I'm driving. Just saying. You can tip-toe across the roof-tops if you like, but I'm taking the easy way."

Smithy's smile spread into a grin. "I already know you're easy."

~*~

"I've got a really upset lady on the phone."

Bec Cartwright looked up from her desk at the young man in front of her, his headphones around his neck. "What's the problem, Eddie?"

"She ordered Burnegy over two weeks ago, and still hasn't received it."

"Okay, did we check her order?"

"Yeah, but it doesn't make sense. I can see the website order, payment's gone through, and it's listed in the inventory …" Eddie shrugged.

"What's the order number, and I'll take a look."

Eddie handed her a scrap of paper, and she entered the details into the system. She toggled screens, then frowned. "I see what you mean. Looks like the order hasn't gone through to the warehouse." She looked up at him. "You'll need to push the order through the system—do you remember how to do that?"

Eddie hesitated, then shook his head. "Not … really."

Bec sighed. "Go back to the customer, and let her know what's happened, and that we'll sort her order out with the warehouse team today, it will be dispatched tomorrow with expedited delivery."

Eddie nodded, and stepped away from her desk, then paused, grimacing. "She's really angry."

Bec eyed him. Part of customer service was taking those difficult calls, but nobody liked being yelled at. "Tell her that you can see there was a problem, you've escalated it to your supervisor, then transfer her to me."

He sighed in relief. "Thanks, Bec."

"And then go offline, and come over—I'll show you how to push that order through."

She donned the wireless earpiece, and switched her phone to available, then smiled as the call came through. Smiling was important in customer service—because clients could hear it down the line, her first trainer, all those years ago, had taught her, and the woman was right.

Within minutes she'd calmed the woman down and explained how her order had been held up, and what steps they were taking to resolve it, along with an apology for the delay. She jotted the order down in her notebook as she spoke, and when the woman was satisfied, Bec disconnected the call. Eddie stood behind her.

"I don't know how you do it," he told her. "She was so angry with me."

"Customers get angry when we make life difficult for them," she told him. "She's paid a lot of money for something that hasn't arrived yet—we'd be upset, in that position, too. It's a case of empathizing with the customer—but it's got to sound sincere to them. Otherwise it's just placatory bullshit— and nobody wants that."

Eddie nodded, and dragged his chair on wheels over. "Okay, so how do we push this order through?"

"Does anybody ever read those manuals I wrote?" Bec asked, her voice loud enough for the rest of the Optimax online customer care team to hear—and then pretend they didn't.

She sighed. She almost wondered if writing up those step-by-step manuals was a waste of time, seeing as nobody seemed to remember they existed, and treated her like the resident brains trust. She shuffled across so that her agent could see the screen. Within minutes she'd taught him the relevant process, and he was back at his desk, taking more calls. She turned to the order number she'd jotted down in her notebook. She'd have to raise it with the IT team and operations, because somewhere along the new so-called automated processing, something had gone wrong. That was the fourth order in two days she'd noticed. There would be more, but they wouldn't necessarily know about it until customers called, chasing down their orders. She couldn't even pull a report. She eyed the screen in consideration. There had to be a way they could pull that data … but that was just one issue she had to deal with today.

She scanned their list of open cases. Sometimes customers called with their issue, but most of the time they used the online forms. She sighed when she saw the climbing numbers. Ever since the Burnegy product had been released four weeks ago, they'd had a flurry of cases pop up. Some were general queries, others were tracking lost orders, and hung orders, and some were about the product itself. She'd started to compile a report, because this product was pretty much an example case of how *not* to bring a product to market. She and her team had received next to no briefing on it, and apart from the product kits that the general public could access—if they took the time to ferret it out on the website—the Optimax staff had no additional information.

"Don't look now, but our illustrious leader is on his way," Marlena, another customer care agent, murmured as she swiveled in her chair.

Bec looked up. "You mean, our illustrious leader's son," she corrected when she caught sight of the tall man making his way through the open-plan customer care department. Clive Jnr was unmistakable, with his tall frame, light brown hair and blue eyes that sparkled. At least, Bec thought they sparkled. He had a winning smile—at least, it won her over. Not that he'd noticed. He had blond strands in his light brown hair that seemed to glow under the fluorescent lighting as he walked past the desk pods.

"How are we going down here?" Clive Jnr asked, and he smiled.

Oh, my God. He was looking right at her. And *smiling.*

Bec rose from her desk, smoothing her skirt down as she gave the handsome operations manager a friendly, if slightly timid, smile. "We're doing well, thanks," she said, then cleared her throat.

"Great, that's what I like to hear," Clive Jnr stated, then continued to walk past toward the door that led to the accounts area.

"He spoke to you," Marlena breathed in awe, and Bec nodded as she sank back down to her seat.

"Yeah, he did." She bit her lip, trying to keep her smile secret. He'd actually made eye contact. That was a good sign, right? She sighed, her finger tapping her notebook, and she glanced down at it. She frowned. "Shoot. I need to talk to him as well about these dropped orders not going through— they're going to affect his area, too."

Clive Wheeler, Jnr, handled the operations of Optimax. He oversaw the warehouse and logistics, which required coordination with the clinical operations manager.

"You'll just have to arrange a meeting with him," Marlena said, then shimmied in her seat. "Too exciting."

"Yeah, well, I'll have to pull the data—I want to make sure I'm capturing everything. We have to figure out a way to fix this, somehow." Her lips tightened. The IT infrastructure was managed by Tony Merlotti, and he'd personally designed the inventory program the warehouse used. It was his baby, and he didn't appreciate it when she brought problems to him. She suspected he'd designed it as career protection—if anything ever happened to the man, the company would find it incredibly difficult and expensive to transition to a different software program—or IT manager.

So, for now, she was stuck with a version that required constant tweaks.

"Bec, I have a Connie Franks on the phone—I've tried to put her through to the medical hotline, but she's insisting on speaking with you." Adriana, another member of her team, stood up to meet her glance over the desk pod screens.

Bec frowned. "Connie Franks. Connie … Franks." The name sounded familiar. "Do we have any cases under her name?"

She quickly pulled up the online ticket program they used for cases, and did a search. She frowned. There were no cases listed, but Bec was sure she'd spoken to her in the past—the name seemed so familiar. There should be a ticket under the woman's name.

She frowned, puzzled, but nodded at Adriana. "Put her through." Bec flicked her phone to available, and waited for the call to come through.

"Optimax Customer Care, Bec speaking. How can I help you?"

She could hear heavy breathing, and for a moment she thought she was being pranked—until she realized someone was sobbing softly.

"Hello?" Bec inquired gently. "Ms. Franks?"

"He's dead," the woman wailed on the line. "You bastards, you've killed him."

About the author

Shannon Curtis has worked as a copywriter, business consultant, admin manager, customer service rep, logistics coordinator, dangerous goods handler, event planner, switch bitch and betting agent. She decided to try writing a story like those she loved to read when she found herself at home after the birth of her first child. Her books have been nominated finalists for Favourite Romantic Suspense every year from 2011 to 2016, as well as Favourite Continuing Romance Series by the Australian Romance Readers Association. In 2016 she won Favourite Paranormal Romance with her uniquely crafted novel, *Tribal Law*, and in 2017 her novel *Warrior Untamed* won the PRISM award from the FF&P special interest chapter of Romance Writers of America, and her novel *Heart Breaker* won Favourite Romantic Suspense 2017.

She is the first Australian author to be published by Harlequin Nocturne. In 2014 she was invited as part of a select group of authors to write romance novels for *The Bold and The Beautiful* TV series. As a founding member of the first romance publishing cooperative in Australia, she has a comprehensive insight into the world of publishing, and worked for some years as the first ever administrative officer of Romance Writers of Australia.

When she's not working part-time to save her sanity by talking with other real people, she's teaching creative writing to students at the Sydney Community College, and spends the rest of her time daydreaming up strong heroes and heroines and complex, captivating stories. She lives in Sydney, Australia, with her husband and three children, and she loves reading, loves writing, and loves hearing from her readers, so visit her at www.shannoncurtis.com and say hi!